FALLING INTO FOREVER

SINGLETREE, BOOK 5

DELANCEY STEWART

1

PUMPKIN SPICE DAY
MICHAEL

In my experience, Sunday mornings generally sucked. Sure, there were the ones when you got up late, made pancakes and lazed around in flannel pajama bottoms longer than you should. And those were okay, at least when Daniel was with me.

But the Sunday mornings when my son was at his mom's house?

You'd think I'd be happy for the peace and quiet, for the freedom from the expectations and demands of a grumpy pre-pubescent twelve-year old. But you'd be wrong.

That was what I lived for. We'd been divorced almost Dan's whole life, and though I didn't miss the chaos that had been my poorly thought-out and hastily completed marriage, I missed Dan anytime he was with Shelly.

So Sunday mornings when I woke up alone in a quiet house with nothing specific ahead of me felt like purgatory. Like a penance of some kind. Like they were engineered specifically to remind me what my life was supposed to be about—and how I'd failed.

I guzzled a cup of coffee, gave myself a pep talk—hard, since I was not a peppy guy exactly—and headed out to run.

Let's be clear here: running is not something I do. At least not historically. But I need to keep myself healthy for the sake of my kid, plus, it gets me out of the house on days when there's a chance I might just decide to give up and wallow in my bed for the entire day. I've found that the feeling of actually running feels a little bit like running away might. And so on days when I have the chance, I pretend to run away. I pretend to run toward some shimmering version of a life I've already forsaken—one I turned my back on twelve years ago.

It was a crisp fall day, one of those where you can practically smell winter just around the corner. The humidity of the mid-Atlantic had finally given way to cooler air, turning leaves, and that scent that always seemed to accompany the arrival of autumn, full of rich earth, dewy grass and cinnamon spice. That last part might not be so much due to fall as to Lottie Tanner's penchant for baking cinnamon spice everything the second the first hint of fall arrived. The Muffin Tin, Lottie's cafe, occupied one corner of the main square in Singletree, and though I made a point to cross the road instead of running directly past it, cinnamon still wrapped itself around me as I passed.

The Muffin Tin was a popular Singletree locale, but aside from sending Daniel in with a fistful of cash now and then, it wasn't a place I ever went. It was a Tanner establishment, after all, and I'd no sooner enter that place than Lottie or her sister Verda would buy a book at my aunt Veronica's shop. Tuckers and Tanners didn't mix. It was tradition.

I jogged to the top of the hill past the town square, my breath coming hard as I pushed myself up the incline toward the old Easter mansion at the top. There was a time this would have been easy, back when I was pretty sure I was going to college to play soccer. I could run for miles back then. But that was twelve years ago. Now? I was an almost middle-aged dude trying to keep himself sane through sweat and near-death exercise experiences.

The hill leveled off in front of a set of old iron gates, chipped and rusted in spots, but chained securely in front of the creepy old Easter mansion. The place had been beautiful once, I'd bet —all Victorian gardens and turrets, wide sweeping porches and an expansive front lawn. But now it gave me a chill every time I passed it, and I headed away, my lungs screaming.

A group of boys on bikes pedaled past me in the other direction, cackling and hooting about whatever boys Dan's age cackled and hooted about. I ignored them but glanced over my shoulder to see them drop their bikes outside the gates of the dilapidated mansion. They were up to no good, I could feel it, and since I thought I recognized a couple of them as Dan's friends, I felt the urge to keep them out of trouble.

"Hey, you kids!" I turned around and moved faster, upping my flagging pace to intercept them just as they were about to squeeze between the iron bars. The old Easter place was endlessly fascinating to local kids. Especially at this time of year as scary movies and pumpkins were getting brought out. "That's private property, see the 'No Trespassing' signs?"

"Yessir, Mr. Tucker. Sorry." One of the kids had the guts to actually face me, which was reassuring, since I was now definitely sure these were some of Daniel's lesser-known pals.

I waved my arms at them. "Go on, get out of here!"

The kids scrambled, hopping back onto their bikes and shrieking with laughter as they pedaled away, leaving me to realize I'd skipped mid-life and progressed directly into the high-pants-wearing grandfatherly phase of my time here on Earth, where I screamed at people to get off my lawn. And this wasn't even *my* lawn.

I stopped running, leaning over to catch my breath in front of the rusting gates of the big house. I let out a breath feeling disgusted with myself, but not just because I'd stopped some kids from vandalizing a decrepit old house I didn't give a shit about.

No, there were plenty more reasons for me to feel like I was watching my life swirling around the toilet bowl of existence, making a slow but steady spiral toward utter and complete failure. Or maybe not failure as much as stagnancy. I. Was. Going. Nowhere.

Now more literally than usual, since I was just standing here in front of the creepiest house in town, staring at the old Victorian monstrosity when I was supposed to be jogging. But . . . Wait, had I just seen something move in the upstairs window? I was one hundred percent sure the place was deserted, and had been since I was a little kid. A chill ran through me as I squinted up at the darkened windows of the second floor. Creepy.

"Now I'm seriously losing it."

I sighed and turned away, determined to finish my run, even if nothing else in my life had gone according to plan.

2

CROSSWALK TANGO
ADDISON

"Pie me." Mom held her hands out for the lemon meringue that sat on the work table in the kitchen at the Muffin Tin. I'd been hiding in the kitchen for a couple days now, pretending to help, and Mom kept coming back and asking for things—her way of checking on me without really checking on me. I guessed it seemed to her this was better than demanding answers from her thirty-five year old daughter who'd shown up suddenly at her childhood home, refusing to discuss what had happened in her fantastic independent life in New York City.

I'd have to tell her eventually, I knew. But my mother, Lottie Tanner, had an affinity for gossip, even when it was her own. I couldn't really tell her until I was ready for everyone in Single-tree to know what an utter fool I was. For now, only my sister Paige knew what had happened.

"Here." I handed Mom the pie and looked around the small kitchen, gilded in stainless steel and feeling suddenly suffocating in its cleanliness and shine. "I'm going to take a walk, I think."

Mom's eyes widened a touch beneath the perfect steel gray

bob, and she pressed her lips together before saying, "Sure, honey. You go get some air."

Lottie was showing remarkable restraint, which I appreciated. I knew she had thirty thousand questions she was dying to ask, but instead she had welcomed me home with a hug, made up my old room for me, and told me I could stay as long as I liked.

I didn't want to stay at all really, and not just because Mom shared her home with three free-range chinchillas. But I had nowhere else to go. Except back to New York, and I couldn't even think about that yet.

I pushed out through the front door of the cafe, offering friendly smiles to a few of the townspeople who gathered there on Sunday mornings for muffins and coffee.

The air had turned crisp, and I wrapped my arms around myself, wishing I'd thought to pull my jacket from the hook before going out. I didn't want to go back inside though, the cinnamon spice felt almost oppressive with its air of comfort and family togetherness. It reminded me of happier times, of feeling loved, of being where I was supposed to be. But this place wasn't where I was supposed to be. I'd moved on, and coming back here felt like a concession. A failure.

I was moving toward the crosswalk, ready to cross the square to avoid walking in front of the little bookshop a block down from Mom's cafe—I avoided it out of habit, not because I really had any beef with the Tuckers. That was Mom's thing. I thought the old feud was ridiculous, especially since not a single person seemed to know how it had started. But it was better to avoid conflict, I figured, so I didn't walk in front of Veronica Tucker's bookstore, though it was exactly the kind of place I'd love to go lose myself now.

The square was busy for a Sunday morning. There was a man jogging down the other side of the street, looking fit and healthy in a way that made me realize I probably needed to stop self-medicating with Mom's muffins soon, and there was an old woman in the crosswalk, moving at a dying snail's pace across the street. Just as I turned to cross, she stumbled and crumpled to the ground in front of me, and as my heart rushed into my mouth with fear and concern, I rushed to kneel at her side.

"Are you all right?" I asked, the question echoed in deep masculine tones on the other side of the old woman. I looked up to find the runner kneeling on the woman's other side. He must have seen her fall too. I looked a moment longer at him and surprise flooded me as I took in the dark blue eyes, the square jaw and tousled ginger hair. He was a Tucker. Michael, I thought.

"Well," said the little pile of old woman between us. "Well, I don't know."

I didn't see any blood, and the woman seemed to be lucid— those were good signs.

Might-be-Michael helped her come to a sitting position, and she lifted a small wrinkled hand to her head, glancing between us. "Is my hair all right?"

Her hair was arranged in a cloud-like pouf at the back of her head, and it looked unharmed by the fall.

I laughed, recognizing Filene Easter, who was a long-time friend of my mother's and had been my babysitter, once upon a time. "It looks fine, Mrs. Easter. Are you all right, though?"

"Did you hit your head?" The runner asked, and his deep blue eyes were fixed on her face, full of concern. Something about his sincere attention made my heart twist inside my chest.

"Maybe you kind children could just help me up," she suggested, and after exchanging a brief glance, we complied. I felt a little jump of amusement at having been referred to as "children." I wondered if Maybe-Michael-Tucker recognized me —we'd never really known each other, but we'd both been kids in a very small town, so we knew who the other was. If, in fact, this was Michael. Might-be-Mike had gotten handsome, either way. Even if he was possibly a Tucker.

"Let's just sit for a moment," the man suggested, guiding Mrs. Easter to the bench in front of Mom's shop. "You're Addison, right?" he asked me, narrowing his eyes. "Your mom isn't going to, uh . . ." He looked at me questioningly. So he was a Tucker—the trepidation in his eyes confirmed it.

"She's not really part of the 'shoot any Tucker on sight' side of the family," I assured him. Though Mom was part of the "ask a million questions if she catches me out here with a Tucker," side. "And you're Michael?"

"Oh, I see. So she's just part of the 'unleash a thousand crickets in a bookshop' contingent, huh?" he said, bitterness narrowing his eyes. "And yeah, I'm Mike."

Wow. So we were going there? Better not to engage. This was not my fight. I would not get involved. Definitely-Mike was acting like kind of a dick. "Mrs. Easter," I said, addressing the old woman and hoping the Tucker at my side would let it drop. "Does anything hurt?"

She looked between us, a tiny smile playing on her thin lips. "At my age, everything hurts, dear."

Michael chuckled, and I realized that when he wasn't being an ass about a hundred-year-old feud, his smile might have been considered charming—as was his concern for Mrs. Easter as he asked, "How about anything new hurting since falling a few minutes ago?"

She sighed. "My knee hurts a little bit." She leaned forward and pulled the hem of her long skirt up higher, revealing combat boots and tall socks beneath. But she also uncovered a bleeding scrape and a rapidly swelling bump. I winced in sympathy. That looked like it hurt.

Michael sucked in a breath and his eyes flew to mine. He

looked worried, and in that second, I knew we'd both dropped the topic of the feud. "Oh, that's just a bump," he said, in the way one would reassure a worried child.

"Let me give my sister Paige a call," I suggested. Paige was one of the family doctors in town. "I bet she'll fix that right up."

"Oh, no. I don't want to be a bother on a Sunday morning. I'm sure she's enjoying some time with that handsome man of hers."

My stomach twisted a little with envy, thinking that Mrs. Easter was probably right. Paige was probably lounging in bed with Cormac, or enjoying a family breakfast with him and his two adorable little girls. She had a ready-made family, and I— well, that wasn't important right now.

"She won't mind a bit," I assured her, pulling my phone from my pocket. I stepped away and explained the situation to Paige, who agreed to come down and take a quick look. "Why don't we just go inside here and wait for her? Maybe have some tea? It's a little chilly out here."

Mrs. Easter smiled. "That would be nice."

Michael looked hesitant, but to his credit, said nothing about being led into a Tanner-owned establishment.

As we walked through the door, my mother gasped and dropped the coffee cup she'd been pouring for a customer. "Addie, what do you think you're doing?"

The broken cup spun across the floor, and then a cold silence spread through the shop, doused in the scent of cinnamon. Michael froze in place, Mrs. Easter at his side. I pulled out a chair at a table by the window for Mrs. Easter.

"Mrs. Easter fell outside," I said, looking around and feeling like I had to explain myself, not just to my mother but to all the concerned busybodies of Singletree who were staring now, hoping for something to talk about later. "And Michael and I were both right there. Paige is coming to take a look and make sure she's okay, so I suggested we come in here to wait. It's cold outside."

Mom seemed to recover herself, and rushed to Mrs. Easter's side. "Of course! Oh, you poor dear. Come sit. Let's get you some tea." She managed to take the old woman's arm from Michael and turn her back on him rather obviously in the process.

"Maybe I'll just . . ." he said, clearly uncomfortable.

"No, no," Mrs. Easter said. "You stay and sit. If I need to be carried or have questions about farm supplies, I'll need you right here."

Well, that was odd—and it felt like Mrs. Easter had an ulterior motive, but neither of us seemed inclined to question an injured old woman. Michael sighed and sat down next to the old woman, and my mother's annoyance was practically tangible. There would be no holding off the barrage of questions later.

"Lottie, that tea sounds lovely," Mrs. Easter said. Besides the knee, she seemed completely fine. She looked between Michael and me, a little smile pulling at her lips. "You know," she said. "I remember you both from when you were small." Mrs. Easter didn't seem too affected by her fall, and I thought maybe she was actually enjoying the extra attention.

"You do?" I laughed, taking a seat beside her. I remembered her a little bit, but wondered what exactly she remembered about me, the serious Tanner sister, as a child.

"Oh yes, dear," Mrs. Easter said. "I don't know if you remember that I used to run a daycare up at my house when I lived in the big place at the top of the hill. Very informal, of course, nothing fancy. But I always loved being around the little ones. And there was a time, Addie, when you were my little helper."

I had a vague memory of being in that big house when I'd been little. I'd thought it was a kind of fairytale castle—lots of rooms and stairs and wide open wood floors, plus the biggest widest porch I'd ever seen. I had a warm recollection of being happy there.

"And you always helped me with the babies. You were a good helper too, since you had two younger sisters and lots of practice with them. You were a big help with Michael here."

Michael cleared his throat as if this news was somehow embarrassing.

I laughed, trying to imagine the well-built man across from me as a baby. "Really?"

"Oh yes, dear. I wondered back then if the two of you wouldn't be the end of this silly feud right there. When you were near, Michael was happy and calm—and he was the fussiest of fussy babies, let me tell you."

"Wonderful," Michael said under his breath.

"Oh, I loved having the two of you around. So sweet, always laughing together, even though you were so much older, Addison."

I cringed. Even as a little kid, I was practically a spinster.

My sister appeared at the curb, pulling her car to a stop and then stepping out, one hand adjusting her bouncy brown ponytail. She smiled at me through the window, and a little surge of relief ran through me.

"Here's Paige," I said, happy to see my sister coming through the door and eager for a change of subject.

Paige looked between Michael and me with a question written on her face, but she was in doctor mode, so didn't ask questions except of Mrs. Easter and about the fall. A few minutes later, she had her patched up, had given her a prescription for an anti-inflammatory, and had scheduled her a follow-up appointment for Tuesday.

And just as suddenly as the odd little meeting of old daycare companions had begun, it was over.

"Uh, I guess I'll see you," Michael said, standing.

He might have been a Tucker, but he sure was pretty to look at, all muscles and golden-red hair with those deep blue eyes and a tiny cleft in his perfect square chin. But still, he was a Tucker, through and through.

"I won't expect to see you back in here," Mom said, coming to stand in front of him, arms crossed.

"Mom," I hissed, appalled. We could feud without saying rude things, I thought.

"No need to worry, ma'am. My uncle would kill me if he knew I'd set foot in here," Michael assured her, his face hardening. "Glad to see you got the place put back in order though."

"If you're referring to that stunt your cousins pulled, you should know it took two days to get all the furniture off the ceiling and the plaster repairs up there cost a fortune," Mom's voice had turned to ice.

Paige pressed her lips together hard, trying not to laugh. I hadn't seen it in person, but Paige had sent me photos of the cafe turned literally upside down. I still didn't know how the Tuckers had managed to fasten all the furniture to the ceiling like that. It was a feat. If it hadn't been so costly to repair, it would have been pretty funny.

"Well, it looks all right now. I'll see you around," Michael said, clearly enjoying Mom's distress. Jerk.

"Better not," I said, not wanting my mother to have a heart attack here on the spot.

"A lot of silliness," Mrs. Easter chimed in. "And time for it to end."

Mom let out a little "hmph," spun on her heel, and returned to her spot behind the counter.

The feud had gone on so long, I doubted it was ever going to end. But as I watched Michael head out the door and break back into a jog, a little part of me wanted it to.

EMPLOYEE OF THE MONTH
MICHAEL

"Can you stack that feed?" I called back to Virgil, my cousin—who also happened to be my employee.

"Stack it yourself, asshole." Virgil was not winning employee of the month this month. Or this century. He and his brother Emmett were bent over the register counter, heads together, with a pad of paper between them and an aura of no-fucking-good wafting off them like thick morning fog.

I dropped a heavy hand on Virgil's shoulder, pulling him to face me. I had at least thirty pounds on the guy, who was barely twenty-one, and his brother was a year older and about three inches shorter. "Listen up, Virge. I'm not 'asshole' around here. I'm the boss, and if you want to keep pulling the deposit that's keeping you in Half-Cat Whiskey and cheap beer, you'd do well to remember that."

Virgil didn't look the least bit chastised.

"Same goes for you, Emmett."

His brother had the intelligence to nod his head, as if he agreed with me.

I would have liked to get some actual employees in here, but my father made some kind of deal with his brother Victor before he died, and these guys had been handed down to me along with ownership of the store. There'd been a time when I'd had plans for this place, when I could envision it becoming something I was excited about running, owning. But that was when I thought I'd be going to college and coming back for it, maybe getting a few years of pro soccer under my belt and my wild dreams out of my system.

"What the hell are you two cackling about over here anyway?" I asked, already regretting the question as a wicked smile overtook Virgil's face.

"Remember the moose?"

Simple question, really. And for most people, a question like this would trigger an obvious memory, if they did, in fact, have a moose-related memory. Sadly, I had about thirteen moose-related memories, and none of them were good.

"Yes," I said, not wanting to be drawn too far into a conversation that generally ended with me agreeing to put the bucket on the heavy-duty tractor on my back lot and close my eyes to whatever happened next.

"This time, we're gonna set him *inside* the Muffin Tin." Virgil's voice got high and squeaky with excitement, and Emmett nodded his agreement, rubbing his hands together. Emmett did a lot of nodding, and not a lot of speaking. That was probably thanks to the lisp he'd always had, for which he'd been relentlessly teased as a kid. Now he let Virgil do all the talking, which was a shame, because Virgil's brain usually caught up to his mouth about three days later.

"I don't think so," I said, crossing my arms and pulling myself to my full height.

The moose sat in Verda Tanner's garden most of the time. It was a monstrous bronze thing, cast solid and just about to scale, so all told, it weighed somewhere around a ton. It was a bit of an oversized lawn ornament, most of the town agreed, but Verda's late sculptor husband had cast the thing during his "bronze age" and she loved it. I'd overheard her talk about it once (after the moose had been relocated to sit beneath the huge tree in the town square wearing a shirt that read: *Tanners. They're not smart, but at least they're ugly.* She'd cried and moaned, and even flung her arms around the moose and talked to it as if it was her dead husband. It kind of reminded me of an old episode of *Sanford & Sons* I'd seen once, where the old man played by Redd Foxx would look to the heavens and talk to his dead wife. I felt a little guilty, thinking about it.

Point was, the woman loved the moose, and moving it around town was a huge hassle. And thinking about the feud now made me think of Addison Tanner, and her pretty brown hair and sad dark eyes. She had a bit of a smart mouth, maybe, but I didn't feel any animosity toward her. In fact the idea of hurting her—even a little—made my own heart ache a bit for no explicable reason. It just seemed like maybe she'd been hurt already. And moose-related antics might hurt her more—even if not directly. Verda was her aunt, after all.

"C'mon, Mike," Virgil pleaded. "I'll move all the feed you want if you let us borrow the tractor tonight."

"No." I sighed as a beat-up blue Camry pulled into the lot out front. "And you'll move all the feed right now because I'm paying you to do it."

Virgil and Emmett exchanged a look, but they headed off to the back of the store together, hopefully to start hauling feed. But probably not.

I turned to the front as the bell over the door rang out, and forced a smile for my ex-wife, who looked upset and frazzled as ever, Daniel trailing behind her. Fridays were kid-trade days. I had Dan every other week, Friday to Friday.

"Hey, Shell," I said, trying to make my voice light and happy.

She'd broken down in tears a few times before when I hadn't sounded happy enough to see her.

"Oh, God, Mike," she started, her voice already a wail as she dropped her keys on my counter and leaned heavily on her forearms, bowing her head. "It's been such a day."

I smiled over her head at Daniel, who looked pretty unfazed by "the day," and when he stepped behind the counter, I pulled him into a bear hug. "Missed you, little man," I told him as something inside me snapped closed. I felt loose and incomplete when he wasn't around. It was always a relief to have him back. "Where's your stuff?" I glanced around for his pack, his schoolwork.

"That's what I'm trying to tell you," Shelly wailed. She lifted her head, and I saw tears standing in the eyes I'd once thought could change the world. I knew now those bright blue eyes only had the power to change my life, and not necessarily for the better. She was still pretty, and if you'd put her in a cheerleader uniform, she'd look a lot like the girl I couldn't quit thinking about at sixteen. But now? Now I'd take one look and realize none of that—the blond hair and high voice—mattered to me anymore. I'd been young and impulsive back then, and I hoped I was wiser now.

I didn't need bright blue eyes and a pretty little rosebud mouth.

I didn't need the tight little body wrapped in a low-cut shirt or a cheerleader's top.

I needed to focus on being a responsible father to my son. And that was all I needed. All other paths led to ruin. I'd already proven that.

"We were running so late, and Daniel was dragging his feet, like always, playing that stupid game on the computer and everything, and I'm already late for work now." Shelly's litany of excuses wasn't new.

"We can swing by your place on our way home and grab his stuff, okay?"

She huffed. "You can't just walk into my house whenever you want, Mike."

Daniel sidled away, disappearing between a couple aisles, undoubtedly sensing a fight coming on. "I don't want to go to your house, Shell," I told her in as calm a voice as I could muster. "But Daniel needs his homework so he's prepared on Monday. And I can grab his clothes and wash them so you don't have to." It was couched in the form of a generous offer, but the truth was that Shelly just never bothered to wash Daniel's clothes, and half the time I got him back as some disheveled version of the stinky kid at school.

Shelly's priorities weren't quite aligned with my own, as it turned out.

"You don't have to," she said, dropping my gaze. "The maid should be coming tomorrow."

Shelly did not have a maid. She had very little in the way of resources, and she had lost her last two jobs, and was now working at The Shack as a waitress. I could do a little laundry if it made my son's life better. And hers.

We were not a good couple in the long run. But that didn't mean I wanted to see her suffering. It was just hard not to resent her a little when I felt like my son wasn't being taken care of properly. But Daniel loved his mom, and none of her sins were egregious—just a little lazy. It wasn't perfect, but it worked.

"Okay, well, we'll just grab his stuff then."

"I'm late for work," she said, looking relieved. "Bye Dan!" she called to the store at large.

"Bye Mom," came Dan's voice from the back of the store.

I was just about to head back and see how he was doing when the store phone rang.

"Tucker Feed and Farm," I answered automatically. I'd been

delivering that greeting since I was twelve.

"Ah, yes, hello. I'm looking for Michael Tucker?"

"Well then, it's your lucky day. Speaking."

"Sir, my name is Augustus Anders. I'm an attorney here in Singletree. I represent Filene Easter."

Oh shit. What was this? Was the old lady suing me for helping her out of the street? My stomach soured. This had the Tanner stink on it.

"Go on," I said, managing to sound civil.

"Would you possibly be able to come to my office this afternoon, sir? Maybe around five?"

"Can you tell me what this is about?"

"Mrs. Easter passed away two days ago," he said, and my mind stopped spinning, frozen suddenly with an image of the sweet old face I'd looked into just a few days before. "And she set up a trust before she died. You are one of the co-trustees."

"Um." That made no sense at all. My mind was spinning. A trust? What?

"By law, it will be thirty days before the will can be read in full, but the trust is already established and passes directly to the trustees upon the death of the administrator."

"Um." I was a fount of intelligent questions. And my heart had begun to ache a little—I hadn't known Mrs. Easter well, but I'd seen her just a few days ago, and she'd been spry and bright in her combat boots and poufy white hair. I sighed, feeling suddenly sad and exhausted. "Okay."

"So you'll come?"

I'd already forgotten his original question. "Come?"

"To my office. Today? At five?"

"Oh. Sure, okay. Can you text me the address?" I gave him my cell phone number and hung up, staring out the window for a long moment after. What in the world would Filene Easter have put into a trust for me? It made no sense at all.

4

TUCKERS SMELL
ADDISON

"I cannot bake another cookie," I moaned, wiping my hands on my jeans and sinking into the single hard chair Mom kept in the kitchen at The Muffin Tin. "I don't know how you do this all day every day."

Mom smiled at me and turned back to the batter she was beating in the standing mixer. "It's my calling," she said, and I knew she was right. Baking and running The Tin made my mother happy, and I was glad. She deserved to be happy.

The atmosphere in the back had improved slightly—we'd learned that morning that Filene Easter had died in her sleep a few days ago, and for the first part of the day, it was hard to believe. I'd just seen her—she'd sat in Mom's shop and drank tea!

"She was very old," Mom had said, consoling us both as we tried not to cry over the loss of one of the town's most entertaining matriarchs. Mom took it harder than I did—Mrs. Easter came into the Tin often. But I'd just seen her, had just talked with her. Her and Michael Tucker. For some reason, that day had lodged in my mind in a strange way, as if it held some kind of meaning I didn't understand.

But most of my life lately seemed to be just a collection of unfortunate events, none of them meant anything, I guessed. And Mom was right, Mrs. Easter was very old. We'd been told that she died peacefully in her sleep, and that her housekeeper had found her in bed the following morning—that she was even smiling.

It made me glad to hear that she'd died happy. Maybe she'd been in the midst of a wonderful dream. I hoped so.

My little sister Amberlynn turned from a bowl of cookie dough. She was a high school teacher, but Fridays were often early release days, and today she'd had time to come to the cafe after her meetings. "You should have seen Mom the week they had to close the place to get all the furniture off the ceiling. Mom not baking is like having a rabid Tasmanian Devil around."

"Oh, you," Mom said, swatting at my sister's shoulder.

"Well, I wish I had your energy," I said. "Maybe I could figure out what the hell I'm supposed to do with my life."

Mom stopped bustling around and looked at me, undoubtedly wondering if I was finally going to tell her what had brought me home, broken and crying at thirty-five, when she'd believed I had it all.

I did have it all. Or at least I thought I did.

The kick-ass career in finance.

The swanky co-op apartment overlooking the Hudson.

The hot musician boyfriend. (Not the rock star kind, if you're wondering. Luke was a violinist.)

An eight-year relationship that seemed destined for permanence.

It's crazy how one person in a relationship can believe it's one thing while the other can see something completely different.

Because clearly, one person was an idiot. And the other person was busy planning a whole separate life.

Mom sighed after waiting a few minutes for me to spill, and said, "It will all work out, Addie. You're a strong, smart girl." And then she bustled right back out to the front counter, leaving the silver kitchen door swinging in her wake.

"Are you ever going to tell us what happened?" Amberlynn asked.

"Maybe not," I said. "I just don't want to even hear myself saying it all—I know it's real. I know it's over. But I just feel like such a fool about it."

"Still in the denial phase, then," my little sister quipped, sliding a tray of cookies into the oven. "Let me guess." She leaned against one of the work tables, bracing her hands behind her as she looked at me. "So it's over with you and Luke. And based on your weepy eyes and general 'poor me' attitude, I'm guessing he ended it."

Ouch.

"And . . ." She drew this word out, pulling her lip between her teeth in thought. "I'm guessing you quit your job or something, since you don't seem in a hurry to get back. Considering you haven't even visited in three years because of that job, that much is pretty clear."

Another direct hit.

"So . . ." Whatever she was going to say next was interrupted by the ringing of the shop phone, which she swung around and answered, her voice bright and cheery. "Muffin Tin."

"Oh," she said then, her eyes falling on me and then narrowing. "Yes, she's here." She held out the phone.

"Hello?" My stupid heart leapt with hope that it would be Luke, that he had finally realized what we had was valuable.

"Miss Tanner?" Not Luke said on the other end.

I slumped. "Yes, this is Addison Tanner."

The man on the other end was a lawyer for Mrs. Easter, and he asked me to meet him at his office at five but didn't explain why.

"There are Tuckers involved, I can smell it," Mom said when I told her about the call. "You should never have spoken to that Michael Tucker, Addie. I don't care how hot his ass looked in his shorts."

"Mom!" Amberlynn laughed.

I couldn't pretend I hadn't noticed. His ass did look pretty nice. And so did the rest of him, really. But Mom was right. He was a Tucker. Better to stay far, far away.

"It's probably nothing," I said, having no idea why Mrs. Easter's lawyer would want to see me. "I'll go find out and tell you later." I checked the clock over the doorway to see it was almost five now. I took off the half-apron I wore and picked up my bag. "Be back soon," I said, heading outside.

The cool fall air was a relief. Sometimes too much time with Mom was overwhelming, and I'd been with her day and night for the better part of two weeks now.

5

DON'T TRUST THE TRUST
MICHAEL

"D id you know her really well, Dad?" Daniel was full of questions as we drove from the store into Singletree Square to meet with Filene Easter's lawyer and find out what, exactly, was in this trust. Considering I hadn't spoken to her at all over the years except for a few words last week when she'd fallen, I couldn't imagine it would be much. Based on the few words she'd said—about watching me when I was a baby and everything—I did get the sense she was a little sentimental, so maybe it was some old photographs of me or something.

"No, not really."

"Maybe she left you a ton of money, and then you can get me a Corvette." he said hopefully.

"Even if I had a ton of money, you would not be getting a Corvette," I assured him. "And she didn't leave me a ton of money, I'm sure."

"Maybe she left you a Corvette." Optimism never flagged in this one.

"I never noticed her driving around town in a Corvette, Dan."

"It was probably really nice, so she kept it in a garage and only took it out on special occasions."

I smiled over at my grinning son. "And if that was the case, you're pretty sure this car is destined to be yours one way or another, huh?"

"Well, you're such a nice dad, and I know you want me to be happy."

Wasn't that the truth? "I do, buddy. And that's why I wouldn't give you a Corvette, even if I had one."

We parked near the address Anders had given me. His office, it seemed, was next door to The Shack. I hoped we wouldn't have a run-in with my ex. The last thing I needed was for Dan to tell her I'd been left a Corvette, though whatever was in this trust, I had no doubt Shelly would know about it sooner or later.

I held the glass door open for my son, and together we climbed the stairs just inside the small entryway. When we reached the landing, I was surprised to find Addison Tanner standing just outside the suite we were looking for, looking a tiny bit lost. She wore slim jeans with a longer shirt, and something about the casual but put together look appealed to me, making me hope I looked okay. I realized it was dumb—it didn't matter what this woman thought of me. That didn't stop my hand from going to my hair though, hoping it wasn't sticking up in thirty directions.

"Hi," I said. "What are you doing here?"

Maybe asking that question wasn't the right move. Her open expression shuttered, and her brows lowered over those dark sad eyes. Her mouth opened, but before she spoke, her eyes slid sideways to take in Daniel, and apparently she thought better of whatever she'd been about to say.

"I got a call from this guy, Anders about poor Mrs. Easter. I have a meeting with him at five."

"Us too," Dan volunteered.

Addison's brows rose now, and she looked between us.

"Did you knock?" I asked.

She crossed her arms. "No, is that how these door contraptions work?"

Dan grinned, but I was not going to respond to that question. I could play the sarcasm game too, but since he was here, it was my job to model good behavior. I knocked on the door. Hard. The sound of my knuckles rapping echoed around the small space at the top of the stairs.

"Thank God you were here to take care of that. Whatever would I have done?" Addison said.

I bit my tongue, but I also had to hide a smile. I liked her fire. More than I should have.

Daniel was snickering, and I poked a finger in his shoulder to shut him up. I was about to knock again when the door behind us flew open to reveal a short round man with little round glasses perched at the end of his nose.

"Well hello there," he said, looking between us. "I'm afraid Dr. Kelly goes home by five each day. No one home, as it were." He chuckled and took a step back. "Just popped out to make sure you weren't knocking on my door. I'm expecting folks." He moved to close the door, and I was relieved when Addison piped up.

"You're not Augustus Anders, by any chance?"

"Why yes, last I checked, I was indeed." He smiled and dropped his eyes, rocking a bit on his feet as if he was bashful about delivering this news.

"We're your appointment," I told him. "You said you were in Suite 2A."

"Oh, no. I'm in 2B." He pointed to the clearly marked suite number on the door. He didn't appear to be older than fifty or so, but I was starting to wonder if he might be losing a few marbles.

"I'm Addison Tanner, and this is Michael Tucker, and his . . . son?" Addie looked at me, uncertain.

"Daniel," I confirmed. "It's my week, so he had to come along."

"Sorry to be such a burden," Dan muttered.

"That isn't what I meant, and you know it," I told him. I could have phrased that better, but Dan knew how much I enjoyed having him.

Addie was smiling at him warmly, and even Daniel's surly pre-teen heart seemed to feel the effects. "Nice to meet you, Dan," she said. As my son smiled at Addison Tanner, a little twinge of admiration swelled in me for her. I liked people who spoke directly to my son instead of talking around him, like so many adults did to children.

"Well, well. Come in then," said the lawyer. "Not sure why you didn't just knock on my door." He shook his head as if in disbelief at our stupidity. This was Mrs. Easter's trusted attorney? I was becoming a little skeptical—he'd probably called the wrong people altogether. Of course Mrs. Easter did not leave anything in trust for me. She barely knew me. This guy had made a mistake—it appeared he might make them regularly.

We followed him into a small lobby and then through a door to an office with a window overlooking the square below. It was a nice view, and for a second I wondered what it would be like, to have an office job, to have chosen for myself. But as Anders settled himself behind the desk, his roly-poly physique propping him in his cushioned chair, I realized that a little hard work was probably good for me.

"Sit please," he said, motioning to the chairs. Addison, Dan and I sat down. Addison seemed nervous, her hands fidgeting in her lap.

"As you know then, we are here to discuss the trust set up for the two of you by Mrs. Filene Easter," he began.

A noise of surprise escaped Addison before she turned to give me a wide-eyed look, confusion clear on her face, "What?"

"Yes, yes," the lawyer said, waving away this interruption.

"Wait," Addison said, leaning forward and dropping a hand on the edge of his desk. "This is about Mrs. Easter? A trust?"

He looked at her as if she were a curiosity, something he hadn't encountered before, blinking his big eyes behind the lenses of his glasses. "Why yes, didn't I mention that on the phone?"

"Yes," I said, at the same exact moment that Addison said, "No, you definitely did not."

Then she slumped back in her chair, one hand resting over her mouth as if she could contain whatever sorrow might fly out. "Oh, poor Mrs. Easter. But a trust? Why would she leave anything to us?"

"Filene was ninety-three years old," the lawyer said. "Natural causes, Ms. Tanner. Nothing to worry about."

Addison nodded, still looking sad. I had felt a little down on hearing the news too, but the guy had a point. Ninety-three wasn't exactly a shocking age at which to die. Only, she had seemed pretty spry last week.

"May I continue?" The lawyer looked between us. Suddenly Anders looked like a guy who had thirty clients waiting in the lobby and no time for this type of interruption.

"Sure," Dan said, clearly eager to hear about the Corvettes coming our way.

"Mrs. Easter visited me just last Monday to set up this trust," Anders said. "Very strange, really. She'd had no direct descendants, so had previously had plans to disburse her belongings to various charitable organizations—the Institute for Tasteful Taxidermy, the Chocolate Lab Rescue of Southern Maryland, and the like.

"However, last week she popped by and made a significant

change to her final wishes, and that's what I'd like to discuss with you now." He looked up at us as if waiting for permission.

"Ah, okay?" I tried.

"Yeah, I guess," Addison said.

Dan was practically bouncing in his chair. "Settle," I whispered, and he stilled.

I hated myself for it, but the idea of having some unexpected cash to put toward the business wasn't a completely unwelcome idea. I needed to build some extra space to house the growing custom furniture selection, and I knew if I could merchandise it correctly, I just might be able to shift the focus of the business. Farm supplies weren't really my passion, but seeing the furniture I'd made by hand heading out the door to sit in people's homes? That was what I wanted.

"Ahem." Augustus cleared his throat and began to read. "This document represents the statement of the trust of Filene Josephine Tucker Easter."

Addison let out an audible gasp beside me. "Mrs. Easter was a Tucker?"

The lawyer looked up, his eyebrows disappearing beneath the brim of the little hat he wore. "Mrs. Easter's mother was a Tanner, but her father was a Tucker. And when she married, her name changed to Easter."

I wasn't sure Augustus understood why this news was so surprising to both of us, but figured maybe his impartiality in the age-old feud was what made him a good choice of attorney. The news was surprising to me too, though, and it gave me a new way to look at the strange things Mrs. Easter had said that day—about Addison and me, about the feud needing to end. Had she decided to end the feud herself? Was that what this was all about?

He continued reading, covering all the legal information,

discussed Mrs. Easter's lack of direct descendants, and then came the interesting part.

"This trust passes down my worldly goods, including the house at 54 Maple Lane and all of its contents, to Addison Agnes Tanner and Michael Joseph Tucker jointly."

I felt my whole body go still. She'd left us a house? An entire house? Together? I shook my head in disbelief. Why? And what the hell were we supposed to do with it?

"The house, as it stands, requires improvements before it can be sold."

That was an understatement. I thought of the old house behind the iron gates, the way the front porch sagged and the darkened windows sat cracked and eerie in the shadows of over-grown trees. Still, it was a big house, undoubtedly valuable. I could do a lot of the work myself and then sell the place to fund my store expansion. I didn't like to capitalize on someone's death, but this could be exactly what I needed.

The lawyer went on, ". . . and neither party named in this document may begin efforts to sell the property or its contents until such time as both have resided in the home for a minimum of six months."

My eager thoughts crashed into a solid brick wall. What? She wanted us to live in the house? For six months each? Why?

"Once both parties have lived at 54 Maple Lane for six months or more, either separately or concurrently, and the required improvements have been made (see inclusion one for an itemized list of required and suggested repairs), then the house may be sold through whatever means the parties named herein deem appropriate, if that is their desire."

I stared at the lawyer as Dan bounced at my side. Addison must have been just as shocked, because she wasn't moving either.

Augustus put the document down and looked at us expectantly.

Addie's mouth opened, but she didn't say anything immediately, and I had no idea what to say. It made no sense at all. Of course we couldn't jointly own and sell a house. We didn't even know each other. Not to mention the underlying fact that we kind of hated one another.

"Wait," Daniel said, rising to his feet and leaning over the desk. "She gave them her house? Together? That's so weird. Isn't that pretty weird? You're a lawyer. Is that normal will stuff? To tell people they have to live together?" Daniel's words were coming fast in his excitement and amusement, and the attorney kept trying to begin answering as Daniel kept forming new queries.

"Dan," I whispered, and my son stopped talking.

"It's unusual, yes," Augustus said. "But not unheard of. And she doesn't stipulate that you must both live in the house at the same time, exactly," he pointed out.

Relief washed through me. Right. We didn't have to live together. Why was part of me a little disappointed?

"But we have to live there for six months to sell it?" Addison asked.

"Correct. Or a full year if you do not live there concurrently."

"Together," Addison clarified.

"Yes."

She looked at me then, as if evaluating my potential as a roommate. I stiffened. Why was some part of me wishing she'd decide that she did want to live with me? I definitely didn't want to live with her.

"And this house," I began, already knowing the answer. "54 Maple Lane . . ."

"Oh, man," Daniel breathed, a chuckle beneath the words. "That's the haunted house in the middle of town!" Daniel laughed out loud now, rubbing his hands together with excitement. "You guys own the haunted house! That place is so creepy!"

"That's enough," I said, making my voice stern and hard, and then regretting being harsh with him. This was a lot for all of us to process.

Dan sat back down, but a second later he was speaking again. "And doesn't it say anything in there about a car?"

I elbowed him in the ribs, but Anders dropped his head back down to examine the document. "Oh, yes, you're right young man. There is a car. Part of the property."

Dan's head whipped around to look at me, excitement in his wide eyes. I tried to give him a stern parental look. We'd discuss Corvettes later.

For a moment, no one said anything. Then Addison stood. "Why would Mrs. Easter leave her house to us?" she asked. "It doesn't make sense."

The attorney sat back, causing his chair to emit a whining protest, and he rubbed one hand down his chin. "Filene had no children or close family. She was part of both the Tanner and Tucker families, so perhaps this decision felt like the right thing. Keeping the property inside the family."

I shook my head. "Do you think she knew what she was doing? Giving something so big to both families? These particular families?"

"I assure you, she was quite lucid when we last spoke. Mrs. Easter was not suffering dementia."

"I just don't get it," Addison said, sitting back down.

"There's one other thing here," the lawyer said, picking up the document and reading again. "A sum of two-hundred and fifty thousand dollars will convey with the house, to be used for the express purpose of enacting the repairs needed. This account is at the Singletree Credit Union and carries the names of both parties named herein. In the event the parties do not accept dispensation of the house and the sum, both shall be donated to the Singletree Historical Society with specific contents to be given to the Institute for Tasteful Taxidermy and the Chocolate Lab Rescue."

I let out a whistle, long and low. That was a shit-ton of money.

"Would you like to dispute the trust?" Augustus asked.

For the first time since his pronouncement, Addie turned to face me, and as our eyes met. Something inside me wished fervently for her to say no. I didn't understand why, but having Addison tied into something with me, even something this odd, gave me an unbidden sense of hope. Like I'd turned a corner in my life somehow.

But that was crazy. It had to be about the house, the money, the way it could change my life.

"I mean . . ." She said, trailing off.

"Maybe we should at least go see the house?" I suggested, looking for a way to prevent her rejecting this insane idea immediately. I was already envisioning the new addition to the store, my improved workshop, my furniture on display.

Her face cleared, the troubled furrow disappearing from between her brows. "Yes," she turned back to Augustus. "Can we see the house?"

"Of course," he said. "The house is yours," he explained. He dug around in his pocket for a set of keys, leaned down to unlock a drawer in his desk, and pulled out a flat plastic bag. "In here is the deed, with both your names on it here"—he pointed to the line that listed our names—"and these are the keys." My name was there, next to Addison's on the deed to the house. It was surreal. Two sets of dark iron keys lay next to the document. "A little old fashioned maybe. Fitting, I'd say."

"Great," Addie said, reaching out for a set of keys. "Can you hold the deed for a bit? Maybe until we've had a chance to think? And talk." She looked at me as she said this last part, and a warm thrill rose in my throat.

What a weird day.

"Let's go check out the haunted house!" Daniel practically yelled, bounding to the door. "This is awesome."

We headed back outside and without deciding out loud, the three of us began walking toward the end of the town center, where 54 Maple Lane sat dark and foreboding behind its iron gates on the hill.

6

'EFFIN CREEPY

ADDISON

We walked together past the town square and up the hill that led to 54 Maple Street. As we got closer to the dilapidated iron gates that stood sheltered under the heavy drapery of neglected trees, I could see the old house standing beyond, quiet and still in the midst of the old overgrown property.

A strange little thrill went through me as I turned over the idea that this was my house. I'd thought I had a house in New York—an apartment, actually—but it had never really been mine. It had been Luke's, and he'd decided to sell it without even consulting me. As a newly homeless individual, owning a house, even a dilapidated creepy house, was a big deal. But still, none of this made any sense at all. And I didn't know the first thing about home improvement. Michael didn't seem hesitant though.

The house was a Victorian, with a turret and a sweep of front porch that made me wish I could remember it better from my childhood. Today, it was gray and sad looking, with dark windows—some of which held cracked glass—and an eerie still-ness hanging around it.

I didn't remember ever being inside, though Mom said that I had spent a summer here when she opened The Muffin Tin— that Mrs. Easter had watched me and a few other kids from town. Including Michael. Mom said the house was somewhat dilapidated even then, and that Mrs. Easter moved out right after that summer, taking a smaller cottage in town. And since then, this place had sat empty—thirty years of neglect, and probably many more before that. There was no way a woman on her own—especially one in her sixties as Mrs. Easter would have been then—could handle all the maintenance required by a place like this.

Owning a home was something I'd imagined lots of times. But in none of my fantasies did the house sit, dark and foreboding, up on an overgrown hill behind a set of iron gates, and neither did my fantasy include any members of the Tucker clan. Luke, maybe. Although I was coming to see that there had been a lot of red flags in my relationship with Luke, and we were probably never headed in the direction of joint home owner-ship. Not really.

"Wow," I heard myself breathe as we stood outside the gates, looking into the vine-covered yard.

"Yeah," Michael said behind me. His voice was low, almost trepidatious.

Daniel, on the other hand, was practically giddy. "Let me see that key, Dad."

As the boy fit the huge iron key into the rusty lock on the gate, Michael and I stared up at the old house, side by side. Having him at my shoulder made me feel a little better about approaching the house I'd thought of for so long as haunted and foreboding. Even if he was a Tucker, Michael was sturdy and strong. He wouldn't let anything happen to us, and especially to his son. I wasn't really scared, but I figured it wouldn't hurt to stay close to Dan as we checked out the place.

The house had been beautiful once, I could see that much. Three stories rose up from what might have once been lovingly tended gardens and a manicured lawn. The paint appeared a weathered and peeling grey now, but it might once have been lavender, with white trim and sage accents. The huge porch that spanned the front and one side of the house was grand, I thought, and I could almost imagine early townspeople resting there in rocking chairs, fanning themselves against the humid Maryland summers.

Daniel worked the lock, and after a moment, the gate opened inward with a groan I felt inside my bones.

What were we doing? Was this really ours?

Walking across the overgrown lawn of the house I'd always thought of as haunted felt a lot like trespassing, or tempting fate, at least. As we wound our way up what had once been a flagstone path to the front steps, the sun slipped behind gray clouds overhead and a distant rumble of thunder rolled in warning.

"Shit," Michael breathed, and his voice was so low, I wondered if he'd meant to speak out loud.

"Dude," Daniel practically sang with glee. "This is so effin' creepy!"

"Language," came Michael's stern reply.

"Dad, I said—"

"We heard you. I don't want to hear it again."

I smiled, despite the creepy ambiance. Michael was clearly a good dad, and Daniel obviously respected him. I envied them a little. Like home ownership, I had kind of thought I was destined for parenthood at some point. I didn't think people left children in trusts though, so my chances were probably pretty slim.

You could almost hear Dan's eye roll at his dad's reprimand, but he was too busy creeping his way up the front steps, wisely testing each to see if it might be rotted, to reply.

"You think this place is safe?" I asked, eyeing a hole in one of the risers skeptically. It was so shadowed beneath the overhang of the broad front porch that it was dark as night. I glanced back toward the iron gates behind us, part of me longing for the sunlight and open spaces of the town that felt centuries away now. A little chill ran through me.

"Wouldn't they have had to check it before she could pass it on? Make sure it shouldn't be condemned instead?" Michael asked.

I thought about that. He was probably right, it must be at least structurally safe. But could I actually live here? I was scared just standing on the front porch—I'd always been a little on the jumpy side. I did not see myself living here for six months just to sell the place. Though it would be a relief to get out of my mother's house. I loved her, but Lottie Tanner had a way of suffocating people with attention. It was one of the reasons I'd gone to New York in the first place.

But my life in New York seemed to be over for now. Since Luke had sold the apartment, I was homeless, and though I had a bit of money saved up, it wasn't enough to buy a place, or even put down the deposit on a rental.

We stepped carefully across the dusty old porch, which was scattered with pine needles and fallen leaves from the trees that grew dense around the upper floors of the house.

"Ready?" Daniel asked us, key poised in the lock of the enormous front door.

An ominous dread swept through me, and something made me swing my gaze to the front window. As soon as my eyes hit the darkened glass, I thought I saw something move just behind it, but it was so shadowy and dim it was impossible to tell. "Did you see that?" I asked Michael, my voice a whisper now.

He looked at me, his eyebrows drawn low over those blue eyes, and then turned to follow my gaze to the window. "Oh yeah, the crack there? That's leaded glass, too. It'd be expensive to replace."

I decided not to let him in on my paranoia and nodded my head. Yeah, that's right. I was talking about the cost of repairs. Not the creepy thing I saw move in the window of our new house. Our hundred and fifty year old haunted new house.

"Go ahead, Dan." Michael put a hand on his son's shoulder.

The lock turned and Daniel gripped the handle, pushing the front door open with a low grinding sound as the bottom of the door departed the debris-strewn threshold.

"Holy," came Dan's voice as he stepped inside.

The entryway was a wide low space, with a stairway at one side just past a door, a long hallway extending before us, and a fireplace on the other wall. The old wood floor was covered in dried leaves and dirt, and the walls were dingy and smeared. Still, you could see the grandeur beneath—the high dark wood moldings, the built-in bench that might have held visitors as they removed outer things and came to warm their hands at the entry fire.

"Who puts a fireplace by the front door?" Daniel asked, shaking his head as if those old Victorians were just too stupid for words.

"I guess they wanted to give guests a warm welcome," Michael said, grinning.

Dad jokes. Huh. I smiled at Michael behind his son's shaking head. I hadn't heard one in a long time, and something about the boy's feigned disgust at the corny joke was charming. They were cute together, this man and his son. And despite the tension that I figured was natural whenever a pre-teen was in that stretch for independence while still under the guiding thumb of a parent, I could tell there was a deep fierce affection between them.

A tiny spark of excitement filled me as I gazed around me.

I'd always loved old houses, and especially loved seeing them decorated and shined up. I collected design magazines and had even fancied myself a bit of a decorator, though Luke had taken charge of decorating our New York place. And his taste, if you asked me, was essentially non-existent. He mixed centuries and styles, creating a mess that he referred to as eclectic. For a split second, before I recognized that the entire idea was ludicrous, I imagined myself getting to decorate this house. But I was not going to go through with this. It was crazy.

We turned right, into the room that occupied the rounded sweep of the turret we'd seen from the front. Another fireplace sat in this room, and though there was a terrible jagged hole in one wall, the space was charming. I could picture it repaired and glowing with a warm fire, someone wrapped up on the couch, sipping tea by those big windows.

"The parlor?" Michael mused.

Wallpaper hung from the wall in tatters, and one low upholstered chaise sat in the middle of the room. There was a wooden door at the back of this room that hung at a diagonal —meant to slide into the wall around it to reveal a dining room behind. We walked through, each of us quietly gazing around us. Something about the air was thick and heavy, and whatever it was forestalled conversation or commentary for now. The sun seemed to have come back out, and light streamed in through high windows on one side of the room. A massive dining table sat in the center of the space, no chairs around it.

As we entered the space, a long low screeching whine came from the back of the house, and my heart gunned out a machine-gun rhythm as my breath caught in my throat. I turned my head in the direction of the sound.

"What was that?" I asked, unable to keep the fear from my voice as the sun fizzled again outside. There was something very eerie and ghostly inside this house. I decided I absolutely wouldn't want to be here alone.

I followed Michael through the side door and back into the entry hallway, one hand on his arm. I didn't know the man, and he probably hated me, but holding onto something strong was my only option for not freaking out completely, and his arm felt solid and strong under my touch. He didn't say anything about it, and I tightened my grip.

The kitchen lay just behind the dining room, a long space with a broad work table in its center, a hefty chandelier dangling just above it. The stove sat on one wall, cast iron and sturdy, and it was flanked by built in cabinetry. One corner held a small table with benches built into the walls behind it, and a back door led into a utility room with a pantry to one side that held floor to ceiling shelving with a collection of old canned goods still waiting for someone to pick one up. My heart twisted a bit —this space would be amazing if we could modernize it but hang on to the Victorian charm. I knew exactly how I'd do it— antique copper tile on the ceiling, shiny subway tile for the backsplash and a huge apron front farm sink beneath the window.

The current sink sat beneath the window in the kitchen, and Michael went over to investigate the drip coming steadily from the spout. I released his arm, and warmth spread through me when Daniel took my other arm in its place. He gave me a reassuring smile. What a nice kid.

Michael turned the cold water handle once, and a low steady groan came from the pipes, making me shiver. The sound was not the same as the screeching we'd heard. But I was willing to believe that had been the noise. Because otherwise . . . I didn't want to consider it.

"This needs some attention. Air trapped in the pipes probably," he said, twisting the handle back the other way to turn the water off.

"I think the whole place needs attention," I said.

"Upstairs?" Michael asked.

I nodded, and Daniel dropped my arm and led the way as we passed through a sitting room on our way back to the stairs. I glanced at the window where I'd seen something move earlier, but there was nothing there now. A harsh breath escaped me, but it wasn't relief. I'd definitely seen something.

Upstairs we found four bedrooms and a single bathroom, along with a creepy staircase inside a closet that Michael said probably went up to the attic. I opted not to climb it, and Michael talked Daniel out of it.

"We can do it next time," he said.

A little jolt went through me. Next time? So he was planning to go through with this? There was part of me that was thinking of the place as mine too, but I didn't think the terms of the trust were going to work. No one could possibly live here. Could they? And I needed to make a plan to get back to New York. At the moment I'd thought I could work for Mom for a few weeks until I didn't feel quite so desperate, and then maybe she could give me a loan for the apartment. Of course, if we did fix this place up and sell it, I wouldn't need a loan. And I'd have enough to replenish the savings account that Luke had slowly squandered over our time together.

But this house. Yikes.

We spent a little time in the master bedroom, admiring the rounded sitting area inside the turret. The windows looked down over the gardens outside, and I could already imagine the little sitting area I'd make there, the overstuffed chair with its comfy throw, the ottoman. The room was better kept than the rest of the house, and I had a strange sensation there of invading someone's privacy, of being in a space where I hadn't been invited. Had Mrs. Easter slept in this room? Or did I feel the lingering presence of someone much older? I shivered.

Finally, we let ourselves back out onto the porch, and I took in the huge sprawl of overgrown yard. We descended the steps and wandered through the weed-filled garden and I imagined it trimmed and well kempt. It could be beautiful. Maybe if Michael worried about the structural things inside the house, I could fix up the garden. There was a wrought iron bench at one edge of the space that was pretty clear, so we sat for a moment, Michael and me side by side as Daniel prowled the yard. It was strange in a way—we'd just sat down side by side as if it was the most natural thing in the world. And now, with Michael next to me, sitting so close, I had warring emotions suddenly bouncing around inside me. I hated him. He was a Tucker and that was what I'd been taught to do. But really, I didn't hate him at all. I actually felt myself drawn to him, to his confidence, his warm but firm guidance of his son.

"This is weird, right?" Michael said, one hand rubbing the stubble at his chin as he turned to look at me.

I let my gaze trace his face—the cleft in his chin, the strong jaw, the hesitant smile—before landing on his deep blue eyes. "I think that's a pretty significant understatement."

"What do you think we should do? I mean . . ."

"Neither one of us planned for inheriting a worn-down house. Together."

"Yeah," he chuckled. "So we could sell it, I guess."

"Except for that stipulation about having to live in it." I shook my head. I couldn't imagine living here. I'd never sleep. I'd lie there at night, waiting for whatever spectral thing lived there now to come whisper "red rum" in my ear or for Freddy to appear in my dreams as soon as I drifted off. This place was a horror movie waiting to happen.

"It's probably worth some money though, to the right

buyer." I could hear him considering it, his voice slow and thoughtful. He didn't seem to be thinking about axe murderers or ghosts.

"Right, but . . . It needs a lot of work."

He nodded. "If I live here for a bit and fix some things up, maybe you could move in second, and then, after a year we could sell."

I couldn't imagine what I'd be doing next month, but I knew that in a year I was not going to be living in this creepy old house alone just so we could sell it. If I was going to collect whatever we could get out of this place, it would have to be as quickly as possible. And there was no way I could live with Mom for another six months. I'd lose my mind while gaining thirty pounds in muffin fat. "I don't think that will work. I'm not staying that long."

"Oh, right, sure." He sounded disappointed, his gaze moving to the dark edges of the yard. "You have to get back to . . ."

"New York. Work. My actual life." Although not much of my actual life still existed. At least not the man, or the place to live. I wasn't totally sure about my job.

"Right. Of course."

We sat in silence for a long minute, each of us lost in thought. It was strangely quiet here, considering how near to the town center we really were. If the garden hadn't been so lush or the vines so thick, I probably could have seen Mom's cafe from where we sat—we were a straight shot down the hill to the square.

"Well, I guess we can go back and talk to Augustus, see what our other options are," Michael said, standing.

I stood too, confused as a stab of disappointment winged through me.

"Daniel!" he called, taking a few steps back toward the gate.

No answer came.

"Daniel!" he called out again, an edge of something a little more urgent in his voice.

We were met by silence, thick and heavy, all around us.

"Shit," Michael said, and without speaking, we went in opposite directions, searching the masses of greenery around us for his son.

7

GNOMES IN THE GARDEN
MICHAEL

In the long list of crap I'd screwed up in my life, even I realized that losing my son on the grounds of a dangerously run-down and potentially haunted house was going to be up there. Shelly would have a field day with this one—she was usually the less responsible parent, and she loved any opportunity to point out one of my failings.

"Daniel!" I called his name as I circled the house, wading through a decrepit rose garden, past a cellar door (locked) and across a weedy patio out back, where I ran into Addison again. Her wide eyes and worried expression told me she hadn't found my son on her half of the search either.

"Daniel!" I shouted again, a twinge of desperation edging my voice. "Where the hell could he have gone?" I asked.

Addison shook her head, and we both turned back to face the house. The kitchen door stood ajar, as if beckoning to us, and without speaking, we went back inside. Had we come out that way? Did we leave it open? I hoped Daniel was inside, though there was plenty in the run-down house to worry about.

The house was like a different world. The second we crossed the threshold, the atmosphere around me took on a dampened feeling, rich with the whispers of memory and decaying things, dust and layers of time. It felt wrong to disturb it all by yelling inside the house, but I was increasingly worried about my son.

"Dan!" I called out, moving back to the bottom of the big staircase.

"Upstairs!" His voice came back, sending my heart galloping with relief, and Addison and I exchanged wide-eyed expressions before heading back up the stairs, sending little clouds of dust swirling at our feet.

On the second floor, I could hear creaking from the ceiling over the master bedroom, and I realized exactly where he'd gone. Telling Daniel no, or we'll look later, had never been especially effective. He was an impulsive, live-for-the-moment kind of kid, and he usually found ways to get what he wanted. He was in the attic. Anger threatened, but it was shadowed by the relief I felt to hear Dan's voice, to know he was okay. We'd need to chat about disobeying directions.

"Upstairs," I shrugged, opening the closet door and eyeing the narrow stairs skeptically. "You coming?"

"Sure," Addison said, sounding less than sure. I didn't blame her. The whole house was creepy, but the narrow stairway-in-a-closet was creepy times ten.

"You go first," I said, trying to be chivalrous.

She narrowed her eyes at me, as if maybe sending her up first was some kind of grand Tucker plan of mine, but after a second she seemed to realize I was just trying to be a gentleman.

Of course a true gentleman wouldn't ogle her ass as she climbed the narrow risers just ahead of me. But it was impossible not to. She wore jeans that hugged her curves perfectly, and climbing stairs put it all right at eye level. Her ass was round and tight, swaying back and forth as she climbed, and I had to work pretty damned hard not to focus on the very inappropriate thoughts racing through my mind at the sight of it.

Once she'd reached the top and stepped out into the attic, I heard Daniel's voice. "Look at this."

A second later, I moved into the tight narrow space with them. The attic was a long wood-planked room with sloping ceilings and a lot of stuff sitting around in piles here and there. A bookcase stood at one end, stuffed with shoe boxes. A couple of trunks that looked like they might have been brought from another continent via ocean liner sat at the other end. In between there was an ancient sewing machine table and stool next to some kind of mannequin thing, a record player with the big horn part I'd never exactly understood or seen up close in real life, and a collection of garden pots scattered across the floor, some of them broken. There were scatters of dirt and leaves up here too, as if a window had been broken at some point, but they all appeared intact now. I sighed. This was one more part of the house that was going to need work.

Daniel crouched on the ground, holding something in his lap and rubbing it with one hand, pushing dirt from the surface. "Check it out, Dad." He held up the object, and I realized it was a garden gnome, but it was pretty far from the cute kind with the little rosy cheeks and brightly colored coat. This one had an expression on its pointed face that could only be described as menacing, despite the smile. The little creature was hunched and its hands were crafted to appear as if they were rubbing one another. The thing looked like it was plotting, and it gave me a very creepy feeling.

"Uh, let's just leave that where you found it."

"No way, this is Thaddius," Daniel said, holding the hideous thing up for us to see. "He's coming home with me."

I exchanged a look with Addison, whose nose was adorably wrinkled. A little stirring of warmth rushed through me at her expression, and I had to stomp it down. This—if it was anything —was a business arrangement at best, with someone I didn't actually like much. No warm fluttery feelings just because she had a nice butt and a cute nose and seemed charmed by my kid.

"Thaddius?" Addison asked. "How do you know?"

"Just a feeling," Daniel said, and I'll be honest. That creeped me right the fuck out.

"Let's get going," I suggested, casting glances around the rapidly dimming space. "It's getting dark."

I didn't say anything else as Daniel descended the stairs, the evil gnome in his arms, but I had a feeling I couldn't quite shake —like the house had an opinion of us, of what we'd done here, what we'd said. Like maybe if we stayed here any longer as the place was subsumed by evening shadow, it might share its opinions with us—and I didn't want that.

Addison pressed a button on the wall in the room that held the attic stairs—the light switches were all the old two button kind—but it didn't do anything.

"We'll get the power back on," I mumbled, heading for the stairway with a bit more focus and speed than that with which we'd initially explored. I didn't think any of us wanted to be here after dark.

When we finally stood on the sidewalk once again, outside the gates of the big house, we all paused, looking back.

"Did you see the garage, Dad? We didn't get a chance to look inside." Daniel's voice was colored with the kind of hope only a kid that age can hang onto.

"I don't think Mrs. Easter had a Corvette, kid," I told him. I felt like I would have remembered Mrs. Easter zipping around town in a sports car.

Addison laughed. "The lawyer said there is a car in there though."

"We'll save that surprise for another day," I suggested. I was curious, but it was almost full dark in the wild jungle of a yard, and I didn't want to risk anyone tripping into poison ivy or falling over Thaddius's abandoned evil sister out there.

"So . . ." Addison trailed off, her eyes studying my face in a way that sent a self-conscious wave through me. "Are you really considering doing this?"

I sighed. This was the most interesting thing that had happened to me in about twelve years, and selling this place would generate money that would allow me to finally have the means to pursue the tiny dream I'd been holding onto. I would expand the store, sell things that mattered to me, things I'd made.

"Yeah, I'd like to."

Daniel let out a whoop and lifted the hideous Thaddius up in the air. I shot him a look, worried he might be too excited too soon. There was a lot to figure out.

"You up for it?" I wanted her to say yes. We'd work out the details later—including how members of two feuding families could renovate a huge old house without killing each other.

Addison looked uncertain, and glanced between me, Daniel and the old house. "I don't know," she said. "Can I sleep on it?"

"Yeah, of course."

We walked back to the square slowly, and I had the sense we were all lost in our thoughts. Except Thaddius, whose expression suggested his thoughts were pure evil. I shuddered and insisted Daniel put him in the trunk on the way home.

8

SISTERLY SARCASM
ADDISON

I didn't want to discuss the house with my mother. She would have four million ideas and thoughts and emotions she would insist on sharing, and I had too many of my own to handle at the moment. And so after I said goodbye to Michael and Daniel in the square, I pulled my phone out of my pocket and called my sister Paige instead. I needed to talk to someone.

"Hey," I said, my eyes lingering on the darkened Muffin Tin across the square. I wrapped my free arm around myself and shivered. Fall had definitely arrived even though it was only the beginning of September. "You guys busy tonight?"

"No, actually. The girls are running around with the dogs and I'm just sitting here having a drink with Cormac."

"Oh," I said, immediately feeling like an intruder. Compared to my planned evening of avoiding Lottie and maybe watching *Upload* or *Younger* again on my laptop, Paige did sound pretty busy.

"Come over for a drink?" she suggested.

"I really don't want to intrude." I totally wanted to intrude. And I needed to talk to someone rational. But Paige and Cormac were the illustration of everything I wished I had, and getting an up-close view of the life I thought I'd been heading for with Luke—but clearly had missed by miles—might be a little hard to take. Still, I couldn't avoid going over to see Paige the whole time I was here just because she had a family I envied. I swallowed hard. "But I'd love to," I added.

"Good! Come whenever. It's open. We're out back." I hung up, relieved. I had somewhere to go, for now, and someone to bounce this off. I thrived on having a plan. A car would have been nice too.

Living in New York City for years meant I'd lived without things most people took for granted. A car, for instance. And while my mother was generous with her aging Toyota, she'd left the bakery and driven it home already. I hugged myself a little tighter and set out for Paige's place. The nice thing about a very small town, I guessed, was that nothing was ever too far away. Depending on what the "thing" was. We didn't have a lot of the big stores and restaurants in Singletree that other places had. We weren't really a suburb of anything, so the town was really a self-contained collection of smaller versions of all the things people near bigger cities were used to. And while it was quiet and quaint, I missed a restaurant on every corner, a bodega around the block, and I missed my old life.

Anger flared in me as I thought again about how my old life had come to a screeching halt. It hadn't been much of a life after all, I guessed. More of an illusion. The thought left me cold and tired, and I felt more thankful than before that I was about to see someone who loved me.

An early fall breeze was picking up as I walked and the streets were nearly dark by the time I reached Paige's door. I didn't bother knocking, but let myself into the sweet little cottage and tried hard to avert my gaze from all the signs of Paige's perfect family life as I made my way back to the patio. The two pairs of little galoshes lined up by the door. The kid-sized armchairs positioned next to the couch. The life-sized kangaroo standing in the corner of the living room. Wait, the—?

I screamed, and that brought a furious round of barking and scrabbling as the the dogs raced inside to see what the noise was about. They were followed by a tall, dark-haired man with friendly eyes and a worried expression on his face who found me still standing face to face with a very large marsupial.

"Hey, Addie," Cormac said, looking me up and down as if he might be able to figure out why I'd walked into my sister's house and screamed. The dogs were leaping around me now, and I felt like I'd activated a circus. "Settle down, Luke. Bobo, quit it." Both dogs quit jumping and exchanged a look, as if agreeing that they would resume immediately if the moment seemed to call for it again. They sauntered back outside. "You okay?" Cormac asked me.

My heart was racing and it took me a second to answer. Maybe exploring the haunted house had put my nerves a little on edge. "I hadn't expected the six-foot kangaroo in the corner is all." Or for Paige's dog to be named after my ex.

"That's Frederick. He's friendly."

"Sure." I gave the huge thing another once-over, wondering if Cormac was the cause of Paige's deteriorating decorating skills or if there was something about enormous taxidermy I just couldn't appreciate. Was this something Joanna Gaines was into now? I needed to watch more television.

"Hey you!" Paige called as I stepped out to the patio.

"Hey," I returned, my eyes falling on the two little girls in fairy dresses twirling on the lawn with what looked like electric sparklers. Wands, I realized. They had wands. In the gloaming light with the dusky night settling around us, the girls really did look like little fairies, and their sweet laughter floated on the breeze and made tears prick at my eyes for some reason. "Hey," I said again quietly as Paige stood to hug me.

"You okay?" She held me out by my upper arms, frowning at me. "What's going on? Wait, wine first."

"I'm on it," Cormac said, turning back around and heading into the house.

"Everything okay, Ads? Do I need to get rid of the man so we can talk?"

We sank into chairs side by side. "No, he can stay. I do need to talk though. It's not exactly girl stuff. It's more, just ... "

Paige angled her chair toward me, but at the same moment, the little girls seemed to realize they had company, and the tiny one came scooting over, fairy wings fluttering behind her as she approached. She dropped a still-pudgy hand on Paige's knee as she regarded me through huge blue eyes. "Maddie, this is my sister, Addison."

"I have a sister," the little girl told me, her voice earnest and strong.

"Is that her?" I asked, pointing at the older girl, leaping across the lawn.

"Yes. Taylor."

"You are both very pretty fairies," I told the little girl, my heart squeezing painfully as she smiled with pride.

Cormac reappeared with three glasses of wine, and as he handed me one he said, "Do you need your sister alone for a bit? I can take the girls in for a bath."

I shook my head. "No, actually. I could use as many rational adult opinions on this as I can get."

His eyebrows rose, but he sat and pulled a chair closer.

I told them about my very strange day, beginning with the part Paige already knew about Mrs. Easter's fall in the street last week.

"I can't believe she's gone," Paige said, and I knew her doctor brain was working through what she might have missed, trying to figure out if there was something she could have done.

"The lawyer assured us it was natural," I told her. "In her sleep. Totally peaceful."

Paige nodded, her eyes sad.

"So a house, huh?" Cormac said, his head angled to one side. "That's crazy. And the money too."

"And you can't just, like, sell the house and take the money?" Paige asked.

"It's all tied up together. And everything is built around Michael Tucker and I each spending six months living at the property."

"Ew," Paige said. "That place is so creepy. And so are the Tuckers."

"It is all creepy," I agreed. "Especially the house. Cool too though. I mean, it's one of the oldest houses in town, right? The design of the place, though—it's so pretty. It could be amazing if we could really get it solid again. I'd kill to have free rein to choose all the finishes. And there's so much history there. Up in the attic there were all these ancient trunks and a bookshelf with shoeboxes and papers stacked up. Kind of a mess, really, but I bet there's some interesting stuff in there."

"Right," Cormac said, sounding thoughtful. "But I guess what I'm wondering, is what was Mrs. Easter's purpose in throwing you and Michael Tucker together like this? She knew about the feud. Why you?"

"I'm not totally sure," I answered. "But she said something that day when we said goodbye, about it being time to end the feud. Her mother was a Tanner and her father was a Tucker—did you know that?"

Paige shook her head. "How did that even happen? It must've been like Romeo and Juliet!"

"It's kind of romantic," Cormac said, gazing fondly at my sister. By now, the little girls had come and climbed onto the arms of his Adirondack chair, and they were both watching me with open interest.

"Everyone dies in that story," Taylor, Cormac's older daughter said. "It's not romantic."

"That is an excellent point," I said, agreeing with the sage words of a child. "And nothing good can come from Tuckers and Tanners hanging out together."

"Except maybe Mrs. Easter was right," Paige said. "I mean, better you than me—I've been poisoned by proximity to Mom's constant concern that a Tucker is going to redecorate The Tin again, or steal Verda's moose."

"What do you mean, better me than you?" I asked.

"The feud is ridiculous. No one even knows why we hate Tuckers, just that we do. I mean, this isn't eighteen hundred. Let's end it already. You should totally do this—end the feud for us all by realizing that Mrs. Easter was basically matchmaking." Paige looked proud of herself for having figured this out.

Matchmaking? Had Mrs. Easter really had that in her mind when she'd put this together? I wasn't so sure. I could see her wanting to end the feud, I doubted she cared about my love life. And how did she even know either of us was single? "I don't think that's what she's doing."

"Maybe she just wanted the two sides of her family to get back together," Cormac suggested.

"That makes more sense to me," I said, letting my eyes slide shut as I thought about the house. "I could actually get excited about renovating the place, being allowed to choose all the colors and surfaces and everything. But I'm not sure at all about the moving in part."

Cormac chuckled. "Because the place is most likely haunted?"

"No," I said too quickly, thinking that my hesitation was exactly because the place was probably haunted, but I didn't want to seem like I couldn't handle a little fear. "Because it's old. And I'm used to modern conveniences."

"Wasn't your building in New York a pre-war building?" Paige piped up.

"They renovated!" I said, defending myself. "We had working toilets and showers, and no ghosts that I knew about. I'm just not sure I could live there with Michael Tucker. And if we each do six months, I have to stay here for a year before we can sell."

"The place is big, right?" Paige asked.

"Yeah, pretty big, especially compared to a New York apartment."

"Couldn't you both live there at the same time without being on top of each other? There's more than one bedroom, right?"

I nodded, thinking about sleeping with handsome Michael Tucker just down the hall. That'd be strange, wouldn't it? And Dan would be there too, because Michael had joint custody. I couldn't figure out quite how I felt about that—would I be an intruder in their family life? I didn't like that idea.

"One sec?" Cormac said, his face taking a serious cast. "How well do we know this guy? You're going to move into a house with him? Is that a good idea?"

"I mean . . . the Tuckers have been in town forever," I pointed out. "It isn't like he's a stranger. I've known him since he was a baby."

"Still," Paige said. "There's one more thing to consider. Mom will hate this."

I thought of Lottie, back in her little house, where my childhood bedroom was just waiting for me to return so it could stifle me with all the hopes and dreams I'd never fulfill under my mother's painfully sympathetic gaze. I had to get out of there either way. "Yeah. You're right," I said. "But I think I'm going to do it anyway."

MONDAY MORNING, I met Michael at the lawyer's office again. Augustus had called to find out if we had questions and to tell us he had something else for us.

"What do you suppose this will be?" I asked Michael as we met on the sidewalk outside.

"Well, it's unlikely to be as surprising as the first time we visited," he said. Michael smiled at me, and in the sun shining over the square, his hair glowed golden red and his blue eyes sparkled. He might have been a Tucker, but on a purely aesthetic level, the man was hot.

I ignored his dazzling looks and my own unbidden reaction to them and cleared my throat. "Let's go find out."

We climbed the stairs and knocked on the door to the lawyer's office, and Anders greeted us wearing the same strange round hat he'd had on the previous week.

"Hello, hello," he said, waving us in.

When we were seated, he looked between us. "You've seen the house, yes?"

"Yes," we agreed.

"Then I am bound by the terms of Mrs. Easter's last wishes to give you this." He slid an envelope across the desk to us.

The crisp white paper had our names written on it in a spindly hand, and for a moment we both stared at it.

"X-ray vision, is it?" Anders asked us, sounding a little impatient.

I glanced up at him. "What?"

"Most folks need to open an envelope to make out what's inside. But maybe you're honing your X-ray vision?"

Michael chuckled as his eyes met mine, and I ignored the warm rush of familiarity I felt as I looked at him smiling. "May I?" he asked, gesturing to the document.

I nodded and waited as he opened up what appeared to be a hand-written letter. Surely this would explain everything and give us a clear idea what we were supposed to do. Michael read out loud:

Dear Addison and Michael:

I'm sure you have convinced yourselves that I was a doddering old woman, losing my faculties. I am not, I assure you. I do feel, however, that I'm losing my grip on life and suspect you'll be reading this sooner rather than later.

At this point, you have heard my final wishes and have visited the house at Maple Lane.

You should know that house holds many fond memories for me, and for my family—which perhaps you have gleaned by now is your family too. Both of you.

I left it to you for two reasons. Number one, that house is both the root and the end of the feud between the Tanners and the Tuckers—or that's what I hope. I'll leave that last part to you two. Number two, you are the only people I could think of who also have history there—albeit short-lived—since you both spent time there as children. I hope that maybe you can see past the overgrown gardens and dusty rooms to find and restore the true beauty of my childhood home.

Finally, I believe you will enjoy the experience. The house holds ghosts between its walls, history and heartache, joy and devastation. I hope you will find something for yourselves there—your pasts, and maybe, your futures too.

Sincerely,

Your Cousin, Filene Easter

"That's it?" I asked. I wasn't sure what I'd been expecting, but the letter hadn't exactly cleared everything up.

"That's the whole letter."

"So what have you decided to do?" Anders asked. "Will you take possession of the house?"

"What happens if we don't take it?" Michael asked.

"If you don't take the house, it'll be donated to those causes Mrs. Easter designated. And as soon as it deteriorates to the point where it can be condemned, it will be demolished so the land can be sold for proceeds to divide between them."

"That sounds kind of awful," I said, imagining the grand old house being pushed over by bulldozers, the contents and history lost forever as it was turned into the soil of those lush gardens.

"Right," Michael agreed. "But you and I just walk away. So really, it wouldn't change much. The house is just sitting there rotting now anyway."

"But . . ." I trailed off, unsure what I was about to say.

"You have too much on your plate already." Michael's eyes met mine again as he suggested this, and I could see hope there. He wanted this.

I lifted a shoulder, considering his words. Did I have a lot on my plate? Not really. I did have—before . . . but now? I had almost nothing. I had Mom hovering and questioning and opining about things, I had work at the Muffin Tin, and I had the scattered rubble of my old life waiting for me to come sweep it up. "I think I want to do this," I said, surprising myself.

"You do?" Michael sounded excited, and part of me felt happy to have made him happy.

"I think I do."

9

MICE IN THE MATTRESS
MICHAEL

"You're doing what? Hell no." Shelly crossed her arms over her chest, lifted her pointy chin and gave me her entitled cheerleader stare. The one that used to intimidate the hell out of me. I'd gone to talk to her on her lunch break at The Shack on Wednesday, to tell her about our plans to move into the house.

That had gone over as expected. Like a wagon full of manure.

"It's not actually your decision," I pointed out, keeping my voice low as other people wandered past the corner of the bar where we were chatting.

"My son is not going to live in that haunted house. Did you know some teenager was murdered in there?" Her blue eyes widened with conviction.

That story had been going around since Shelly and I had been kids. It was just one of many stories told about the old house, which was the center of hundreds of ghost tales in Singletree. "That's not true, it's just a story we used to tell each other to scare ourselves."

"Daniel told me his friends knew the girl who died."

This was pure Shelly. Zero rational thought, one hundred

percent reaction. I needed to have a chat with Daniel about telling his mother stories. "It's not true, Shell. Don't you think there would have been a police investigation we would have noticed? And it's a small enough town—we would have known the family. Plus, that story has been going around since we were in school, remember?"

"It's haunted," she said defiantly.

"It might be, I guess." I didn't know that it wasn't. I suspected ghosts were not real and that the house suffered mostly from neglect rather than an infestation of otherworldly spooks.

"It's dangerous."

She might have a point on that one. "I won't let Daniel wander, and it'll be a good chance for him to learn how to fix a few things around the house." I had already thought about how Dan could help patch drywall and replace fixtures. I'd thought that part through. This was a great chance to teach Dan things, to work on a real project side by side and to grow our relationship. I was excited about it.

She sighed. "I don't like it. What's wrong with the house you have now?"

The house I had now was a two-bedroom bungalow I'd bought after things fell apart with Shelly. It was a bachelor pad for the most part. But I think Shelly liked me being there, knowing I was staying put in the remnants of the failed life I'd once had. If she couldn't move forward, she didn't want me to. Or maybe that was just me, assigning my life's failures to someone else. Either way, I was ready for a change, and this opportunity felt like an offering from a universe that had previously offered me only lost dreams.

"It's going to be fine, Shelly. I'll look out for Dan."

Her shoulders rounded, the fight leaving her. "Fine."

I sighed, turning to leave, and wished fervently that somehow things had worked out differently. For us, for Dan. For me. But these pseudo-fights with Shelly were just reminders of the mistakes of my past, the life I'd failed. And I would bear them because the only real obligation I had now was to my son. To make sure his life went a different way, that he had every opportunity I could give him.

I headed for the truck, where I'd already piled my duffle bags and the few scant pieces of furniture I thought I'd move. There had been beds in all the rooms, but I brought along an air mattress and sleeping bag for me and Dan just in case. I wasn't sure how long that furniture had been there or what kind of condition it was in, and there was a good chance the mattresses needed to go out.

Today I drove around back, to the street entrance of the property. There was a one-car garage covered in vines, and a driveway that had once been paved but was now mostly rubble. I pulled the truck in, and shut off the engine, peering through the overgrown trees up at the old house, standing silent against a blaze of bright blue sky. A little shudder ran through me, but I wasn't sure if it was excitement or foreboding.

"Here we go," I said to myself, stepping out of the car and grabbing a couple of my bags.

I stopped to gaze through the dark windows of the little garage, but I couldn't see a thing through the dirt-streaked glass, most of which was cracked and disintegrating. Whatever vehicle sat inside was undoubtedly in as bad of shape as the rest of the garage.

It only took an hour to get my room set up inside. I had taken one of the smaller bedrooms, figuring I'd let Addie have the master, not that it was really any better. En suite bathrooms had not been a thing when this house was built, and no matter where we each slept, we'd be sharing the single bathroom in the hall upstairs. I'd managed to get the power turned on with a call after we'd seen Anders Monday, so that was a start. But the place was dusty and creepy, and there wasn't much I could do about that right away.

I was expecting Addison to arrive at any moment—she'd said Wednesday afternoon—and I thought I heard the door downstairs open a few times and then slam shut. Once I thought I'd even heard her walking around down there as I dusted the room I'd chosen for myself, but when I called down, no answer came.

That time, I'd bolted down the stairs, certain someone was in the house, but the place had been empty, the front door shut firmly. I refused to let the place creep me out, though. It was just a house. An old creaky house.

Finally, around four, I heard a car in the driveway outside, and peered out the back window to see the silver Toyota I knew Lottie drove pull up next to my truck.

Addison stepped out, her dark hair gleaming in the afternoon sun as she pushed her sunglasses to the top of her head and gazed up at the house. I wasn't sure if she could see me in the window, so I waved, but she didn't wave back.

I found myself hurrying down the stairs and out the back door, more excited than I should have been to have her here.

"Let me help you," I said as I arrived to greet her.

"I don't have much. I think I've got it." Addison pulled two suitcases from the back of the car and then shut the trunk again.

"That's it?" I asked. Part of me was a little disappointed she could come and go so easily—it might mean she wouldn't find it hard to bolt at the first sign that this house was more than she wanted to take on.

"The house is furnished." She shrugged. "I brought some clean sheets."

I'd checked out the beds while I'd been poking around. The mattresses were destroyed by whatever had been living in the house since people had cleared out. "I don't think you want to sleep on the mattresses up there."

She frowned. "Why not?"

"Mice love mattresses when people aren't around."

Addison's eyebrows shot up and her eyes filled with horror. "Mice?"

"'Fraid so."

She took a step back, like maybe that single word was going to make her change her mind about the whole plan.

"We'll catch the mice," I said, thinking of the traps I had at the store. "And don't worry about the beds. I brought an air mattress and sleeping bag," I told her. "I actually brought a second one for Dan that you can use tonight. He's sleeping over with a friend until tomorrow."

Her eyes slid from the big foreboding house to me and back again as she thought about this, a little frown line appearing between her eyes. "I don't really camp."

"Figures." The word slipped out before I thought about it—and her face darkened. I hadn't meant anything really, I was just so used to being petty when it came to Tanners that my brain was still searching for opportunities to drop little daggers.

"What is that supposed to mean?" She asked.

"Nothing, sorry. Only, that you're a city girl. Nothing about you screams I'm-the-camping type." Her frown told me I hadn't managed to make that any better at all. "Sorry," I said again.

She sighed. "I guess I can sleep on the floor for one night. I'll figure something else out tomorrow." I decided not to mention the wealth of bugs and dirt that would be joining us on the floor tonight.

"Great," I said, and as I followed her down the path next to the garage and back toward the back door of the big house, I felt an unfamiliar glimmer of hope, or maybe excitement at the prospect of a new opportunity, spring to life inside me.

10

LACK OF AIR
ADDISON

Something about the way Michael was leading me into the house—our house—was rubbing me wrong. The fact he had moved in first, had been here all afternoon doing whatever it was he'd been doing . . . it made it feel like this was his house, his project, and I was just a guest. One who had to sleep on the floor in a room inhabited by mice. Ew. But Lottie had needed a lot of convincing, and she'd demanded help with her famous pumpkin spice muffins before she'd let me go. Technically, she reminded me, I was still working at the Tin part time.

At least at the Tin there were no mice.

Living in New York City had made me pretty immune to—or at least used to—things like rodents and cockroaches. But it sure didn't mean I enjoyed sharing space with them. Still, I'd never been the squealing type unless confronted by enormous kangaroos, and I wasn't giving Michael the satisfaction of seeing me afraid.

We were partners in this insanity, and I needed it. I needed to get out of Mom's house for a bit, get some space to think, and to figure out what to do about my past life, which felt like it was standing just around the corner, waiting for me. The problem was that it was tarnished and ruined. And expensive. Very expensive. But I didn't know if I wanted it back. Everything about my life in New York had hinged on a fantasy—my belief in the love Luke and I shared. And it turned out, we'd shared that in the same way we always shared fries—I'd take one and savor it, and when I went for more, they were gone. That wasn't sharing at all.

"I guess I'll leave you to get settled?" Michael stood in the doorway of the biggest bedroom, the one with the window seat in the turret, shifting his weight from one foot to another. He had on a long-sleeved navy-blue T-shirt and dark jeans, and his ginger hair was pushed back from his face in an annoyingly perfect kind of way. He looked uncertain, though, like now that this was officially my bedroom, he'd be intruding to cross the threshold. That was fine with me.

"Yeah, I guess." I looked around. Michael had handed me the air mattress and sleeping bag, and I dropped them next to the window that overlooked the yard. "Not really that much to do. Are there projects we can start on today?" The sooner we got everything done, the sooner we could both get on with our lives. As long as it had been six months, that was.

"There are. Meet me in the dining room in a few minutes, and I'll show you the project plan I've been working on?"

He made a project plan? I wasn't sure why that bothered me, except if this was our project, if we were equal partners, then the idea that he was somehow leading the charge was annoying.

"Okay," I said, unable to keep the irritation out of my voice.

He left me then, and I stood in the center of the dusty old room and looked around. The space was nice, and it was flooded with late-afternoon light, giving it a golden glow. But it felt stale and stagnant, and smelled like ancient ammonia and old clothes. Not dirty, but not clean. Just . . . old. And not quite empty, either.

Maybe it was the old sleigh bed pushed against the wall, its rolling headboard standing strong in contrast to the wallpaper tattering around it, but it felt like someone else's space. Like I was an intruder. It made me shiver slightly, so I busied myself rolling out the air mattress and putting the sleeping bag on top of it.

"This is the flattest air mattress I've ever seen," I grumbled. The thing was anemic, flattened and thin. I looked for a spout to blow into, but didn't find one. There was some kind of doodad on the corner, a plastic protrusion, but its use was not obvious. I tried blowing into it, but it did nothing. "Great. This one's broken." I glanced back toward the door, not especially wanting to look helpless or needy in front of Michael Tucker.

I sighed, and smoothed the sleeping bag on top of it. It was going to be a long night. Glancing back at the bed, I wondered how horrible it would really be to sleep on mouse-eaten foam rubber or cotton. Maybe I could just sneak back to Mom's for the night. But I didn't want to explain that to her or to Michael. And not sleeping in the house wasn't really living in it, and probably wouldn't fulfill the terms of the trust. Anders had promised he'd be by now and then per the terms to check on us.

One night wouldn't kill me. I'd figure something out for tomorrow. brushed my hands on the legs of my jeans and headed downstairs to meet Michael.

He was sitting at the dining room table, a laptop open in front of him, and an empty chair pulled to his side.

"Hey," he said, looking uncertain as I stepped into the room. "Will you come take a look at the plan I put together?"

I bit my tongue, feeling a tiny bit snippy and irritable, and instead moved the chair just slightly away from him and sat in it, peering at the screen. It was a spreadsheet, filled with projects, costs, calculations and estimates. It reminded me of my job—I'd been in finance my whole life. My fingers itched to take the mouse and keyboard, to analyze his work, to make it better, more precise. But I sat still, my hands in my lap. "What's this?"

"I was just trying to get us organized, figure out how best to apply the renovation funds to all the things that need doing in the house."

"I see." That was smart. That was exactly what needed doing. I sighed. I felt useless once again, and it reminded me of everything else in my life—living in limbo here in Singletree, Luke, who had clearly moved on to something or someone better, and my job, which I really needed to check on. I was used to being the person who did the things that needed doing. Now somehow I'd been relegated to incapable of blowing up camping mattresses and watching other people build spreadsheets. Maybe I was somehow overreacting, but it felt warranted. I was tired of having to depend on everyone else.

"This is the list of projects here, and they're broken into subprojects, with estimates where I got them from inspectors who came in to look or who I spoke to on the phone over the last couple days. And then here are some of the estimates I made myself"—he pointed to another column—"and this stuff here is pure guesswork."

"You did all this yourself?" My voice was flat, emotionless. Useless. I did not want to be so useless.

Michael turned to look at me, those dark blue eyes open and friendly—until they met mine. "Are you angry about something?"

"You know this is basically what I do for work, right?" Of course he didn't. Why would he know that?

"Renovate ancient houses?" A tiny smile lifted the corners of his mouth, but even his charm couldn't charm me out of the bad mood I'd worked myself into.

"No, analyze and valuate companies. Organize budgets and estimates. Calculate risk based on numbers." My voice was cold, partly because the indignant and overconfident career woman inside me wished she had done this work, or been asked to, but partly because having that part of me rear up, angry and possessive, was confusing.

"I didn't know that."

"You just went ahead without me." I stared at his work. "There's an error here." I pointed to the screen.

"Oh," he said, leaning in closer. "Yeah. Thanks." He fixed the number and then turned to face me, worry written in the wrinkle between his dark red brows. "Listen, Addison. We're going to have to work together. And agree on things."

"Yes."

"So if you're pissed at something I've done already, I guess you should tell me and we'll figure it out."

I let out a long breath. I wasn't mad at him, not really. I was unhappy with the situation, with everything external to this, and a little bit with this. "I think I'm frustrated about a lot of things. Things that maybe don't have to do with this." I waved my hand at the laptop. "But also, I want to be real partners. We're in this together, right?" I let my eyes find his, and the warmth and patience I found there took a bit of the steam out of my anger.

"Right, and I was trying to offer something to the team, to bring some value, get us started." He was being patient and kind, and I felt like I was in the middle of some kind of mild adult tantrum.

I sighed. "Okay."

"Okay?"

"Fine."

"In my experience, when a woman says 'fine,' it's like an iceberg."

I narrowed my eyes and jutted my head forward, furrowing my brows. "What?"

"Fine is just the tip. Everything looming below that fine is so not fine it'll sink you."

"Well, we're as fine as we're going to be for now," I said, leaning back and crossing my arms. "If you really want to get into icebergs and whatever other Titanic references you need to bring up, we can do it tomorrow. I'm grumpy and not in the mood for allusions to enormous chunks of floating sea ice."

He tilted his head sideways, just a tad. "Bad day?"

I let my eyes slide shut, reeling the day back to my argument with Mom, who had made herself into a human doorstop and literally refused to let me out of the Tin when I told her I would be sleeping somewhere else from then on. "Lottie doesn't like this idea at all."

"Not shocked. My uncle was pretty pissed about it too, though he seemed to think it would be a good chance for me to kill you off, make it look like a freak construction accident, and collect the property for the Tucker clan." He shook his head as my blood turned to ice in my veins. I hadn't even thought of that. I narrowed my eyes, evaluating him the best I could. From what I could read on his face, he didn't seem to be buying into that plan.

"If you did that, my evil cousins would probably come out of feud retirement." I had two distant cousins on Mom's side —Eunice and Esther, who were both over seventy, unmarried, and united in their hatred of the Tucker clan. But since Eunice's fall last time they were spray painting "Tuckers are Fuckers" in the road in front of Michael's feed and farm store, they'd declared themselves too old to carry on with tradition.

"How's Eunice's hip?" He actually sounded concerned. After seeing him with Mrs. Easter, I wouldn't have been surprised to find out that he'd been kind to Aunt Eunice that day, despite her evil intentions.

"She uses a walker now," I said, shrugging. "It was nice of you to call the ambulance."

"Discovering old ladies who've fallen in the street is kind of becoming my thing," he said, closing the laptop and smiling. "Eunice fell on top of the 'F' she'd just finished painting, so at first I didn't realize exactly what the girls were up to."

"Did you think it said 'Tuckers are Cluckers?'" I laughed.

"Uncle Ernie was a trucker once. I figured the girls were old enough to remember that."

"Ooh, burn. Tuckers are Truckers." I chuckled, some of my tension falling away.

"Not everyone respects the art of long-haul transport." He tried to look mildly offended, but the lines around the corners of his eyes gave away his amusement.

"Not everyone does," I agreed, finding myself smiling and more relaxed than I could remember being. As soon as I realized it, however, I felt the tension tighten up my shoulders again. "Don't suppose you have a plan for food tonight? My brain only got me as far as how to escape the Muffin Tin with Lottie physically trying to keep me inside. I didn't even bring muffins."

Michael smiled then, a white-toothed sparkling thing that made the chin cleft deepen and his eyes actually twinkle. My stomach did an annoying little flip, and I realized suddenly that living here with Michael could be dangerous. Distracting. He was very good looking, and that smile was practically a weapon. "I brought a tray of enchiladas I made yesterday."

"You cook?" I couldn't keep the admiration from my voice. *Dammit, Addie. He doesn't need to know you're impressed. You're supposed to hate him, remember?*

"A little." He stood, and leaned over slightly to scoop the laptop off the table, putting his ass right at eye level. It was nice, from what I could tell through the jeans—round and firm, probably. I thought about Luke—he was a musician, and that was sexy in a different way. But he did not have the body that Michael appeared to be sporting beneath his clothes, and a little part of me wondered what it would be like to be with someone as fit as Michael Tucker appeared to be.

I stood up quickly, to get my eyes back to level with his. I felt a flush creeping up my neck and tried to mentally douse my inappropriate self with cold water. "Great."

We went together into the kitchen, and I watched, feeling useless again, as Michael pulled a tray of enchiladas from the refrigerator and figured out how to heat the wood oven. He'd obviously planned for this too.

"Not sure how long they need to go in the oven," he said. "I don't have a lot of experience cooking with wood. But they really just need to get warm, so we should be good."

"Okay," I felt a little stupid, standing there just inside the door from the hallway, watching Michael put dinner together so proficiently. I was mostly adept at storing and sorting takeout menus. I was out of my element here. And it wasn't just in the kitchen, in the realm of meal preparation. I knew nothing about renovating houses, nothing that would help us manage to bring this sagging old house up to modern standards. I could pick out tile and granite, but the current state of this place was so far from that, I could only visualize the potential end result, but had no idea how to get it there.

"There's some silverware in there," Michael pointed to a drawer. "Set the table?"

I glanced at the little table against the far wall and had a sudden memory of sitting there as a kid, having graham crackers with Mrs. Easter. The same yellow plastic tablecloth hung over the table now, faded and worn. I wiped it down gently with a sponge, and then put out silverware, my chest warm as I considered the woman who'd left us this place. She had always been kind, from what I could remember. And a little spunky, as evidenced by the combat boots we'd seen the day of her fall. Tears threatened, but I pushed them away. I hadn't known Mrs. Easter very well really. And Michael didn't need to see me crying now.

When I opened the fridge looking for drinks, I found a six pack of Mexican beer, and put one at each setting. Michael had thought of everything.

"Were you a Boy Scout, by chance?"

"What?" He looked over his shoulder at me, smiling. "No, why?"

"You've got everything all set here. The salad, the enchiladas, beer. Very prepared."

"It's called being a single dad," he said, no bitterness in his voice. "Since I fucked up everything else about my life, I decided I was going to be good at that. Part of the gig is feeding the kid, making sure everything is ready at the right time and not forgetting things. I keep a lot of lists."

That stopped me in my tracks, it was so honest and endearing. And I didn't know a lot of men who would be willing to try so hard—even in Michael's circumstances. Of course, the truth was that I just didn't know a whole lot of men in general. But I still thought Michael might be special in this way. "I think you might be more organized than Lottie, and that's saying something."

"Thanks." He put a plate in front of me and sat down with one in front of his place. "Do you always call your mom by her first name?"

"Only when pointing out her more annoying traits."

He nodded, and I recalled that he didn't have his parents anymore—I couldn't remember when they'd passed, but I knew he'd been young, at least when his mom died. Guilt flooded me —he probably thought I took Lottie for granted.

"I mean, we all love her to pieces," I said quickly.

"I know, Addison. It's just funny, that's all." He smiled at me, warmth in his expression, and I relaxed a bit.

"Where's Daniel tonight?" I asked him, realizing he'd said he had the boy every other week. Was it his week off? He'd had him on Friday.

"I asked Shelly to take him for a couple extra days. I wanted to make sure the house was safe before we had him here."

That was smart. Michael was a really good father, I realized. "He's coming tomorrow?"

Michael nodded, and part of me felt happy to imagine Dan here, exploring and just adding one more bit of life to the empty old house.

We ate in silence for a few minutes, the house emitting creaks and groans here and there as the lawn outside the windowpanes in the back door went from green to taupe to black with the fading light of the sun. As we finished up, I started to relax a little bit. The house felt like a whole world apart from everything I'd known before, its own universe of worn fabric, ruined wallpaper and creaky old floors. Even with a Tucker here, the place felt comforting in some way, and despite my need to pull together some funds and jumpstart my life in New York again, I found myself taking a deep breath and relaxing a little bit.

"So," Michael said as we sat in relative silence, eating. "Finance, huh? Has that always been your calling?"

I thought about that. Did I have a calling? "Honestly? No. I wanted a job that would pay well. I knew I wanted to live in a big city, to make my own way, and finance seemed appropriate since math and numbers had always come easily to me."

He nodded, his fork poised in the air as his eyes held mine. "And if you hadn't had to think about money, if you could have chosen anything, what would you have done, Addison?"

"Call me Addie, please."

"Okay. What would you do if you could do anything, Addie?" His head tilted slightly to the side, and I realized he was really listening, waiting for my answer. When was the last time I'd felt that kind of rapt attention from Luke? Maybe never. Our lives were about his life, mostly.

I let my mind roll back to dreams I'd had as a kid, before I knew how important money was going to be in my life. "I used to want to be a decorator. Or an interior designer." It sounded so vapid to me now. "Silly."

Michael was still watching me intently. "Why is that silly? That's a real job. And not many people have the kind of foresight to know what works together in a space. I definitely don't."

I lifted a shoulder, suddenly a little uncomfortable at his validation of my one-time dream. I had dismissed it, set it away from me as unworthy of my lofty city goals. I knew there were interior designers in big cities, but I had never been sure how to approach that, how I would build clientele, get my footing. I didn't think that kind of job came with the same starting salary as mergers and acquisitions work. "It just always seemed insubstantial to me, I guess. Like it would be something fun. Not work."

"That sounds like the perfect kind of work to me." He smiled at me, his eyes lingering on my face, dropping from my eyes to my lips for a split second before suddenly clearing his throat and scooting his chair back from the table to clear his dish.

As I carried my plate to the sink, considering his statement, a shrill scream came from somewhere above us and my heart skittered to a halt and then took off at a gallop inside my chest.

What. The hell. Was that?

11

OLD HOUSES AND UNEARTHLY SCREAMS
MICHAEL

I t wasn't like me to believe in things I couldn't see or touch, but I was beginning to think maybe Daniel and his friends were right. This place was haunted.

The scream that came from upstairs had not been human, that much was sure. And it seemed to reverberate inside the walls long after the actual noise had faded back into the gauzy silence of the place. Addie was frozen over the sink, her eyes huge as she stared at me, and I wished I could stand up and offer some comfort.

Don't worry, I'd say. These old houses are often plagued by sub-human screeches that make your skin crawl right off your bones. Part of their charm. Nothing to worry about.

But I didn't know what the noise had been, and it had been creepy as fuck. My skin was prickled in gooseflesh and for a second my mind had screamed too, telling me to run.

Once silence had settled again, I tried to appear calm. Brave. I was about to address the sound we'd heard when another noise crashed through the house—a single distinct impact, like something hitting the floor above us, hard. I swallowed, forcing my feet to stay planted, my lungs to continue to breathe normally.

"Those weren't just old house noises," Addie said, her face white and her knuckles matching it as she gripped the edge of the counter.

"No," I agreed. Had someone broken in? Maybe the noises I'd heard earlier before Addie arrive had been someone coming inside. Had they been hiding all this time? Waiting for what, exactly?

"So we should . . . " She looked around the kitchen, as if she might stumble onto a handbook we'd missed: *How To Handle Oneself in a Haunted House*. There was nothing.

"I guess I could, ah . . ." I trailed off, wishing chivalry was actually dead. "I could go check it out." I cringed inwardly while trying to look self-assured on the surface. Being in possession of a set of balls didn't seem like a good reason to have to be the one to investigate any and all terrifying noises. I picked up a cast iron pan that I'd found earlier in a cabinet.

"Um, no." Addie said, shaking her head. "You can't go alone. You'll go up there, and then if something happens to you, I'll have to go up. Or whatever kills you will know I'm alone and come down looking for me."

"You think I'm going to die?" I was trying for light, but the question came off dire. There was definitely something up there, maybe it was a real possibility.

"I've seen a lot of movies," she said, looking uncertain about my impending demise. "We shouldn't split up."

"Maybe it was nothing," I suggested, knowing that saying it would not make it true. I was going to have to go up there.

"A nothing that screams and then crashes onto the floor." Her face was pale and her body looked as if it was completely stiff. No one was sleeping here tonight if we didn't figure this out.

I sighed, gripping the frying pan tighter and running a hand through my hair, undoubtedly sending it standing on end and pointing in all directions. "Okay. I guess we go up, then?"

She wiped her hands down the front of her jeans, took a deep breath and then met my gaze. "Let's go." She turned around quickly and picked up a butter knife. I didn't comment. But I didn't think the threat of being buttered was going to frighten even the wariest of intruders.

I turned toward the back stairway, and her arm caught my shoulder. Despite my fear, there was something nice about the way she grabbed me, the idea that she needed me.

"Hey, wait. All the lights are on now, right?"

"Power's back on, yeah," I answered.

"Good," she said, whispering now, like she didn't want whatever was up there to hear us discussing the house's utilities. "Maybe we should take the main stairs."

"You don't want to surprise the murderous thing that is probably going to kill me?"

"I just . . ." She squeezed my arm, as if pleading with me silently. "It feels safer. The back stairs are so dark and narrow."

"Sure." I didn't think it mattered much one way or the other.

Darkness hovered just outside the streaky windows of the first floor as we moved, and it felt almost like an entity watching us from out there. We moved to the foot of the stairs, the house moaning and complaining around us with each step as I shivered with anticipation and not a little fear. There was really no sneaking through this creaky old place.

Addison's hand slipped from my shoulder to my elbow as I climbed the first stair, and she set herself right against my side. I turned to look at her, unsure whether to be charmed or annoyed by her appropriation of my arm, but she looked so frightened when she returned my gaze with those huge dark eyes, I just tried for a reassuring smile.

"Sorry," she whispered.

"It's fine," I told her, and together, we moved as quietly as we could up the stairs. At the landing, darkness stretched itself down the hallway and crept into each of the four bedrooms. I reached for the switch, but nothing happened when I pressed it. I cursed myself for not trying all the switches earlier.

"Bulbs are out," I suggested, wishing I felt half as sure as I was acting. Addie pulled her cellphone from her pocket and switched on the flashlight. The hallway was empty. Creepy as hell, but empty.

We continued toward the nearest bedroom, and I flicked the light on as we entered. I was relieved the electricity wasn't out on the entire floor. The room looked exactly as it had earlier—dusty, but empty, the sagging old bed sitting against the wall looking sad. Nothing was amiss, and there was no ghostly presence screaming at us. I felt tension mount in my shoulders, wishing we could just find an easy explanation and get on with it.

We turned and investigated the next bedroom over, which was also empty of deadly ghosts or scary screaming things. The room I'd chosen as mine was in order, and the last bedroom—the master, where Addison would sleep—appeared undisturbed, except that her suitcase had fallen from the end of the bed where she'd set it, and the contents were scattered across the floor. The stress in my body dissolved.

"That explains the crash," I said.

"How would that happen?" She stared at her upended bag.

"I guess it just slid off. The mattress probably isn't flat, and the house shifts a little now and then, I suppose."

She did not look sold on this suggestion, and if I was honest, it seemed far-fetched to me too. But what other explanation was there? Ghosts had pushed her things to the floor? I couldn't believe that.

Addison dropped my elbow and moved to put a few of her

things back into the bag. I caught sight of a flimsy-looking piece of pink silk tucked among her clothes and my stupid mind went off on a tangent, wondering exactly what that was and what it might look like on her.

I stood still, watching her move around the room nervously, righting her belongings.

"Hey, you know these work better if you inflate them?" I pointed to the air mattress that lay flat beneath the sleeping bag she'd unrolled.

"I couldn't make it inflate. I felt stupid and didn't want to ask for help." She looked so sad as she told me this that my heart crumpled a little in my chest. Was I that much of a dick that she hadn't felt comfortable asking for help with the air mattress? I stepped over to it and unscrewed the valve. The mattress made a gentle hissing sound as air began to push inside.

"Thanks." She turned to face me, wringing her hands before her narrow waist. "So, what now?"

"Um . . . I guess we could plan which projects we're going to approach tomorrow?"

She nodded. "So we're going to pretend that whole screaming thing didn't happen?"

"I'll just check the attic."

She waited at the bottom of the stairs as I checked the space above, and she seemed as relieved as I was that there was nothing there.

We went back down to the dining room, but the tension that had lain between us earlier had vanished. Instead, we fell into a comfortable togetherness, discussing the many projects ahead of us and talking about what would be involved in each. It was nice, if one could overlook the creepy factor of everything that had just happened. I had the sense that Addison and I worked well together, that we were compatible partners. It was nice— enjoyable, almost—not to feel challenged at every turn, which was how I'd spent my whole relationship and very short marriage to Shelly.

"So I guess it makes the most sense to get the place livable first," she said, recapping what we'd been discussing.

"Tomorrow, we'll clean. Once we can see what we're really dealing with, we'll get into the bigger tasks and figure out what we can do ourselves and what we'll need to pay for."

"Cleaning, I can probably handle," she said, one side of her mouth pulling down doubtfully. "But I've never done any kind of . . . manual labor."

There was something charming about her admission that she wasn't much of a do-it-yourselfer, and I couldn't help the smile that took over my face. I hadn't really pictured Addison Tanner hanging drywall or pouring concrete anyway, but the fact she thought she should apologize for not knowing how to do any of that was cute. "That's okay."

"I mean, I guess I'm saying I feel like I might not be very helpful. Might not really pull my weight."

"Maybe this is the perfect opportunity to learn a few new skills."

She wrinkled her nose. "Yeah, I guess."

"I mean, I can't imagine you'll need to learn to lay tile or anything for your life in New York."

She hesitated, her chest rising and falling with a deep breath. "I'm not sure I have a life in New York anymore."

She hadn't told me much about her life, or why she'd left, but it didn't feel like the right time to ask. "If you're really interested in design and décor, you could definitely head up that department. I'm clueless on that stuff," I told her.

She frowned. "I don't really have experience though. I don't want to screw things up."

"This is the perfect opportunity to learn. It can't get worse than it is," I said, giving her what I hoped was an encouraging smile. "Nowhere to go but up, right?" I stood and folded up the laptop. "Should we head up?"

Addie gazed uncertainly at the stairs through the doorway. "Yeah, I guess so."

We switched off the lights, and made our way together up the grand staircase of the old house. As we took turns in the single bathroom and said our goodnights, I tried to keep my mind focused on the work that lay before us. Not on the beautiful woman who would be settling down to sleep just a room away.

Not on the fact that she'd have to change her clothes just on the other side of that wall.

And definitely not on the fact that whatever feelings I had about Addison Tanner had shifted in the very little time I'd spent with her. I didn't want to think about how easy it was to be with her, or how pretty her dark wide eyes were, or how nice it had felt when she'd gripped my arm.

I sighed deeply, laid down on the air mattress on the floor, and closed my eyes.

12

THUMPS IN THE NIGHT
ADDISON

I was not exactly a fanciful teenager, eager to believe the stories I'd heard my whole life about the Easter Mansion being haunted. But I'd also never expected to find myself stretched out on the floor in said mansion, trying to fall asleep to the dulcet tones of creaking floors, swollen pipes, and potentially miserably ghostly entities. And while we'd spent a surprisingly nice evening after the otherworldly scream and the upending of my suitcase, this place was still super creepy. The odds of me drifting peacefully off to sleep seemed very low.

But maybe making decisions about changing your entire life on what some might call a whim was more tiring that I'd considered. Because a few minutes after stretching out on the surprisingly comfortable air mattress Michael had loaned me—after he'd shown me how to inflate it, I found myself sinking into sleep. But my dreams weren't peaceful.

I dreamt of dark dusty rooms filled with fog and shadow, movement in the periphery of my vision that disappeared as soon as I turned to look, and someone crying in some distant room of the house—a baby.

Though I slept, I was aware of my body's restlessness, and so

I lingered in that half-waking state where dreams mixed with reality and my brain never quite shut off, as if it knew that remaining vigilant would be the best plan when sleeping in a creepy old house some lady willed you just to try to end a feud.

The scream that cut the air, catapulting me violently out of my half-sleep was one hundred percent inhuman, that much I knew.

I was on my feet without making a conscious decision to get there, and those same feet were already carrying me to Michael, though I definitely didn't make a decision about that. I burst through his closed door, panting and gripping my pillow to my chest, to find him sitting up and looking around, the light on his phone illuminating the room.

"What was that?" I asked, my voice a panicky whisper.

"Same thing we heard earlier, I guess." Michael had clearly been sleeping, and his hair stuck up on end, giving him an adorably disheveled little boy look that was contrasted sharply by his bare chest, which was well muscled and dusted with light hair. "You okay?" He asked.

I came back to myself slowly then, realizing too late that I was standing in his room, half dressed in only a long ragged T-shirt I'd gotten for attending some corporate event years ago. It wasn't the way I'd normally present myself to a near-stranger. "Uh, yeah. Sorry to barge in. I was asleep," I said, feeling abashed.

"It's okay." He stood, revealing a pair of loose flannel pajama pants and bare feet. "Want me to check it out?"

"If it's the same thing as earlier, we won't find anything," I said, late-night cynicism and fear making a less-than-optimistic combination.

"Sounded the same." He sounded as tired and resigned as I felt. Would we live with this screaming fear for six months? Were we already so willing to accept it?

I sighed, relaxing the tension that had me gripping my pillow tightly to my chest, and my shoulders fell as I met his gaze. He must've seen my hesitation to go back to my room alone, my understanding that there was no way I'd be able to sleep now. Not alone.

"I'll help you move your stuff in here if you want." He sounded neither generous or annoyed, just tired.

I debated as deliberately as one can do in a state of terror in the middle of the night. Mom would not like me sleeping in the same room as a Tucker. But if he was going to kill me, he could just as easily walk down the hall to do it, and the man did not seem inclined to take the feud to that level. He'd actually been very kind so far. "Yeah, okay."

We went to my room and gathered the sleeping bag and air mattress, laying them in the room Michael had been sleeping in, situating me against the wall farthest from him in order to preserve at least the feeling of privacy. I tried to tell myself it wasn't comforting to see his things there, to know I wasn't alone.

"This okay?" He asked, smoothing the bag and standing to look down at it.

I dropped the pillow to the head of the bag and gazed up at him. "Yeah. Thank you."

"It's fine," he said. His voice was toneless, and I still couldn't tell how he felt about having me crashing into his room in the middle of the night like a terrified toddler. At least I wasn't demanding a story or to sleep with him.

A few minutes later, we were both on the ground in the dark, the not-quiet of the old house settling around us again as I tried to forget the high-pitched misery of the scream I'd heard. I didn't know what it was, but I was more willing than I'd ever been before to believe in ghosts. Shrieky, wailing ghosts.

The rest of the night passed eventually, the long hours of my wakefulness consumed by my thoughts of the choices I'd made recently, and those that had been made for me, punctuated by the steady sound of Michael's soft breathing. Something about the constant and reassuring sound gave me the space I needed to consider all that had happened in my life. Luke's departure after so many years together. My near-breakdown in my boss's office. My decision to come back to Singletree. And now this. The choice to move into a deserted and dilapidated house with a man I didn't know and had been bred to detest.

Life was strange, and mine recently had been a steady string of disappointment, but I thought that was because I'd allowed myself to depend completely on someone else to fulfill me, to make me happy. A man.

And I would never make that mistake again. I'd find my own happiness without having to depend on anyone else—especially a man. I'd learn a few things working on this house, sell it as fast as was possible, and take the money right back to New York to fund the life I should have been living. On my own. Independent.

When shades of orange and red filtered across the walls as the sun rose through the dense trees outside, I heard Michael begin to stir. After a few minutes, he whispered across the room.

"You awake?"

"Good morning," I returned.

There was something intimate and fragile about whispering through the quiet morning air, and I found myself liking it.

"Did you sleep?"

"Not really."

"I did," he said, and I could hear the rustle of his sleeping bag as he stretched. "No more screaming, right?"

"I didn't hear any more."

"That's good. We'll figure out what it is," he said. "It's probably just some bird outside or something."

Except we both knew perfectly well that sound had been inside the house. Still, it was sweet of him to try to comfort me.

We each lay quietly for a few moments, soaking in the sleepy atmosphere of morning, of that fuzzy border between sleep and wakefulness.

"Addie?" Michael said after a few minutes of silence.

"Yeah?"

"I'm glad we're doing this," he said.

And though I didn't answer, his simple statement and the honesty it contained made me happy in some inexplicable way.

I actually managed to doze for another half hour or so, and Michael must've been content to do the same, because when I woke again, it was to him pulling clothes from a duffle bag, bent over a chest beneath the window.

I sat up, surprised to have fallen back asleep. "What time is it?" I asked.

He straightened and shot me a lopsided grin. "Almost nine. We slept in." The sun caught his hair from behind, and lit it in shades of dark red laced with gold. I had a sudden urge to put my hand into it, feel the thick burnished strands with my fingers. I swallowed hard.

"I guess I should get up." Suddenly, I felt shy in my night-shirt, as if I'd come back to my senses and realized that exposing half my body to a near-stranger wasn't exactly considered good manners. I huddled in the sleeping bag, waiting for Michael to leave the room.

"I need to check in at the store," he told me. "But I'll be back by noon and I'll bring supplies for cleaning. You'll be okay until then?"

"Yeah," I said, doubting seriously whether I'd be okay if I stayed here alone. I already knew I'd be right behind him. I'd return Mom's car and probably spend my morning at Mom's shop until he came back. Enduring an inquisition, but it'd still be better than being here alone. "Um, Michael?"

He straightened and turned to face me. "Yeah?"

"I'm really sorry about barging in here last night. It won't happen again. Just . . . I got scared. Sorry."

His face rearranged itself into an expression I expected he must've used with Daniel when he was small—his eyes were soft and his lips turned up at the corners. "It's no problem. Although," he cleared his throat, his face hardening a bit. "Daniel will be joining us tomorrow. He might think . . ."

"Oh, no," I interrupted. "He won't need to think a thing. I'll be fine. I'm going to get my own air mattress thingy today, and maybe some ear plugs or something, and I'll be just fine in the other room."

Michael looked a bit skeptical, his half-smile sliding side-ways, but he said, "Okay. Great."

As he pulled on a T-shirt and picked up a few other things from his bag, he spoke again. "Oh, hey. I forgot to show this to you." He turned and crossed the room, handing me a box. It was dusty and faded, and looked like a shoebox.

"What's this?"

"When I first got in here, I looked inside the chest there before I dropped my bag on it. This was in there. There's a bunch of letters inside."

"Letters?" My conversational skills were not finely tuned in the morning. Lack of sleep would do that to a person.

"Yeah." He was looking at me as if he thought I might regain my power of comprehension if he just waited long enough. "I don't know who from or to, I didn't have time to look. But if you wanted to look at them while I'm at work—there could be some-thing in there."

"Sure," I said, lifting the lid to find the box tightly packed with paper. It would actually give me something to focus on besides the ghosts when I got back from Mom's place.

"I'm gonna see if I can grab a quick shower," he said, and headed out of the room.

I used the opportunity to go back to my own room and dress, and then ventured down the wide staircase and to the kitchen, seeking the house's second bathroom, and then coffee. There was a Keurig machine on the counter I hadn't noticed the previous night, and I realized Michael must've brought it with him. A quick search through the cupboards revealed a few mismatched mugs too. I put two out and made myself a cup of coffee, and then turned to the box of old letters I'd brought down with me.

I pulled one from the box, scanning the address, which was written in swooping cursive and addressed to Private Robert Tucker, AEF, 29th Division, 58th Brigade, 115th Regiment, France. The letter was dated September 1918.

Robert Tucker? I didn't know anything about Filene Easter's family history, so I wasn't sure who this particular Tucker would be to her. But a glance at the return address added a bit of insight.

Miss Lucille Tanner, Number Three, Canterbury Lane, Singletree, Maryland, USA.

I felt like I'd heard the name Lucille a few times before. Mom had some old family documents—had this been in there? Could these have been Filene's parents? The lawyer had said that she was born a Tucker and that she was descended from both families.

Feeling like I was breaking some kind of law, or at the very least violating someone's privacy in a big way, I pulled the thin sheets from the envelope, letting my greedy eyes devour the missive within.

My Dearest Robert:

Thank you for your last. I never know when your letters will arrive, and though my heart burns during the long waits between receiving them, each one is celebrated and cherished.

Life here continues as ever. Mother goes on about the way your father stole her birthright and Uncle Lester continues to plot and scheme—for he is even more fixated than Mother. They are both relieved you are gone, since they clearly think distance will lead me to forget about the love we share, or allow me to become distracted with someone else. Though, honestly, all the boys are with you over there and the town feels sad and empty. I miss you, and hope you know I will never love another. I am waiting for you. We will deal with our parents when you return.

We are doing well otherwise, though as the fall sets in again I find my mind always on you, on your location, your duties. I bide my time until you return to me, my love, and eagerly await the day when I might be held in your arms once again.

Stay safe and come home soon to me.

Yours ever,

Lucille

"WHAT'S THAT? One of the letters?" Michael asked, striding into the kitchen, his hair damp and his skin freshly shaven. He smelled clean as he came to stand beside me, like soap and spring and fresh laundry. I wanted to lean into him, breathe deeply, relax.

"Yeah. They're love letters."

He chuckled. "Really? Whose?"

"Robert Tucker and Lucille Tanner. Dated 1918. And Robert must've been deployed overseas. Look." I showed him the front of the envelope and Michael stared at it for a moment.

"I've heard of Robert. We talk about him like a war hero in our family. But I was never sure quite how we were related."

"I guess maybe he was Filene's dad."

We exchanged a glance, and I sensed he was as interested and curious about our shared history as I was, and then Michael skimmed the letter. "World War I," he said. Then his eyes darted to me and his lips pressed into a line, almost as if he was deciding whether or not to tell me something. "The 29th Division saw some major action at the end of the war. They fought in Meuse-Argonne. It was a bloody battle."

I smiled up at him, surprised. "Bit of a history buff, are we?"

"It was this guy. Knowing we had a hero in the family, a vet. I did a bunch of research when I was about Daniel's age."

"Well, he must've made it home," I mused. "No mention here of a baby. I don't think they'd gotten married yet."

Michael folded the letter back up carefully and tucked it into the envelope, setting it gingerly onto the table in front of me. He eyed the box of letters with something like longing, his inner history buff no doubt curious about what else was tucked into these old envelopes. "I better get going. See you in a few hours?"

"Okay," I said. And as he picked up his keys and headed out the back door, I was hit with a strange wave of emotion. Longing? Familiarity? I could see this same scene playing out in another lifetime—me saying goodbye to my husband as he headed out the door to work.

I pushed down the sentimental idea. That was not what this was. This was a business arrangement. And I needed to focus. Today I'd call my supervisor and inform him that my leave of absence would be at least six months. Perhaps that would have been a wise thing to do before diving headlong into this agreement, but wise had not been my strong suit lately. Then I'd read a couple more letters if I was brave enough to be in the house, and then I'd go to Mom's. After that, I'd figure out what I needed to sleep in the room upstairs without running to Michael every night.

13

TANNER TROUBLE

MICHAEL

The store was a bit of a disaster, since I hadn't been there all day the day prior. Technically, Virgil was assistant manager, and some days (against my better judgment), I left him in charge. And it sometimes turned out just fine.

But this morning there were deliveries piled in the warehouse at the back of the store, an enormous line of customers was waiting, and signs plastered on everything that said, "HUGE SALE - CLOSING - EVERYTHING MUST GO." What were my cousins up to now? Fury began to pipe a hot path through my veins.

I noticed that the entire selection of gas grills off to one side of the counter was also marked "FREE - TAKE WHAT YOU CAN CARRY!" Why on Earth would we be giving away some of the most expensive and popular items in the store? This was not happening.

I ripped down the signs that lined the aisle as I approached my cousins, who both stood behind the counter, looking nonchalant as ever, despite the chaos.

"Are we having a sale?" I asked, trying to contain the anger threatening to spill out of me.

"Guess so," Virgil said. "You know, a little notice next time would be good, boss."

"Yeah, Mike." Emmett chimed in. He spoke so rarely it caught me off guard and I stared at his round ruddy face for a beat, wondering if he was going to say more, but that was it.

Virgil pulled a hand down his long spiky beard. "I mean—I don't even know how to ring half this shit up." He motioned to a customer standing in front of him holding our entire inventory of weed blocker in rolls in his arms. "He says the sign said it was free."

I stepped behind the counter, trying to push down the panic rising in me at the thought of people just walking out with inventory. Our margins were thin as it was. I tried to keep prices fair—these folks were my neighbors, after all, but I couldn't just give everything away. I looked out at the line of people, who in total were standing there, ready to relieve me of thousands of dollars-worth of merchandise. I wondered what Virge and Emmett had sent out the door already this morning.

"Folks, hi there. Hi. Can you give me a second here and listen?"

The crowd grumbled into silence, the line stilling as people held their treasures, hoping for a ridiculous deal I couldn't offer. This had the Tanner stink on it, and anger welled inside me, making it tough to speak. Had Addie known about this? Had she been playing sweet while her family tried to ruin me?

"Thanks. So, listen, there's been some kind of mistake here, and I hate telling you that, but I'm guessing this is a prank, and I'm pretty sure if we could just locate a member of the Tanner clan, we could probably get confirmation of that."

Helen Manchester pushed a huge wheeled barbecue from the line and glared at me. "This grill is free. Says so right here."

I liked old Mrs. Manchester, usually. She was great comic relief, but she was also irrational, belligerent and sometimes altogether terrifying. Today she wore a hat that said, "Give me a reason to shoot." I looked behind her, hoping maybe one of her granddaughters was accompanying her, but didn't see anyone that seemed to be in charge of the ninety-something woman trying to steal my most expensive barbecue.

"I wish it was, Helen," I told her. "I wish I could give you all the things you want and need, but I'd be out of business by tonight if I did that." The crowd grumbled, but a few people moved to put their items back, which was a relief. "What I can do," I announced, "is offer you all ten percent off whatever you have in your hands right now." It pained me to do it, but I had been planning some big holiday promotions anyway, maybe volume would make up for the loss. The Tanners had managed to get more people into the store than I'd seen in months.

"Better'n nothing," came a man's voice from the back of the line.

Some people shot me dirty looks and left the store, dropping work gloves and shovels, bags of mulch and feed right where they'd been standing. So much for being kind to our neighbors. Others seemed happy to get a discount. Helen Manchester made for the door with the grill, but I was happy to see her grand-daughter Tess arriving just beyond the glass, exasperation etched into her features. "Gran!" She said. "What are you doing? We already have a great grill."

"This one is free!" The old woman shot me a look over her shoulder, daring me to contradict her.

Tess met my eyes then and I shook my head.

"We'll just put this back over here," she said, wheeling the grill off to the side of the front doors. "And I'll treat you to a Manhattan at the Shack before lunch, okay?"

The old woman crossed her thin arms, but said, "It's the least you could do." I wished I had a stiff drink right about then.

I spent the rest of the morning offering discounts, and when the people just kept coming, I figured out there was also a huge sign planted in the town square advertising the liquidation of my inventory. By mid-afternoon, the mess was somewhat sorted, and I had a few minutes to breathe.

"It was those sisters, I bet," Virgil said, as we tried to figure out which members of the Tanner family might've pulled this particular prank.

"Who, Addie and Paige? Amberlynn?" I couldn't imagine Addie's sisters doing this. I'd met Paige a few times, and she seemed very rational, the type to remain impartial in a fight. Or a feud. Amberlynn was younger, and I didn't know her as well. I supposed it could have been her, but not alone.

"No," Virgil shook his head. "The one with the walker and the other one."

The image almost made me laugh, except he might have been right. "They've got that cousin, too, right? Lottie's older brother or something?" I could see Virgil working himself up to revenge.

I nodded. There was a Tanner who'd come back to town recently. Arthur, I thought. And he would have been pretty loyal to Lottie, who had been the most recent feud victim. "That might be it. I'll ask Addie about it." I'd know by her expression if she had been involved, I thought. She didn't seem like a great liar—her face was too open, too trusting, with those huge brown eyes and that sad smile. I forced myself not to think about how scared and vulnerable—and hot—she'd looked the night before, clutching her pillow to her chest, miles of bare legs coming from the very short hem of an old T-shirt. If I hadn't been slightly terrified I might have tried to talk her into my own sleeping bag instead of helping her set up hers.

"Forget asking Addie," Virgil said. "Time to plot revenge."

"I wish you wouldn't," I said, feeling exhausted by the whole idea. Yeah, I'd just lost thousands of dollars, but what if we took revenge. What would we lose next time? "Can't we just let it die?"

Emmett and Virgil shook their heads resolutely. They lived for this feud. I knew I couldn't stop them.

"No one gets hurt, okay?" I reminded them. Back in the day, I'd heard stories about much more dangerous activities—tampering with brakes and setting fires. At least the feud had civilized to some degree. I couldn't imagine losing a family member to something so ridiculous, though it would certainly fuel the anger that had kept the feud going this long.

I hadn't planned to hang around the store long, but it took longer than I'd hoped to put the place back in order, and I wasn't completely sure I could trust my cousins to be here on their own, but by mid-afternoon, I felt like it would be okay for me to leave, but this time I gave explicit instructions about what needed to happen in my absence. When Virgil and Emmett were sufficiently busy, I headed back toward the old house on the top of the hill. I was already exhausted, and cleaning would not normally have been something I looked forward to. But Addie was here, and for some reason I was looking forward to seeing her again, despite the feud.

Driving around the house to the back, I encountered a sight I had certainly not been expecting—four different cars were parked on the overgrown drive, blocking the little garage and making it look like Addie had decided to have a party in my absence.

"What is going on?" I wondered aloud as I pulled my truck up behind a VW beetle that was painted a frightening shade of pink and in questionable condition. I'd seen the car around town, but had no idea who it belonged to. I supposed I was about to find out.

"Addie?" I called, stepping through the back door and into the kitchen. There was a thick aroma of something hanging in the air, something I couldn't quite identify. There were also numerous pots on the stovetop filled with liquids of various shades, and voices coming from upstairs. Did she invite people over to make soup? As I followed the voices and the footsteps, the smell became stronger, and when I finally reached the master bedroom, the source revealed itself.

Three women stood around the room with Addie, all of them gray-haired and draped in layers of baggy clothing that looked like it might have been made from old curtains or maybe lampshades. Their wrists jangled with metal bracelets, they wore slippers that they might have stolen from Aladdin himself, and they were holding smoking sticks in the air and chanting. Addie stood at the edge of their small circle, wringing her hands and looking worried. The sight of her looking so upset made me feel upset, but it was also a little confusing to find this scene—and even Addie didn't look like she knew exactly what was going on here.

"Uh . . ." I wasn't sure exactly what was happening, and I was less sure how to interrupt it to get an explanation.

"Michael," Addie said, spotting me. "Hi." Her face slipped into a glowing smile before quickly turning wary.

"Um. Hi?" I glanced at the three women, who still had their eyes closed and were ignoring me with a tenacity I'd only witnessed previously in my ex-wife.

"They're cleansing," Addie said, gesturing at the women.

This was unlike any scrubbing technique I'd seen before and I greatly preferred the scent of lemons or even bleach to whatever this pungent smoky smell was.

"I brought some Lysol from the store," I said. "Would that work better?"

"Young man, do you mind?" One of the women snapped, turning to glare at me.

"I'm not sure. I might mind. What exactly are you doing?"

The woman sighed and looked at Addie before explaining to me, in the same tone she might use with a repeatedly disobedient puppy, "We are cleansing the house."

I had an inkling what this was about, based on the chanting and the skeptical look on Addie's face. I'd seen movies about witches before. "Of?"

"Spirits, of course," the woman said. "But now you've interrupted and we'll have to begin again. I honestly don't know if this will be effective at this point." She looked pretty exasperated, so I figured it might be best to just let her and nutty buddies finish up. I motioned to Addie and she followed me out into the hallway.

"What's going on?"

"They confirmed that the house is haunted. We're trying to clear it of spirits." She sounded like she believed in this about as much as I did.

"With burning sticks and fashion from the seventies?"

"They're smudging sage." Addie crossed her arms defensively.

"A proven technique for making the house smell funny, for sure."

"And for cleansing negative energy."

I watched her face, looking for any sign that she actually believed this would work. Her manner was defensive, but her face made me think she wasn't buying into it. Her intelligent eyes looked tired, a little glazed. "How's it going so far?"

"I don't know. They've been here for hours." She dropped her arms and looked up from beneath dark lashes. "I didn't know what else to do, Michael. I went to Mom's but she told me she didn't need me this morning, so I came back up here. I was trying to clean the bathroom upstairs when that screaming noise echoed through the house. It scared me to death. I called my mom from the driveway, and she sent these ladies over. They're proven spirit whisperers from Center County."

This felt like one more part of the feud, except Lottie wouldn't have pranked her own daughter just to get me, would she? "How does Lottie know about spirit cleansing?"

"I think she found them on the internet, actually. But they were on that Ghost Hunters show. They're legit."

One of the women took this opportunity to raise her warbling chanting to an impressively high note, causing me to cringe. They were legitimately kooky, that was for sure. "Are you paying these people?"

Addie nodded, looking sheepish.

"A lot?"

She raised a shoulder. "I mean, I don't really know what the going rate is for this kind of service. I was desperate, Michael. I can't stay here and be terrified all the time!"

I didn't believe for one second that brewing potions and waving a stinky stick around the house would stop whatever was making the screaming noises, but if it made Addie feel better about staying in the house, I guessed it wouldn't hurt.

"Fine," I said, resigned to whatever it was the crazy ladies were doing in there. "Hey, do you know anything about my store? About a sale I was supposedly having today?"

Addie looked completely confused, which secured my confidence that she had not been involved in the attempted liquidation of my stock. "What?"

"I'll tell you later," I said.

"We have finished," said one of the old women, appearing in the hallway. "Lucrecia will finish the perimeter of salt outside and we'll hang the talisman on the front door. Do not disturb it until you are sure your spirits have departed." I hoped all the chanting and smelly smoke hadn't pissed our ghosts off more.

"Oh, thank you," Addie said. "And you're sure they're gone?"

"The spirit world is mysterious," the woman said, narrowing her eyes at us. "I conversed with your spirit, but she will have to choose to leave on her own."

"You talked to the ghost?" This was a little much for me.

The woman's spine stiffened. "I did."

"What did it say?"

"*She* told me that this is her beloved family home and that she is uncertain about the intentions of the intruders."

I stifled my irritated laugh.

"That's us?" Addie asked.

"Correct." The woman bobbed her head.

"Okey dokey, then," I said, ushering the spirit sisters down the stairs and to the back door. "Be careful out there on the porch when you're hanging the voodoo doll or whatever. Some of those boards are rotten."

"I see you are a non-believer, sir," the woman said, squinting up at me.

"Yep."

"Then you have more trouble here than I'd imagined," she said to Addie. "Good luck to you." With that, she bustled out the back door, calling over her shoulder, "I'll invoice the rest on Venmo! Don't forget to review us on Yelp!"

Addie avoided me for the next half hour, tidying up the things the spooky sisters had used around the house. I took a quick shower and changed out of my dirty work clothes, and then went down to the kitchen, planning to eat something before I dove into cleaning the old-fashioned way.

"So," I started, "do you think it worked?"

Addie stopped wiping down the counter and sighed, turning to face me, arms crossed. "I don't need you making fun of me, okay?"

I hadn't planned to make fun of her. Or at least not a lot. "Sorry," I said, sitting at the little table. She watched me warily for a moment, and then crossed the space to take the seat across from me.

Outside the sun was beginning its fall through the turning leaves and it cast the little kitchen in a warm glow.

"Do you really believe in ghosts, though?" I asked, figuring this could actually impact the speed at which we could get through the projects ahead of us.

She nodded. "Yeah, I do. I know you probably think that's stupid."

"No, I don't." I thought for a moment about what I really believed, Addie's dark eyes watching me. "I guess I just have a hard time believing in things I can't see. Or prove."

Addie traced a circle on the old wooden tabletop, a scar from a long-ago glass of water or lemonade. "I get that," she said. "I just don't think everything can be explained easily."

"So if ghosts are real," I ventured. "What do you think causes a person to become a ghost? Does everyone's spirit stick around when they die?" I'd always wondered about the logic governing this topic.

Her eyes met mine across the table then, and I could feel her measuring, weighing whether she wanted to talk about this. There was something wary in her look, and I wondered if someone had hurt her before after she'd admitted to believing in something they didn't. I had a defensive spark light up inside me on her behalf—I didn't like the idea of anyone hurting Addie.

"No, I don't think everyone's spirit stays," she said finally. "I'm not an expert, but what people seem to think is that ghosts stick around because they had something unfinished when they died. Something they needed to complete."

"Like a jigsaw puzzle?" I smiled as I said this so she'd know I wasn't really poking fun.

Addie rolled her eyes at me, but the corners of her lips

curled up slightly, and the almost-smile had me wanting to work harder to make it happen again.

"No, not like a puzzle. Like important life stuff. An apology, or a declaration of love, or revenge. Stuff like that."

"Speaking of revenge," I said, "you wouldn't happen to know anything about a giant sign in the town square advertising liquidation of all the inventory at my store, would you?"

She sat up straighter, her eyes widening. "What? Is this what you were talking about earlier?"

"Yeah, whoever put up the sign also got into the store and put signs on everything that said, 'free' and 'clearance, everything must go.'"

"Oh no, Michael. That's awful." Addie's wide eyes were full of sympathy. There was no way she knew about this.

"Seems like a Tanner thing."

She frowned but didn't deny it. "I can find out."

"Thanks. It doesn't really matter who it was, though."

"You planning some revenge?" Addie sat back in the chair and crossed her arms. Her long dark hair was arranged behind her head in some kind of knot, and one long strand fell to the side of her face. In the sun's fading light, she looked beautiful, like a goddess in a painting.

"No," I said. "But I can't speak for Emmett and Virgil."

"You know your cousins are basically criminals, right?"

That got my attention. My cousins were townies for sure, and maybe not at the top of the haystack in terms of intelligence, but they weren't criminals. "What?"

"What they did in Mom's cafe was vandalism. You're lucky she didn't press charges."

"And what about what happened in my store today?" I asked, feeling my blood heat. "I spent the entire day offering discounts when the place barely breaks even as it is."

"You didn't have to do that." She dismissed me with a wave of her hand and my exhaustion and anger boiled over.

"I was trying to avoid a riot!" I stood, my anger over the stupid prank spilling out of me now. I hadn't really had time all day to process how pointless and mean-spirited it really was. "Someone broke into my store and set this up. And I don't know why I'm a target. I've never once done anything to any of you!"

"Any of us? Like we're some other breed of human?"

"You know what I mean. *Tanners.*"

Addie rolled her eyes again. "Right."

"What does that mean?" I was vibrating with anger, and while I knew Addie didn't really deserve any of it, I couldn't help myself. This feud was ridiculous, and today it had hurt business. I didn't have a lot of spare money lying around.

"As if the Tuckers are so much better than us, like we started this whole thing."

"I have no idea who started it," I fumed. "And I don't care! What I do care about is that today I lost thousands of dollars from a business I don't have any interest in running in the first place! Is it too much to ask that I at least don't go bankrupt because of someone else's stupidity? I can fail perfectly well all on my own."

Addie's eyes widened as I spat these words at her, and she stood up from the table, her expression less imperious than it had been a second before. "Look, Michael, I'm really sorry for what happened. But—"

"I don't really want to talk about it anymore," I said. I'd told her far more than I intended and now I wished I could just reel the words back in. I felt my face flush, with embarrassment and anger—at the prank, but also at the state of my life and the fact I'd just given a beautiful, successful women a bird's eye view of my pointless existence.

"Okay," she said, her shoulders slumping slightly. "Well, I

think I'm just going to walk down to the square and get some dinner at the Shack."

I stood there, feeling stupid for a beat too long, and Addie turned to pick up her purse from the hook by the back door. I watched her pull her coat on, letting the anger dissipate from the atmosphere around me. Just as she put her hand on the knob, I managed to find my voice again. "I'll walk you."

"I'm fine," she said, the dark eyes finding me as she turned her head over her shoulder. "You don't have to."

"Do you mind the company? I'm hungry."

She turned to face me, her smile tentative and those wide eyes questioning. "As long as we don't talk about the feud."

"Deal," I said. I'd had more than enough of it anyway, and I knew it was Shelly's night off, but I also knew she'd have words for me about eating at her place of work with a woman. At that moment, I didn't care. "Let's go."

We stepped out the back door and walked around to the front gates, leaving the old house standing in shadow for the ghosts to claim for the evening.

14

OLD BAY STRIKES AGAIN
ADDISON

I f you'd told me a month ago that I'd be sitting at The Shack in Singletree with Michael Tucker, eating fried clams out of a bucket today, I wouldn't have believed you. Partly because my life was all planned out already, and there was no room in it for my tiny hometown, and certainly not for anyone named Tucker, no matter how handsome he looked with his dark red hair glinting under the glowing lights of the bar. But the other reason I would have said this was impossible was because I was in the middle of an eight-year-long delusion that involved my long-time boyfriend finally sacking up and proposing. It involved kids and a bigger apartment and some form of happily ever after.

But now, I was here. In a place where food was served in a bucket.

"I didn't miss the Old Bay," I confided, holding yet another fried clam before my lips.

"Doesn't seem to be putting you off these too much," Michael observed, watching me devour another.

"I can handle it," I told him. "Just wouldn't be my first choice of spice blend, that's all."

"Do you have a first choice in spice blends?"

I had to think about that. "I mean . . . what are the choices, really? There's Allspice, right?"

"Not great on clams probably."

"Maybe not. There's Italian." I shrugged, knowing this one was a stretch.

"That's a culture, not a spice blend."

"You can buy a little bottle in the store that says 'Italian Spice.'" When he just stared at me, I added, "I see that you are absorbing this new information."

"No, I'm just sad."

I dropped my latest clam onto my plate. "Sad? About Italian Spice?"

He shook his head, and though his face was a mask of disappointment, there was a little glint in those dark blue eyes that both told me he was kidding with me, and sent a little pulse of giddiness through my stomach. "I'm sad that you think that's a valid spice blend."

"Fine, what's your favorite?" I asked him.

"I'm partial to Garam Masala," he said, and I kicked myself, wishing I'd thought of that one. "But my all-time favorite? Cinnamon sugar." He smiled as if he'd won some kind of contest.

"That's not a blend. That's just two spices that you're naming."

"And they are delicious together. Which makes them a blend."

"Not."

"I bet Lottie would agree with me." He raised his eyebrows and gave me a smug smile before taking another sip of the Half Cat Whiskey he'd ordered.

"Do not bring my mother into this." I took a sip of my beer

and sat back into my chair. Despite the company and the weird train of conversation, I found myself relaxing in his company, enjoying it even.

"But you and your mom are close, right?"

"Like she'd give me any other choice."

He cocked his head to the side and narrowed his eyes at me, and I had the oddest sensation as he did it. Michael Tucker was listening to me. Really listening. A warm wave of emotion passed over me. I liked it.

"Tell me about it," he said. "About life with your mom and sisters."

I considered giving him a flip response, turning off this line of questioning before it could really get rolling. But hadn't I spent the last many years wishing Luke would really listen to me? Not that I was comparing Michael and Luke, not at all. Luke was my boyfriend—my lover. And Michael was . . . so handsome as he sat and waited patiently for me to respond. His squared jaw was stubbled with fine golden hairs and his forearm, where it rested on the tabletop next to his glass, was tanned and muscular. He didn't have the same fine hands that Luke had—a musician's hands—but Michael's looked strong and capable. My mind began to picture those hands at work, and maybe in the shower. Without meaning to, I imagined what that big firm hand might look like wrapped around my breast, or his cock—

I nearly spit out the sip of beer I'd just taken as I realized where my mind had gone. I felt heat rise in my cheeks, and still, Michael just watched me with those penetrating eyes.

"Life with Lottie," I started, trying to cover the very inappropriate thoughts I'd been having with zero provocation at all. "Well, I'm the oldest," I said. "So that means all the parenting practice happened on me. When I was little and my dad was still around, things were good. They were strict, but it was good, I think. But after Dad died, and Mom was so sad for such a long time. And by then, we had Paige and Amberlynn, and it was almost like I had to be the parent. She checked out." Lottie would kill me for sharing so much with anyone, especially a Tucker. But there was something so understanding in Michael's gaze, I didn't think he'd judge us.

"That must have been hard," Michael said quietly. "How old were you?"

"I was ten." I took a sip of my beer, remembering how I'd felt all those years ago, like if I slipped up or screwed up, there was a chance Mom would just leave. She was already so distant in her sadness, sometimes I wondered if she even knew how much I'd been doing to try to help.

"How long was your mom depressed?"

I sighed. It had taken me so many years to realize that Mom had been depressed. "A long time," I said. "As a kid though, I didn't understand that's what it was."

"Of course not."

"I just thought that maybe without Dad around, Mom wasn't interested in being a parent anymore." A shadow of the fear and sadness I had felt as a little girl awoke inside me and I tried to press it down. I had purposely put those feelings away. It was odd that I was talking to Michael about something I'd never even mentioned to Luke.

"Well, it wasn't what she signed up for, right? Raising three girls alone?"

"It wasn't what any of us signed up for." A wave of sadness threatened to wash through me, and I ignored it, pasted on a smile.

"And so what about you?" He asked.

I shook my head in confusion. "What?"

"You. You became this super successful career woman. So, no kids for you?"

"You might have missed the part of my super successful career where I had something close to a breakdown and ended up sitting in a shack eating clams out of a bucket."

Michael's face changed then, and I thought I might have offended him. I rushed to apologize.

"I mean, tonight is fun, this isn't what I meant. It's just—"

"Addie, I get it." He smiled, waving away my apology. "If I've learned anything about life, and honestly, I don't think I have learned much—no one's coming to me for tips, at least—but it's this: nothing ever goes the way you want."

"Wow. Cynical much?"

"Yeah. Well, I guess I learned pretty early that making plans is pointless. Or maybe I just suck at execution."

I frowned at him, surprise making the wheels in my head turn as I tried to figure out what he meant. "You own a huge farm supply store. You're your own boss. You have a wonderful son. What plans did you have that went so wrong?"

He sat back in his chair and his face completely changed. He reached out, lifted his glass, and downed the remaining whiskey. "Nothing."

I sensed that we were finished. I felt a little cheated—I'd told him so much, and when it was his turn, he clammed up.

"Should we head back and see if burning a bunch of crap made the spirits decide it smelled too bad to stay in the house?" He asked.

"Funny," I said, though I did feel a little silly about my knee-jerk decision to try to cleanse the house today.

"I don't blame you," he said, his tone softening. "That noise is terrifying. Especially if you're there alone."

"And there's something else," I said, deciding to just tell him. He had to live in the house too.

He cocked his head as he signaled for the check, still listening intently.

"When I was reading those letters, I had this feeling," I said, dropping his gaze because it was just too embarrassing to hold. "Like someone was right there with me, reading over my shoulder. And in a way, I felt like maybe they were mad, like I was invading their privacy or something. That was when the scream came."

He nodded, moving to sign the check. I reached for my purse. "You get the next one," he said, dismissing my gesture. "And I don't blame you at all, Addie. The house is a little spooky. But we'll fix that. We'll make it the most amazing house in Singletree, okay?"

I lifted a shoulder. The house, this project—it was more of a means to an end than anything else. If it ended up looking amazing, it would be good for resale value, but didn't make a difference to me otherwise. "Sure."

"I've got the roofers coming out tomorrow like we talked about."

"Okay."

"So you won't be there alone when I go into the shop."

I was almost embarrassed at the relief I felt at this knowledge.

"And this weekend, we'll start on the floors downstairs, okay? Together."

I nodded, realizing Michael could see every single emotion I felt—I'd never had a poker face. And he was trying to reassure me.

"Thanks," I said, but it was almost a whisper, and I wasn't sure he heard me.

THE NIGHT WAS cool and breezy as we walked back through the square and up the hill to Maple Lane. It was a moonless night, and it was peaceful as we walked side by side, the town settling into slumber around us, pulling the darkness up like a warm quilt. But the dark seemed to gather and convene at the top of the hill, where overgrown oaks and wrought iron formed the foreboding entrance to my new home.

I suppressed a shudder as Michael unlocked the gate and we made our way through the deserted side yard to the back door. A single light glowed over the door and it cast a ragged circle out onto the back lawn, making the dark reaches of the yard feel that much more threatening.

We went inside, each of us saying polite words about dinner and then going our separate ways to get ready for bed.

"Goodnight," Michael said, passing me in the upstairs hallway as we traded places in the bathroom.

"Goodnight," I said.

And then the house was quiet, except for the creaking of the structure itself and the scratch of overgrown branches outside the bedroom window. I had brought an Aerobed from Mom's house when she sent me home from the diner, and it was far more comfortable than the camping setup I'd borrowed from Michael. I thought maybe I'd actually be able to sleep.

I forcefully kept my mind from thoughts of ghostly presences, terrifying shrieks, or angry correspondents, and tried to find something more peaceful to let my mind turn over as I drifted off. Somehow, my thoughts turned to Michael Tucker, to his conflicted face as he told me there was no point in making plans for ourselves, that they'd all get ruined anyway. And then to the strong muscles of his forearms, his hands, the broad shoulders stretching the fabric of his deep green Henley shirt. He might be a Tucker, I told myself, but I could still appreciate his aesthetic appeal. The man was attractive.

I'd just begun to drift into the calm happy place between waking and sleep, when an ear-splitting scream sounded from just beside me. I shot straight up to sitting and searched the darkness around me, terrified to discover a set of beady eyes glowing in the darkness, staring right at me.

The funny thing is, I'd never thought of myself as a screamer. But it turns out, I am. And the scream that I let loose was ten times louder and more terrifying than the one that had frightened me in the first place.

Michael burst into my room, switched the lights on, and rushed to the bed, and putting his arms around me as he pulled me against his chest.

His very bare, very muscled chest.

"Are you all right?" He asked, his voice breathless. "What happened?"

I let him hold me, but my eyes searched the room my cheek pressed against his chest. "Someone was here," I managed.

"In the room? You saw someone?" His grip on me tightened, and his voice had become steely.

I nodded against his shoulder, but as my panic began to recede, other things began to register. He smelled clean. And manly. A little like hay or grass, maybe. But good. Reassuring.

He held me tightly against him, his strong legs to one side of the bed as my heart rate descended. I could feel the beating of his heart against my cheek, and it was comforting.

"Are you okay?" He asked, his voice soft.

"Yeah," I managed.

"I should check the house. See if there's anyone here."

I nodded, though the idea of him wandering through the house if someone was really here was terrifying. "Okay." I climbed out of bed and tugged down my nightshirt, unwilling to let him out of my sight, even if he was about to lead us both to our deaths. Better than sitting here alone, waiting for his screams to echo through the house.

I followed at his heels, creeping through every room in the

old creaking house, flicking on lights and checking closets. And there was no one inside. No one but us. We even checked the creepy attic.

"Do you think maybe you dreamed it?" he asked.

I thought about that. "I had been almost asleep," I said, accepting the glass of water he offered me as we stood in the kitchen. Michael stood next to the sink, completely disregarding the fact he wore nothing but a pair of flannel pajama pants that rested quite low on his hips. I was trying to be just as nonchalant about the fact, but if I was honest, he had the nicest body I'd ever seen up close, all molded muscles and sinew. "But that scream pretty much woke me up."

"Yeah, you screaming woke me right up too."

"Not my scream." I whacked him with the back of my hand, and it felt a little like hitting a cliff face—hard and unyielding. But warm. I pushed away thoughts of being in his embrace. I'd think about how nice that had been later. "That same horrible scream we've been hearing. The sage didn't work at all."

"Shocking."

"Your sarcasm isn't helping right now."

"I know. I'm sorry." He paused, his gaze dropping mine and finding the floor. "Listen, are you going to be okay to go back to bed? I mean—"

"Hey," I said, putting some bravado into my voice that I definitely didn't feel. "Of course. I'm a big girl."

"You can sleep in my room again," he offered. "If you want."

I didn't respond right away, but thought about how I'd feel knowing he was right there, versus trying to be comfortable in the bigger room alone, where I'd most definitely seen a set of eyes in the darkness. "Um. If you're sure?"

"Of course," he said. "We'll get things sorted out tomorrow."

I followed him upstairs, feeling a little sheepish about my

own terror, and climbed into the sleeping bag I'd put back into his room when I'd brought in the Aerobed. "Thanks," I said.

"It's nothing, Addie," he murmured.

And then I lay there in the dark for a long time, listening as his breathing turned even and deep. And finally, I slept.

15

VEGGIE RESTORATION
MICHAEL

I woke to sunlight streaming through the dirty film that covered the windows of the bedroom. The filth gave the light a gauzy quality that seemed to float around the room, ethereal and insubstantial—like a ghost might be, if such things existed.

A shaft of light fell across the woman sleeping three feet away from me, her hair spilling across the white linen of the pillow and onto the floorboards surrounding her. Addison's face was turned toward me, and in sleep she looked innocent and serene. When Addie was awake, she was beautiful, but when she was asleep, there was something in her expression—so unguarded and trusting—that made my heart twist inside my chest when I looked at her.

I lay for longer than I probably should have, resting on my side, my eyes wide open as I considered her. Mrs. Easter had said we were babies together—well, I would have been the baby. Addison was five years older than I was, not that any of that mattered now that we were adults. In the soft possibility of dawn, I searched for any memory of us as children, in this house maybe, but none came. And the realization made me sad, because I thought now that any time I got to spend with such a beautiful woman would be time I'd want to remember forever.

Quietly, I slipped out of my sleeping bag and to my feet, picking up my clothes from atop the old chest as I did so. The roofers would be starting early, and I'd need to wake Addison so I could head down to the store, at least for a bit, but for now I was going to let her sleep. It had been a rough night.

As I brushed my teeth, my mind kept creeping back to the previous night, to the fear and terror I'd felt when I'd heard Addison scream. I didn't remember running to her room, or going to her bed. All I remembered now was holding her, pulling her against me and wrapping my arms tightly around her, fiercely. As if I could protect her from anything that threatened. As if she really needed me to. But in that moment, Addison Tanner had not seemed like the competent and decisive career woman I knew she was. She'd seemed vulnerable and scared, and while I knew there wasn't much I could do for a woman like Addie who could certainly take care of herself, I knew I could at least use my size and strength to give her a fighting chance.

I laughed to myself. A fighting chance? Against what? There was nothing in this house except some really old plumbing and a lot of memories belonging to other people. I didn't believe Addie had seen eyes in the darkness any more than I believed the witchy women who'd stunk up the place the previous day were actually banishing spirits. I pulled open the medicine cabinet, where I'd stashed my razor, and stared inside for a moment, not fully awake.

I reached for the razor on the top shelf, and my fingers brushed something against the back of the cabinet I hadn't noticed before. Removing the razor, I peered inside. And reached in to remove a key. It was old and tarnished, but not ancient looking. Who would hide a key in a medicine cabinet? I might have, when Dan was small, I thought. But a key to what?

When I was downstairs, I slipped the old key onto my keychain and set about making coffee and muffins. Daniel had always loved chocolate chip, and while he wouldn't be here until after school let out, he wasn't picky about eating muffins that had been made hours before. It was my version of giving him an afternoon snack—one I had time to prepare, since he usually met me at the store in the afternoons during my week with him to help out.

Twenty minutes later, I heard the telltale creaking of floor-boards overhead, the groan of pipes in the bathroom, and then Addie's feet on the stairs. For some reason, anticipation built in me over the thought of her coming down to the kitchen, still touched with sleep and whatever strange thing had passed between us the night before. Something in the way I thought about Addison had shifted, and it wasn't an unpleasant feeling. She might have been a Tanner, and I'd been bred to despise those, but more than that, she was Addie.

"Muffins?" she asked, looking around the kitchen in surprise. "I smell muffins?" Her hair was wet from her shower and had been braided into a long plait that hung over one shoulder. Her skin was pink and clean, and those dark eyes were wide and clear. She looked like she belonged in a soap commercial, and for some reason my stomach flipped when her eyes came to rest on me.

"Yeah," I said, a twinge of embarrassment pulling my eyes to the floor for no reason I could fathom. I fought the feeling and forced myself to meet her gaze. "I make them for Dan sometimes."

"Oh, he's coming today, isn't he?"

"Yep. I plan to be back here around one, and he should be

here by four. I'll make dinner for us all tonight if you don't have other plans."

Addie laughed lightly, but the sound was sad. "I have no plans, Michael. Except Sunday dinners with Lottie." She crossed the kitchen, pulling a mug from the open shelf and then turning to the coffee pot. The machine made single pods or a full pot, and it had felt like a full pot kind of day. "May I?"

"Of course," I said, feeling out of place, as if I was hosting this beautiful woman in my house. I took a cup too, mostly to give my hands something to do.

"So roof today, right?"

"Yes," I said, and her reminder had me peering out the windows toward the back, but the old garage would have blocked my view of any arriving work trucks. "They should be here soon. Want to hear a roof joke?"

Addie looked uncertain.

"It's on the house."

"Stop that," she said. "That's terrible." But the corners of her lips turned up in a way that made it feel so much better than terrible.

I shrugged and turned back to the muffins. Dad jokes were in my blood.

"Anything I need to do? To supervise or whatever? I've never had a roof repaired." She wrapped long fingers around her mug and sat at the wood table, those eyes fixed on my face.

"Just be here in case they have a question or find something unexpected."

She nodded, and then sipped at her mug.

"Oh, speaking of unexpected." I pulled out my keys and took a seat across from her, singling the one I'd discovered out from the others. "This was upstairs in the medicine cabinet. Any ideas what it might fit?"

She looked at it, one of her fingers tracing the outline against the wood of the tabletop. "No," she said. "It doesn't look that old."

"I haven't been able to get into the garage," I said. "Maybe it goes to that door. I'll try it on my way out."

She nodded. "Let me know. So while you're gone, I will supervise roofers, and I guess I can clean out this pantry." She angled her head toward the open door at the back of the kitchen. "There are cans in there from nineteen-twenty, I bet."

"Don't throw the old stuff out though," I said, surprising myself. "I'd love to see it."

"Into antique vegetables?"

"I would have said no, but for some reason I want to see the cans."

The oven timer dinged then, and I went to retrieve the muffins with a smile on my face. Addie's wit was a combination of sarcasm and self-deprecation that I enjoyed. She wasn't overly confident—though I couldn't really fathom how a woman like her wasn't—but she was clearly super intelligent, and that made her quick with a joke. I liked it. A lot.

"Wow," she said in a breathy tone as I put a plate of muffins in the center of the table next to a tub of butter. "Don't let Lottie know you can bake like this."

"Think she'll feel threatened?"

She nodded, and the idea of her thinking I was good at something gave me little flush of pleasure. I was good at so few things, it was a nice change.

"Instead of vegetable restoration, you could get the rooms ready for the floor refinishing down here," I suggested.

Addie looked at me, her nose adorably scrunched in confusion. "How would I do that?"

"I brought the drum sander over and stuck it in the parlor. Just need to move the furniture into the dining room and start sanding, really."

"I have no idea how to operate that thing."

"I can show you. It's like a vacuum cleaner. You've used one of those?"

She frowned at me, her eyes narrowing. "Once or twice. But I do appreciate that you didn't jump to the conclusion that I had just because I'm a woman."

"Okay, then you should be good. Just get it scuffed up. The professional guys will do the rest."

Addison was finishing a second muffin as I washed my hands and started getting ready to head to the store, but when her phone rang, I turned to see her answer it.

"S'my mom," she said through a mouthful of muffin. She finished chewing and then answered the phone.

I watched as her face changed from carefree and happy to dark and drawn. Whatever Lottie was saying wasn't good. I crossed my arms and waited for her to hang up, feeling an odd certainty that the call might have something to do with me.

"The moose," Addie said, putting down her phone.

"Oh shit." I sighed. It had to be my cousins. No one else had access to the kind of heavy machinery required to haul that enormous moose around town. "Where'd they put it?"

"Town square," Addie said. "Wearing a tutu, I guess."

I couldn't stifle the laugh that launched from my throat at the image.

The smile vanished from Addie's face and her voice was sharp. "That statue is very dear to my aunt."

"Why a tutu?" I managed to ask between repressed chuckles.

"There was a sign around its neck. 'Tanners are tutu stupid.'"

I sighed. That wasn't very clever. "My cousins are idiots."

"Resourceful idiots," she noted. "That thing must weigh—"

"About a ton," I confirmed. When she lifted an eyebrow at my quick answer, I confessed, "I've helped move it before. In my less educated days. Before we were partners."

"And you weighed it?"

"No, but the equipment I used had one point five ton limit, so I know it's not over that."

She nodded. "I see."

"I'll make sure they return it this morning, okay?"

"My mom is furious." From her tone, I was guessing Lottie wouldn't care how quickly the moose made it home. The damage was done.

I sat down for a minute, gazing at Addie. There had been a time when I would have found this funny, but seeing how her mother's angry call had worn down whatever energy reserves she had made me realize how much even silly pranks could wear on people. "I'm sorry, Addie."

"You didn't do it. I know for a fact where you were all night."

"You're my alibi," I said, smiling without thinking about how I'd almost implied something I hadn't meant to. We'd been together. But we were not together. Not like that. The damned blush threatened again and I cursed my ginger complexion.

"It would be really nice if you could put it back," she said, letting my strange innuendo go.

"Think Verda will retaliate?"

Addie lifted a shoulder. "Lottie might."

"This needs to end."

"I agree," she said. "But maybe it's close. I mean, look at us. A Tanner and a Tucker sitting in a dilapidated old house having muffins."

"We are the future."

She chuckled, and I stood, picking up my keys and heading for the door. "I'll see you later. Do you have my number in case you need to reach me today?"

We exchanged phone numbers, and I tried not to feel like a dude at a bar who'd just scored the pretty girl's digits. Those days were long since past.

16

SANDSTORM
ADDISON

Michael left me with a strange feeling wending through me, one that was not altogether unpleasant, but one that made me wary. It was comfortable, being with him. And sitting in the kitchen of our shared haunted house, eating muffins, had felt very domestic, and normal. It was something I could do every day for the rest of my life and feel content. There were the other things too, the way my stomach leapt when he met my eyes, the way my skin heated when he brushed against me accidentally, the way my mind had gone to very naughty places when he'd held me against his bare chest late at night.

But none of that really mattered.

I was at a decision point in my life, and this interlude was merely that—a way for me to take a breath before getting back to the things I'd chosen. But right now, all those things reminded me of Luke. And a dark chill swept through me when I thought of him. Of how he'd left. Of the fact that I still hadn't heard a word from him.

Eight years had been easy enough for him to brush away like specks of unwanted dust on his sleeve, so why was I struggling so much to let it go?

The odd thing was, I didn't feel heartbroken. At first I had, I thought. But in the wild tangle of emotions Luke left in his wake —shock, disappointment, loneliness—it had been hard to pull one thing from another. And there had seemed to be a few feelings that didn't completely fit the situation too.

Like relief.

Had I persevered in the relationship with Luke mostly because it was habit? Because we'd put in so many years together by the time I might have questioned it that it seemed wasteful to let it all go and move on?

I sighed, picking at the last muffin on my plate as my mind twirled through realities I didn't want to face. One thing was crystal clear, even if everything else was murky and uncertain: I'd trusted Luke, depended on him. And it had been a mistake. I'd ended up hurt and alone, and that was my own fault as much as his. I should never have given him that power over me. And I'd never do it again.

Which was why I needed to decide what I was doing with my life. Six months, I told myself. And then I'd go back to New York and pick up the pieces. I talked to my manager on the phone the day before, and while he sounded uncertain, he hadn't said no. So I thought there was a good chance I'd get my job back. If I wanted it. I'd give the situation with Luke time to flush through me, give myself time to think through next steps. We'd sell the house, I'd have some money, and then I'd go back and begin again.

The roofers arrived at nine-thirty, and seemed to need no direction from me at all. They put up ladders and ropes, and soon the whole exterior was swarming with men climbing up and down, dropping things to the ground and pulling things up.

It was reassuring, having them out there. As if the ghosts that inhabited the place couldn't act if there were witnesses.

While the men outside worked, I moved the scant furniture

from the parlor and entryway. Once the rooms were clear, I eyed the big drum sander Michael had brought from somewhere, wondering if this machine and I were going to be able to work together.

"Use it like a vacuum cleaner," he'd said. "Just go slowly and evenly. Don't linger in one spot too long."

"I can do this," I said, mostly to myself, but I figured the ghosts might appreciate my confidence too. With that, I grabbed the handles and switched the thing on. It hummed to life, vibrating roughly beneath my hands, and I followed Michael's directions, leaving a dusty wake behind me.

The day passed quickly in a haze of sawdust and hammer sounds, and for the first time in weeks, I felt as if I'd accomplished something. When Michael returned—much later than he'd hoped, since returning the moose turned out to be quite difficult once Verda noticed the Tuckers replacing the sculpture out in her garden and called the police—I'd sanded the two rooms I'd cleared.

"You did a good job," he said, wandering through the rooms and looking at my work.

"It wasn't hard with that huge sander, I guess," I said.

"You're pretty strong though," he told me. "That thing tires people out, and you have to be a certain size to handle it."

I flexed one of my arms, making my bicep bunch up beneath the sleeve of my flannel shirt. "Guess all those gym classes paid off then."

The men were wrapping up outside, and we went out to talk to the foreman, who said they'd return on Saturday to finish the work. Already, the house looked fresher, with the very top already sporting new slate tiles. The previous tiles, the roofer had said, had lasted more than a century—something he attributed to the durable nature of slate. That had figured into our decision to spend a small fortune to replace the roof with a fresh layer of slate instead of the less expensive wood shingles he offered.

"It's gonna look good," Michael said.

"Hey, Dad." Daniel appeared then, coming around the back of the property past the little one-car garage, wheeling his bike at his side. "Ms. Tanner."

"Hi Daniel," I said, feeling awkward for no reason I could discern around the boy. I took a step away from Michael and then wondered what in the world had made me do it. "You can call me Addie," I added.

"The house is a disaster," Daniel observed, glancing around the lawn, which was strewn with pieces of old roof tiles.

"They'll clean up when they're done," Michael said. "But watch your step out here, okay?"

Daniel shrugged, leaning his bike against the railing of the back porch and letting himself inside.

Michael offered to cook, but Daniel talked him into ordering pizza, and we ate it around the little table in the kitchen. Daniel told us about school and asked his father a million questions about the moose that had appeared in the town square again.

As the evening wound down, I began to feel awkward—it wasn't like we could all lounge on the couch in front of the television. We didn't have a television. Or a couch. And so I excused myself to my room.

"You'll be okay?" Michael asked me in a way that had Daniel squinting his eyes and looking between us.

"I'll be fine," I assured him, not feeling quite as sure as I sounded. I'd go to my room, get into bed, and read a book, I decided. And I took myself upstairs to get ready for bed. I spent more time than necessary brushing my teeth and washing my face, dragging my feet a bit about the idea of closing myself yet again in the room where I'd awoken to screaming and beady little eyes staring at me from the edge of my mattress. I knew it was ridiculous, that it was likely I'd dreamed the eyes and that the "scream" was just some sort of plumbing issue, but it was hard to convince myself of that completely.

As I stepped into the room, which felt chilly and cold compared the warmth of the little kitchen downstairs, Michael appeared in the hallway. "Hey."

"Hey," I paused, a hand going to my hair, which I'd just piled atop my head in a bun.

"We're gonna watch a movie on Dan's laptop. Wanna join us?"

Relief swept through me. I didn't have to be brave yet. "Sure."

"I'll help you move the air bed so you have somewhere to watch," he said, and with that, we were moving me into his room again, where Daniel already lay on his stomach on his sleeping bag, flicking through movie options.

"The Ring?" He suggested.

"No," Michael said without a pause.

"Friday the Thirteenth."

I cringed.

"Definitely not. No ghosts, serial killers, or knife-wielding psychopaths." Michael peered over Daniel's shoulder.

"That's all the good ones," Daniel complained.

I settled onto my bed as they debated, feeling warm inside and out. I didn't care what we watched—though I agreed that ghosts and killers were not my preference given our current location—I was just happy not to be alone for now.

In the end, we agreed on one of the Avengers movies none of us had seen, and it was perfect. The house creaked softly around us as we lay on our respective makeshift beds in the darkened upstairs room, and I marveled at how much more at home I felt at this moment than I had in at least the last four years.

My life in New York had consisted of waiting for Luke almost constantly. At first, he was good about calling, about texting when rehearsals ran late or when some of his colleagues were going to go out together for a drink after a performance. And in those days, he always seemed excited to return home to me, happy to have my attention and my questions. We traveled together for his performances across the country when my job could spare me, and I would have said we were happy. *He* might have even said we were happy.

But then he began neglecting to call. Neglecting to tell me he had travel coming up. Neglecting me.

And I was too blind to see or too stupid to accept that his life had somehow gone on without me, that I had been relegated to the dark corners of our life like his old practice violin—the one he kept for sentimental reasons, but which he'd said held no real value. Not in comparison to its shiny expensive replacement.

I drifted to sleep before the credits rolled on the movie, and it wasn't until much, much later that I awoke to the sounds of people walking the floors of the attic overhead. At first I wasn't sure what I was hearing, but as I awoke, I realized something was terribly wrong.

Darkness had enveloped the room, and it took me a moment to realize I was still in Michael's room. Who was upstairs? Had Daniel and Michael gone up there? But no. There were two sets of steady breaths coming from nearby.

My groggy mind tried to remember how I'd come to sleep here, when I had fully intended to move back down the hall. What would Daniel think, after all?

But I was grateful to Michael for letting me sleep, for leaving me be. He undoubtedly suspected I would be afraid to go back to sleeping in that room alone—even if my reasons were inherently crazy.

Now though, I thought they weren't crazy. I sat up, squinting my eyes as if it would help my ears better decode what I was hearing. A scuffling noise, followed by silence. Footsteps racing across the floor. More silence. A crash!

A yelp flew from my mouth as I clutched the covers to my chin.

"What was that?" A sleepy voice came from the darkness at my side. Daniel.

"Not sure," I admitted, trying to sound brave, adultly.

He sat up then—I couldn't see him clearly but could feel another wakeful presence in the room. The noises overhead continued.

"Ghosts," he said, and his voice held an edge of fear but also one of awe. "Dad, wake up."

He must have poked Michael because the next sound was a startled and sleepy, "Ow. What?"

"The ghosts," Daniel said, as if this explained things.

"There's no such thing," Michael said, and I heard him roll over. "Go back to sleep."

"Let's go look," Daniel said, his voice holding equal parts fear and excitement. "I can't sleep now." Oh no. I couldn't let him go look alone and Michael did not sound like he was up for attic exploration.

"No." Michael said.

I, for one, did not need to go look. Despite my hesitation to believe there was any such thing as ghosts, the point was that I didn't NOT believe it. And that little edge of possibility was where terror lay.

"I'm going," Daniel said, and I heard him getting out of his sleeping bag.

"Dan," Michael moaned. "No."

"Come on." At this point, Daniel's voice was at the door, and it was clear he was not in the mood to be the obedient son tonight.

"I'll go," I said, slipping out from beneath the blanket I'd snuggled under as we'd watched the movie. Dread filled my chest and I moved slowly toward the door.

Michael made some kind of grumbling noise and shuffled out of his sleeping bag, lighting our way with the flashlight from his phone. In the tiny arc of light, I noticed he was again shirtless, and again wearing the low-slung PJ pants that sent an unfamiliar wave of lust through me. The fear still bolting around inside me banished it easily enough, though. Lust was not the appropriate feeling for a ghost-hunting expedition.

The attic stairs looked especially creepy in the glare of the phone light, the darkness at the top looming as Michael led us forward. Scarier still, the noises continued as we approached in our socked feet.

At the top, Michael made a motion for us to stop, and I waited just behind Daniel, who seemed to have finally gained an appropriate level of fear about the fact that we were about to confront whatever was making all the noise up here. Michael swung his light around, and I heard him sigh heavily.

"Holy cow," he said. "No ghosts, I don't think. They're gone, if they were here. And they must have been really mad. Or maybe they're the spirits of messy toddlers. Come look."

The attic, illuminated in the light of Michael's phone, was a disaster. The boxes that had been stacked into the bookshelf had been pulled out, their contents flung wildly around the space. The dressmaker's form, which had stood eerily in one corner, had been knocked over, and a jagged slash now ran the length of its torso.

What was all this? These ghosts weren't just angry—they were furious! Was the dress form supposed to represent me? My blood iced and my breathing became shallow.

"Creepy," Daniel said, his voice full of awe.

There was also a smell that permeated the space, something that reminded me of wet dog. I tried to slow my breathing.

Hyperventilating would only let me smell more of the fetid perfume the ghosts had left.

"Do ghosts have a smell?" I asked, trying to remember if that was something I'd heard, along the lines of haunted spaces feeling chillier than the rest of a room.

"I guess so," Michael said.

There were no ghosts here now, but clearly something or someone had been here. We had proof. I wasn't crazy. But a search of the house revealed—unsurprisingly—nothing at all.

17

DROOL CAN BE SEXY
MICHAEL

Our late night adventures might have led to a late morning sleeping in, only the sun streaming in through the filmy bedroom windows had us stirring at the crack of seven.

I watched Addie for a few minutes, lying on my side on the floor not far from her bed. The morning light was illuminating her golden skin, and her dark hair spread across the pillow. Her dark lashes fanned across her cheeks, and her lips were rosy as she frowned the tiniest bit in her sleep. The tiniest little drizzle of drool left a dark spot on her pillow, and something about that —about seeing something that reminded me that for all of her seeming perfection, she was very human—it made me feel closer to her.

The dark eyes fluttered open as I watched, and I rolled to my back, stretching and trying hard to pretend I hadn't just been watching her sleep like some kind of creeper.

"Morning," she said softly, her voice still dreamy.

"Good morning," I said.

She glanced at Daniel, who lay sprawled, arms flung over his head, one leg kicked free of his sleeping bag.

"He won't be up for hours," I told her. "His record is two p.m."

"Wow." She chuckled and sat up, stretching her arms overhead in a way that made her long-sleeved T-shirt pull across her chest. I forced my eyes away as she slid from her bed, still in the sweats she'd worn to watch the movie. They were casual and cute, and I had a fleeting feeling that we were playing house, that maybe this is how it would be if we were really together. Not the waking in separate beds part, but waking up together, getting to see one another in those pre-breakfast moments when we are all just human.

"Shall we knock out the rest of the floors?" She asked. "I've totally mastered that sander. Made it my bitch yesterday."

"Oh really?" I asked, laughing at that statement coming out of this particular woman's mouth.

"Totally."

"Breakfast first. Coffee," I said, wishing I could pop out of bed feeling ready to conquer the world. But I was fueled on caffeine, and there wasn't much to be done about that.

"Meet you in the kitchen in ten," she said. And the most impressive thing about Addie Tanner? She let me have the bathroom first.

Ten minutes later, I entered the kitchen, embraced by the scent of coffee and the sight of Addie at the sink, holding a mug and gazing out the window at the side yard.

"Those floors look good," I told her. I'd walked through the parlor and foyer again before coming into the kitchen. Addie had done a good job. "You weren't kidding about telling that sander what's up."

"I never kid about my mastery of power tools. Now I just wish I could master them well enough to get the front porch put back together. I want to drink my coffee out there on a rocking chair."

I laughed at Addie's power-tool confidence. "Really? Have you mastered a lot of power tools? In New York City I can't imagine you were doing a lot of home renovation."

She turned and leaned against the counter as I sipped my coffee. "No, not really," she said. "I'm handy with an electric screwdriver if you need me to put up some curtains, though."

"Might need those to avoid waking at the crack of dawn every weekend."

"I like being up early," she said as I joined her in leaning against the counter. "The day feels like it could still go perfectly."

"And then it gets rolling and you realize that perfect doesn't exist?"

"Something like that." Her words were so leaden with disappointment, I wanted to ask her why. I wanted to know who had let her down so terrifically. I suspected the answer would be the man she'd talked about in New York, and I knew I had no right to ask. But I had come to feel a little bit protective of the woman at my side—Tanner, though she was.

"I like that idea," I said, hoping she might open up a bit more. "That the day is stretched out ahead of us, perfect and full of possibility."

That earned me a smile, but her gaze lingered on my face and the smile turned into a half frown, like she was trying to figure something out.

"What?"

"You're not an optimist by nature," she suggested.

"I haven't found a lot of reasons to be optimistic," I said.

"Someone left you a house out of nowhere. And two hundred thousand dollars to use to fix it."

"Came with a few burdens," I quipped. "Like a Tanner in residence."

Addie elbowed me in the side, and despite the coffee that

sloshed over the rim of my cup, I thrilled at that little familiar touch. "You're not so bad, I guess," I said.

"Oh, thanks." She looked into her own cup. "I'm working on my own optimism. So we can work on it together while we fix the house, I guess."

"Are you a reformed optimist?"

She looked at me, and I could feel the change in the air between us the second she decided to confide in me. "I am. I used to believe the best of people. I believed you could count on them, depend on them if they said you could. But I know better now."

"Who let you down, Addie?" I put down my mug and faced her.

Addie met my eyes, and the depth of sadness there lit a fire inside me. Whoever had turned this pretty, smart, independent woman into a pessimist deserved to be unhappy for the rest of his life.

"His name was Luke. I thought we were going to get married. Have kids. I waited eight years for him to think the same thing."

I sighed. Clearly, it hadn't gone that way. I was sad for Addie, but didn't feel terribly torn up about it really. He clearly didn't deserve her.

"I came home from work one day to a letter. More of a note, actually."

"A note?" Fury stirred inside me, despite the fact I'd had only a half cup of coffee. No asshole should write anyone off with a note.

"He said I was holding him back. That he'd had an opportunity to join a symphony in Europe and had turned it down once already because of me. He took it this time and left."

"Seems like that's more of a conversation after eight years. Not a note."

"Right?" Addie stared into her cup. I could almost feel the

self-doubt that asshole's actions had lodged in her otherwise confident persona.

"Hey," I said, touching her hand. Her skin was warm, soft. "That's on him. That wasn't about you."

"I wasn't enough to make him want to stay." Her expression was so defeated, I felt like I'd do anything to wipe it from her face, change it to a smile.

"You're enough," I said, and stepped closer, pulling Addie into my arms. I hadn't planned it, but the atmosphere between us made it feel so natural, so close. And if ever a woman needed a hug, it was Addie.

Her arms slipped around my waist, and her head dropped to my shoulder, and we just stood there, letting the warmth of our bodies mix. Addie smelled good, and her hair was soft and silky against my cheek. And after a moment, the feel of her breasts pressed against my chest began to become a little bit distracting, and I felt my cock hardening in my jeans. I was about to step back when the kitchen door opened and the last person I wanted to see in the world stepped in.

"Well, this is cozy," Shelly said, crossing her arms over her chest.

Addie practically leapt backward, spinning to face my ex-wife. "Oh, hi! That was, I mean . . . that wasn't what it looked like, it was . . . "

"It was really none of Shelly's business," I interrupted. "Since she walked into our house without even knocking."

"*Our* house?" Shelly asked, looking between us. "Are you two a thing now?"

"Also none of your business," I said, at the same time as Addison said, "No!"

Shelly rolled her eyes—something she was very talented at —and pulled a piece of paper from her purse, unfolding it.

"Daniel left this at home, and I think he needs it for school Monday."

I reached for it, but she didn't hand it to me. "I'll give it to him," she said. "Where is he?"

"He's still asleep," I said, hoping my voice made it clear she wasn't going to go traipsing through the house.

"I'll find him," she said, and she turned and headed up the stairway to the left.

It was my turn to roll my eyes, and I followed her up the narrow back stairs. "We should really let him sleep, Shell, he's growing."

She made a noise that sounded like "Pffft," and continued, turning into the hallway on the second floor. She peeked into the two rooms she passed, and finally pushed open the door to the room where Daniel was sleeping. And then she pulled it shut again and nearly crashed into me.

"What the hell is going on here?" She asked, her eyes wide and angry.

"What do you mean?"

"Are you all sleeping in one room? Together?"

Oh shit. Addie's bed was in my room. "Well, yeah, but not like you think."

"With my son?"

"Our son."

"No. Michael, I've put up with a lot, but this is just too much. He doesn't need to witness you, doing whatever it is you're doing here, in the room where he's sleeping, for God's sake."

Anger and exhaustion combined in me—my usual reaction to Shelly's over-the-top reactions to ordinary things. "That's completely not what's happening here."

"Well, that's what it looks like. And he's twelve. What is he supposed to think?"

"We're all in separate beds, Shell." I rubbed a hand across

the back of my neck, wishing I'd managed to drink about three more cups of coffee before being forced into this conversation.

She continued to glare at me.

"Can we talk about this downstairs?"

"With her? No thank you." A flicker of jealousy flared in Shelly's eyes, and I understood a little bit what this anger might be about.

"Shelly, there is nothing going on with me and Addison Tanner."

"That wasn't what it looked like when I walked in on you in the kitchen."

"Which was rude, by the way. You need to knock."

"This is a construction zone, not a home where you should be shacking up with your new girlfriend."

"She's not—"

"And I don't think it's appropriate for you to have my son living in a construction zone, either. None of this is good for him. You, living in sin, the possibility that he might fall through the floorboards at any moment. All the filth and grime."

I shook my head. Shelly was just grasping at straws. She did this whenever she was unhappy with me. She was irate now, spewing words and waving her hands around.

"I'm going to sue for sole custody, Michael. You clearly aren't responsible enough to be raising our son."

Despite the declaration being baseless—it wasn't the first time I'd heard it—it was still my worst fear. I'd done everything wrong in my life, and I was determined to do right by Daniel. But I wouldn't be able to if Shelly took him from me. And worse, I knew he would be better off with me, or at least with shared custody. Shelly's life was unstable and irregular. For the first time though, I was a tiny bit worried she might have a point. I was living in a construction zone with a woman who was not my wife. Maybe unstable and irregular looked better than dangerous and illicit.

"No, Shelly, I—"

"I don't want to hear it. Give Daniel this paper. I'm going to talk to my lawyer."

I sighed, but Shelly needed to feel like she had some power, so I defaulted to apology, which was what usually appeased her. "Please," I said, genuine worry making my heart pound. Daniel was the only thing I hadn't screwed up. I couldn't lose him.

I followed Shelly back down the stairs, hoping she'd cool off.

"You'll be hearing from my lawyer," Shelly said, walking through the kitchen and shooting Addie a dagger-eyed look as she passed. Then she clattered out the back door and disappeared.

"What was all that?" Addie asked, and the care in her voice, the softness of her tone, made me wish I could pull her into my arms again. But now—especially now—I could not.

"Nothing," I said, refilling my coffee cup. "Let's get to those floors."

18

A MOOSE ON THE LOOSE
ADDISON

S helly left in a huff, and there was a noticeable change in Michael on the heels of her departure. I hadn't missed her threat of a lawyer, and wondered what exactly she was talking about, but Michael's face was closed and he wasn't meeting my eyes. Clearly, the sharing part of our morning was over.

I'd just given him the truth about my own issues and fears—had opened up more than I'd intended. And then he'd taken me in his arms and given me a hug that was at once reassuring and —something else entirely. I hadn't meant to, but I'd let myself consider that hard solid chest I'd seen beneath the T-shirt he wore, had let myself feel those strong hands on my body. And while I took comfort from the gesture, there was something more I couldn't deny. I was turned on.

But it didn't matter. For one thing, my life was not here in Singletree, and I wasn't looking for love. I was coming off the heels of a devastating breakup, and I just needed to regroup and get back to New York. Besides, what in the world would my mother say if I hooked up with a Tucker?

We spent the day working on the house as the roofers finished up overhead, Daniel joining us and Michael remaining terse and distant throughout the effort. At one point, Daniel insisted we go back up to the attic to investigate the ghostly disturbances of the night before, and I thought he was actually quite wise. Nothing would look as terrifying in the light of day. We went up after lunch, picking up the scattered papers and letters, photos and newspapers that had been strewn around by the ghosts.

The letters were the most interesting thing we found, besides the pictures. But without knowing quite who the people in the photos were, it was hard to learn much from them—except that the house had been beautiful once. And I was starting to feel invested in the hope that it would be again. Even a couple days of pouring my energy into the place had made it feel more like mine, like something I cared about.

"This one is totally gushy," Daniel called from the corner of the attic where he sat reading letters. "Listen. 'My love, I cannot imagine what you've had to endure during your time in France. I can only hope that the knowledge of your imminent return home is as much a balm to your soul as to mine, and that the love I have for you will help to heal any wounds your soul may have sustained. I do not care what my father says. We will be together. As you said, it is fated in the stars. I wait for you, always. All my love, Lucille.'"

My heart warmed, imagining Lucille waiting for Robert to return. I'd read through dozens of their letters now, and the love story between Filene's parents touched my soul in the same way a great romantic movie always did. They weren't worried about what their parents thought about Tuckers and Tanners together. Of course, they'd never met Lottie.

"That's a love letter, all right," Michael agreed.

"Gah." Daniel made a little retching noise. "Who's Lucille?"

"Filene's mother," I answered.

"Who's Filene?" Daniel asked.

"Filene Easter," Michael said. "The lady who left us this house."

"This letter is addressed to Robert Tucker," Daniel said. "And it's from Lucille Tanner. So who is Easter?"

"Those were Filene's parents. Easter was her married name," I explained, setting the mannequin back upright as I suppressed a shiver at the gash in its torso.

"So Mrs. Easter was a Tucker?" Daniel asked, looking pleased.

"And a Tanner," I reminded him.

"Oh, that must've made people mad," Daniel said.

"Probably," I agreed. "My mom says the feud has been going on for hundreds of years."

"What started it?" Daniel asked, his freckled face lit by the dusty sunlight coming in from the high round window. He looked so young and innocent in the daylight, and the attic itself looked so harmless and ghost-free.

"I'm not sure."

"I don't think anyone remembers," Michael said. He'd been quiet for a while, sorting newspapers in the far corner.

"Then why don't we give it up?" Daniel asked.

"Old habits, I guess," Michael said. "And people get their feelings hurt and want revenge."

"Aunt Verda's feelings are definitely hurt," I said. Mom had told me that Verda saw moving her moose around town as akin to desecrating her husband's grave. Mom had been pretty upset about it herself, telling me that she was going to help get revenge this time. I'd suggested we could be the bigger family and just let it go. But it didn't sound like that was what Mom had in mind at all.

"Virge and Emmet are so invested in the whole thing," Michael said. "I've tried to get them to just give it up, but they have so little else going on, I guess." Michael had spent the better part of an hour this morning on the phone with them, walking them through what needed to be done at the store in his absence. They didn't sound like the brightest fellows to me, but they were family to Michael and Dan, so I kept my mouth shut.

Eventually, we'd managed to sort the attic back into order, tucking the letters and clippings into boxes and setting them back on the shelves. I swept the space out and even cleaned the windows. By the time we headed back down, the place didn't look ghostly at all, and I found it hard to believe how terrified I'd been the night before. The whole house was starting to feel less haunted and more, just, old.

We finished sanding floors on the main level Saturday evening, falling into bed—me in my own room—and immediately to sleep with no ghostly interference all night. On Sunday, we started upstairs, working through the bedrooms we weren't using. By the lunchtime, the house was almost livable, the company we'd called to complete the job of refinishing the floors would show up Monday. We'd agreed early on to do as much of the work ourselves as we could, but since Michael had a store to run and I had very little home improvement experience, there were limits to what we could do. And we also had the improvement fund to work with.

I was vacuuming up some of the last bits of sawdust from our sanding when Michael stepped in front of me to get my attention. I shut off the vacuum. "What's up?"

"Since the guys are coming in to finish the floors, it probably makes the most sense for us to stay somewhere else, keep off of them until they're done."

I hadn't thought about that. "Somewhere else?"

He shifted his weight, wrapping a hand around the back of his neck, and I sensed the same reluctance in him that I felt in myself. I didn't want to leave the house. In the few days we'd been here, it had begun to feel like an odd kind of home, and we'd gotten along so well it was hard to remember that we weren't actually any kind of family. "Yeah, I thought maybe you could go back to your mom's for a few days? Dan and I could stay at my place. Get him out of the construction zone."

"Oh yeah, sure."

"It should take the guys a day or two to finish prepping and then they'll refinish. I think the hardwood will be cured and dry in a week."

A week with Lottie? I swallowed back my disappointment. "Sure."

I said goodbye to Michael and carried my bag down the hill to the Tin. I went back to Mom's house with her that afternoon.

Sunday dinner with Lottie was always a bit of an inquisition, but this one was particularly painful.

"So you two are getting along?" Mom asked over a forkful of chicken.

All eyes at the table were on me—my sisters, Wiley Blanchard's, and Cormac's. His girls were at his brother's house, so he and Paige were both free to offer opinions and advice about my odd living situation.

"Yeah, we are," I said.

"No in-house pranking? Maybe you could switch the sugar and salt or something. Keep the feud rolling on a smaller scale," Cormac suggested.

"Definitely not," I said. "The feud is ludicrous, and you should all just forget about it."

"Tell that to poor Verda," Mom said. "Her moose got dinged when they moved him back to her garden this time, and now he has a divot right in his privates."

"In his what, Mom?" Amberlynn laughed.

"You know." Mom sniffed, clearly too refined to repeat her comment about moose privates.

"Let me get this straight," Wiley said. "The moose sustained a feud-related groin injury?" He was barely suppressing a grin.

"Yes," Mom said stiffly. "And you know Verda thinks of that moose as representative of Harry. It's almost like those horrible Tuckers kicked Harry in the balls or something."

No one at the table was doing a good job showing the appropriate amount of respect for the idea of Uncle Harry's dearly departed balls at this point.

"I hate seeing Aunt Verda upset," Amberlynn said, and something in her voice made me worry.

"Don't do anything," I warned.

She smiled at me, and I had a very bad feeling that something might already be in the works.

"So what's Michael like?" Paige asked. "He's always kept to himself, seemed pretty private since high school."

"What was he like in school?" I asked. Michael and Shelly had been behind me in school. I hadn't really known them. But they were only a year behind my sister Paige.

"He was popular. Soccer star and all that. Everyone was sure he was going pro."

"And then he got Shelly knocked up and he decided to put a ring on it," Amberlynn added. She'd been a year behind him and Shelly, so had no doubt had a front row seat to the scandal.

"Which was the noble thing to do," I pointed out, even though I was not one of Shelly's greatest admirers, based on her performance at the house.

"The noble thing is to not knock up your high school girl-friend," Wiley suggested. He elbowed Amber at this comment and I had a very unwanted vision of the two of them as teenagers. I knew they'd probably been having sex, but having confirmation of it was more than I needed at Sunday dinner.

"I know none of my girls were being so irresponsible at that early age," Mom said. "But it's just like a Tucker to tempt some poor girl into making terrible decisions." She offered this last bit looking right at me, and I knew she meant the house. If Mom knew about the other horrible decisions I'd been tempted to make when I'd seen Michael without his shirt on!

"Michael didn't tempt me into this thing with the house. Mrs. Easter gave it to us."

"So ridiculous," Mom said.

"Did you know she was both a Tucker and a Tanner?" I asked. "Her parents fell in love when they were teens, and got married when Robert Tucker came home from World War I." Mom actually looked impressed when I shared this information. She loved old family stories, and maybe learning that the house was actually related directly to our family line would convince her the Tuckers weren't all evil.

"That's romantic," Paige said.

"It was," I said, nodding. "Their parents didn't approve of the relationship."

"Very Romeo and Juliet," Cormac said.

"I think it was," I said. "Her letter said they believed their relationship was fated in the stars."

"Lord," Wiley said, leaning back in his chair.

"What?" Amberlynn asked him. "I think that's romantic."

"That's a load of hooey," Wiley said. "Love is a choice. Not something that's fated."

"Hmmm," Mom said, standing. "Clear the plates, girls. I need you to taste some things for dessert." I was glad for the change of subject.

Mom often tried out new cafe ideas on us. "Ooh, what is it this time?" Cormac asked. He said Mom's cherry-themed treats were responsible for him falling in love with Paige.

"Halloween is around the corner," Mom said. "I've got some ghost poofs and goblin toes for you to try."

"Yum," Wiley said sarcastically, and Mom shot him a look.

She was, historically, not the biggest fan of my sister's boyfriend, who embraced sarcasm like religion.

That night, after everyone had left and I was once again lying in my childhood bedroom, I picked up the phone stared at it. I wanted to talk to Michael, but couldn't explain to myself why. I missed him, which I knew made no real sense. I put the phone down and sighed, but the lonely emptiness of my room made me pick it up again. I sighed and texted Michael.

Addie: Did you stop by the house at all? See how the floors are coming? I'm not sure I'll survive a week at Mom's.

There was no immediate reply, and I put the phone down on the nightstand, trying to ignore the swirl of disappointment in my stomach. Michael was not obligated to text with me at night. We weren't boyfriend and girlfriend. Hell, we weren't anything. Why did recognition of that fact make me feel so sad?

19

VIRGE IN LAVENDER
MICHAEL

I waited a long time to respond to Addie's text. Longer than I wanted to, and that was the whole problem. Seeing her note —knowing she was thinking of me at night, feeling like a kid with a crush—all of it was wrong. Shelly was threatening to take the one thing that made my life make sense, and if I let myself think about any of what I wanted with Addie, I was putting everything at risk. I couldn't afford to get distracted. I wouldn't get myself into a situation where I was putting my son any place other than first in my list of priorities. If I let myself become infatuated, if I nursed this misplaced desire I was starting to realize I had for Addie, I might end up failing at the only thing I was managing to do right in my life.

Addie was like a bright spot that had appeared in an otherwise dark sky. I'd wandered through the murk for years, doing what was expected and doing everything in my power to be a good father to my son, because that was all that mattered. But now there was Addie, and some whisper in the back of my mind saying that maybe she mattered to me too, even if she wasn't supposed to. Telling me that maybe I wanted her too, even if I couldn't have her.

The time we'd spent together so far had been special to me, even though most of it had been focused on cleaning up an old house. There was something about her, something that made me want to be near her, learn more of what went on in her head. And it was the most interesting thing I'd encountered in a long time. I didn't want to give her up.

I picked up my phone.

Michael: Haven't been by today but I'll check progress tomorrow. You doing okay?

Addie: Mom is a lot.

Michael: I can imagine. And I mean that in the nicest way possible.

Addie: I'll survive. But when choosing between ghostly shrieking and Mom's questions and judgment, I'm pretty sure ghosts win.

Michael: That's saying something.

Addie: It would probably be hard for anyone to live at home again at 35. Plus, she liked Luke and keeps suggesting I try to work things out with him.

I paused. I hadn't considered that Addie might be thinking of going back to her ex. An unwanted churn of jealousy erupted in my gut.

Michael: Are you considering it?

Addie: Definitely not. Turns out I have a shred of self-respect left.

The jealousy fizzled out.

Michael: Good.

Addie: ?

Crap. I realized I had no say at all in what she did, and offering an opinion about her ex was probably the wrong way to go.

Michael: I just mean that I think you deserve better.

Addie: That's nice.

Did she not believe me?

Michael: There's something about you. You're special. Don't take anything less than you deserve.

I cringed after hitting send, wondering if I'd said way too much. There was a significant pause, and my stomach twisted. Definitely too much.

Then, after a full five minutes:

Addie: Thank you. That means a lot to me. I have similar advice for you, you know.

I wasn't sure what to make of that, but decided I'd already put myself out there enough for one night.

Michael: I'll talk to you tomorrow.

Addie: Good night.

I did talk to the contractors the following day, and learned that we could be in the house again after the floors had a full four days to dry and set. I texted Addie to let her know we could move back in on Friday.

I spent the week at the store, sneaking back to my workshop when I could. I was building a few things for the house, things I probably shouldn't have bothered with. But Addie was on my mind, and while maybe I needed to avoid thinking of her in the attractive-woman-I-had-interest-in kind of way, I could think of her in the friend-I-wanted-to-do-something-nice-for kind of way. No harm in that, right?

On Thursday, I arrived at work to find Emmet and Virgil behind the counter, and the whole place scented like a bath and body shop and not a farm supply store. This stunk, and not just of lavender. My cousins were up to something.

"What's going on?" I asked them.

They exchanged a guilty look, and then faced me with matching blank expressions. "Whatddya mean, 'cuz?" Virgil said.

My suspicions rose even higher. "The smell in here? Did you light candles or something?"

"There's no smell."

"Virge, you can deny a lot of things, but there is definitely a smell. Is it lilac?"

"You can identify the scent of lilacs?" he asked me skeptically.

"I don't know, actually. Probably not. It's like gardenia or something. Floral. Ovewhelmingish."

The brothers exchanged a look. "I told you we didn't get it off," Virgil said, punching his brother in the chest.

"What is it?" I asked, incredibly curious now, despite my better judgement.

"Something happened," Emmett said, dropping his eyes to the floor.

"We got hit," Virgil said.

"Hit?" They'd been pranked. "By what? A bath bomb?"

They exchanged a glance and then Virgil's ruddy face darkened. "Tanners."

Here we went again. "Tanners made you smell like a garden party full of old ladies?"

They nodded. "It's in our apartment," Virgil said. "The smell is literally everywhere. Like a potpourri bomb exploded in there or something. We've been doing laundry all night, and we both took a bunch of showers with super manly soap, but nothing helps."

That was a mental image I didn't need. "Did you try tomato juice? Supposed to help with skunk smell."

"This isn't skunk, Mike. It's worse," Virgil said, looking embarrassed about his womanly scent.

"Lavender," said a woman approaching the counter with a large bag of dog food in her arms. "It's nice," she said, clearly believing we had decided the store needed to upgrade its scent. I doubted the bulk of my customers—who wore work jeans and boots and chewed tobacco would feel similarly.

"Thanks," I said, ringing her up. "Come again."

She smiled and headed out, and I turned back to my cousins. "You guys reek."

"The Tanners will pay for this," Virgil said.

"Or how about if they don't?" I asked, Addie's big dark eyes flashing into my mind. "What if we just let it die here on this very flowery smelling hill? The ball's in the Tucker court. Let's just drop it."

"You're just saying that because you're in bed with a Tanner now," Virgil said, poking a chubby finger into my chest.

I thought for a split second about being in bed with Addie. I'd thought about it back when I was in high school too, I remembered her vaguely from that time—the distant older sister of the two Tanner girls who were closer to my age. She'd been tall and beautiful back then. Way out of my league. But now . . . the thought of it was distracting. But still impossible.

"I am not sleeping with Addie."

"Addie, is it?" Virgil asked, his tone mocking.

"That is her name." This was getting old. I didn't like justifying myself to these guys, but I didn't need them spreading rumors about us, either. Shelly was already fired up, though I was pretty sure she knew there was nothing going on. If she had some reason to think there really was, I'd never hear the end of it.

"Addie is a very fond nickname, I'd think," he said.

"Guys, lay off, okay? There's nothing going on with me and Addie. I just think this feud has run its course. Let's end it."

The brothers exchanged a look and then Virgil nodded. "We'll end it, all right."

Shit.

20

LOTTIE'S LEARNINGS
ADDISON

Mom had begun coming home each day with new tidbits of information about the age-old Tanner-Tucker feud.

"Did you know that house was built in 1828 by a Tucker?" She asked me as we sat in matching recliners in her living room watching a rerun of *Charmed*.

I swiveled my head to regard her. "Is that right?" I was interested in the history of the house. But if Mom was suddenly interested in it, there was a good chance she was up to no good.

"It is." She kept her eyes on me, despite the fact that the *Charmed* sisters were in a very sticky situation with a warlock and a possessed schoolteacher.

"Is there something else you wanted to tell me about the house?" I asked.

She nodded. "The reason it is very interesting that the house was built in 1828 by a Tucker is because there are records of that land being purchased in 1827 by a Tanner."

I felt a bit dense. Like maybe I needed Mom to connect the dots a bit more. "Okay, so they sold the land to the Tuckers?"

"No record of that at all." Mom didn't even have to say that she was extremely interested in this information. Her tone said it all.

"Okay, so what, Mom?"

"So the Tuckers clearly stole the land from us."

I sincerely hoped my mother wasn't considering some kind of legal action over something that had happened hundreds of years ago. I didn't need the extra hassle. I needed her to give up the dumb feud, let me fix up the house, and sell it. "From us? Really? It's 'us' now?"

"The Tanners. Us." She gave a fierce nod to make her point.

"I'm sure there's some other record somewhere that explains what happened next."

"Maybe." She narrowed her eyes at me. "That old Tucker fart has been down poking around in those records too."

"Down where? And which fart?"

"City Hall in the archives where I've been digging. I saw him in there today."

"Who, Mom?"

"Victor Tucker. Your boyfriend's uncle."

A little thrill shot through me at the idea of Michael as my boyfriend, but it was so far from reality I needed to put this to rest immediately. "Michael Tucker is not my boyfriend, Mom."

"You're living together," she pointed out.

"No. I mean, we are, but . . . God, Mom, what's your point?"

"I think Victor is doing what I'm doing."

"And that would be?"

"Trying to prove the house should rightfully belong to the Tanner family, not be left equally to both families."

I stood, *Charmed* completely forgotten in my annoyance over her ridiculousness. "The house, Mom, was not left equally to both families. It was left to two individual people, neither of which has any interest in continuing this ridiculous feud."

"That's easy to say when it hasn't affected you personally."

"You're kidding, right? How many complaint sessions have I sat through with you and Aunt Verda moaning about her moose? How long were we on the phone when your shop was turned upside down?"

"Those things didn't happen to you, Addie. They happened to us."

That stung. Mom had complained for years that I'd run away from the family, that I'd thought I was too big for my britches and had to show off by moving to New York. She'd been so passive aggressive about it for so long that I stopped coming home to visit. And now she was essentially telling me she didn't count me as a Tanner at all. "Yes. And I'm sorry. And if we don't stop, things are going to get worse and someone might end up getting hurt."

Mom sniffed in response and I decided that seven-thirty was not too early for a thirty-five year old woman to go to bed. In the morning, the floors would be finished drying, and I could go back to the house. And to Michael. My not-boyfriend who I lived with.

Maybe Mom had a little bit of a point.

THE FOLLOWING DAY, I went to the house with a fresh load of laundry and a fast belief that ghosts would not be as difficult to handle as my mother. I also had a load of garden supplies I'd bought at Michael's store earlier when I had been disappointed not to find him there. What I did find were his cousins, Virgil and Emmett, who both smelled strangely floral, as if their clothes had been washed with some too-strong detergent.

"Aren't you that Tanner lady?" One of them asked me, narrowing his eyes.

"I am," I agreed, feeling a little on the spot.

"The one Mike is shacked up with." This was said by one cousin to the other, as if explaining the situation.

The other cousin nodded enthusiastically, as if this was the most interesting revelation ever to come his way.

The first one said, "Your sister is Amberlynn, right? High school teacher?"

Now I felt slightly defensive. "She is," I confirmed, wondering what they wanted with my little sister. She might be a pain, but I was in the habit of looking out for her nonetheless.

"She may or may not have broken into our apartment," the speaking cousin told me. I wanted to tell them there was zero chance my upstanding little sister would break and enter. But Amberlynn had gotten pretty invested in the feud. I actually didn't doubt she would if she could.

"Yeah," he went on. "And she may or may not have unleashed some kind of perfume bomb in there."

The scent suddenly made sense. I wanted to smack my sister. She was perpetuating this insanity. With a bulk buy from Bath and Bodyworks, no less. "I see," I said.

"Yeah," the cousin said, agreeing in general, I guessed.

"I'll have a word with her," I promised them. "For the record, I think you smell nice," I added.

"Screw you, Tanner," the one that hadn't spoken yet said. He would now be characterized in my head as the mean one.

"Nice," I said, starting to feel annoyed at these rednecks. "Is Michael here?"

"No," they said together, and it was clear they were not going to tell me anything more.

"Fine," I said. "Bye."

They did not respond, but I could feel their angry glares on my back as I left the store.

I spent the rest of the day in the side yard at the house, pulling weeds and digging out roots where I could find them. I wanted to rescue the rose garden, an idea I'd gotten from the photos we'd found. There had been a woman in a long white dress holding a parasol over her head to shade her from the sun. At her feet were at least twenty blooming rose bushes, forming a beautiful backdrop to the imposing structure of the house. I didn't know much about gardening—it wasn't much of a city pursuit—but I remembered a bit from the time I'd spent weeding with Mom as a kid.

I dug and pulled and sweated most of the afternoon away, and when I was close to finishing up, I was rewarded when I found two rose bushes still holding fast in the damp soil. They'd been overgrown and hidden in vines, but they were still there, and I thought maybe there was enough of them left to thrive.

Something about seeing them still there, still fighting for sun and air, gave me hope. We can all come back from hardship. And even if we think our lives might be one way, it might turn out they'll be even better if we just hang on and open ourselves to alternatives.

"What are you up to out here?" A familiar voice came across the lawn, and my stomach gave a little jump. Michael.

"Just trying to clear out some of the weeds out here," I told him.

"It's looking good," he said, striding across the lawn and coming to stand next to where I was kneeling.

I stood, letting out an accidental groan like a much older woman, and wiping my dirty palms over my jeans. "I've been crouching all day long," I said, stretching.

"You got a lot done," he said. "Did you go inside? How are the floors?"

I'd dropped my things in the kitchen, and then had spent the rest of the day outside. I wasn't quite ready to admit that I was still scared to be in the house alone, but that was the truth of it.

"Well, if you're almost done out here, I brought dinner and a bottle of wine to celebrate a major milestone accomplished."

I raised an eyebrow. "That sounds good," I said. It also sounded kind of like a date, but as I considered pointing that out or protesting, I realized the idea actually made me feel warm and giddy. I closed my mouth and smiled. "I might need to clean up a bit before I'm ready for dinner though."

"No rush," Michael said. "By the way, the guys told me you stopped by the store today."

"Oh, yeah. I needed the tools." I wasn't sure if I should mention that they'd told me to screw off.

"I apologize for whatever stupidity came out of them."

"It's fine," I said as we walked together toward the back door of the house.

"It's probably not, but it's nice of you to say so," Michael said. He glanced at the little garage sitting behind the house and stopped for a minute. "You know, I almost forgot I had this key I found and I wanted to try it on the door over there." We still hadn't gotten into the garage, and I had no doubt it would be filled with more stuff we'd have to deal with.

"Sure," I said, following him to the door. The structure was so overgrown with vines it was hard to even get to the door, and the windows were blackened and much too dusty to see through.

He pulled his keys from his pocket and selected the dirty brass one. He wiggled it around a bit, but ultimately stuck the keys back in his pocket. "Doesn't fit."

"We should ask the lawyer about it," I said. "Maybe he has a key he forgot to give us."

"Maybe," Michael shrugged. "But I think I know why this key doesn't fit in."

"Why?"

"It's too door key." He grinned at me, waiting for me to get it.

"Oh my God, you are the absolute worst."

"You love dad jokes."

"I do," I admitted. I loved his dad jokes, at least. It took a willingness to be vulnerable to tell a truly horrible joke, and I liked that Michael was willing to reveal that part of himself to me. It made me feel closer to him.

We went together into the house, and I took my things upstairs to shower. The newly finished floors gleamed beneath my feet, and the creaking I'd grown used to in the short time I'd been in the house had lessened, since the crew had shored up boards that were loose or damaged. The house was beginning to feel less neglected and spooky, and a little more like a place where I could imagine families once having lived.

21

DORKY
MICHAEL

I shouldn't have felt so happy about being back at the house, about seeing Addie again. But in the few days since we'd been away, I found that I missed her, that the few days we'd spent together working side by side had been the closest thing I'd ever had to the kind of home life I'd always wanted. A man and a woman with similar goals, working together. I knew it was a stretch to put us into that little stereotype I had in my head, but I couldn't really shake the feeling of semi-domestic bliss that I'd had while we'd been together in the house.

It didn't hurt that my lawyer had assured me Shelly had no chance at winning a bid for sole custody. I'd spoken to him about my fears and been honest about the situation at the house, and he'd told me that while it would be best if Addie and I maintained separate bedrooms—at least while Daniel was around, there was no real cause for concern.

So I'd felt like there were a lot of reasons to celebrate as I had come back up the hill to Maple Lane tonight. And when Addie had appeared as I'd come up the garden path, I'd felt a little surge of excitement bubble within me. It might not have been real, and maybe it wasn't right. But it felt good.

In the kitchen, I opened the bottle of pinot noir I'd brought, and put together the bulgogi. I set the table with two settings, and brought the old sterling candle holders in from the dining room, where they'd been perched on the mantle over the fireplace. I even managed to find two candles in a kitchen drawer, but then thought better of it. I heard Addison on the stairs as I rushed to take the candles away. I didn't want to make her think I was expecting anything. This wasn't a date.

I picked up the heavy silver bases and turned to carry them back into the dining room, just as Addie appeared in the kitchen doorway.

"Mr. Tucker, in the kitchen, with the candlestick!" She said triumphantly.

"Very funny."

"Those are pretty. Were they the ones in the dining room?"

I nodded and turned back around, placing them on the table again.

"Good idea," she said, and when I turned to look at her again, her smile banished all the nervous worry I'd been feeling. I'd forgotten how things were with us. Easy. Comfortable. Natural.

She smelled like soap, and her hair hung in loose waves around her face, still damp. She wore a soft-looking pumpkin colored sweater and faded jeans, and she had socks on her feet. I wanted to pick her up and snuggle her. I wanted to do much, much more than that.

"You ready to eat?" I asked her.

"If we are going to eat whatever it is I smell, then absolutely yes."

I poured two glasses of wine and handed her one as she came to sit at the table. I took one myself. "To the house," I suggested, holding out my globe.

"To the house," she said. "And to being out from under

Lottie's scrutiny." She took a sizable swig and leaned back into the bench behind her, looking relaxed and happy.

"Was it that bad?" I asked, still standing.

"No," she said. "Not really, but it's just a lot of pressure, you know? To prove that I'm okay, that she did a good job raising me and she can relax now."

I thought about that. "I guess I get it. I mean, I can't imagine ever not worrying about Dan."

"I guess so," she said. "I'm not a parent. I don't really know how that works."

"And I don't have adult parents still worrying over me, so I guess I don't know the other side either," I said. I missed my parents every day, but I'd never really thought about having them worry about me even as an adult. It would be an extra layer of stress.

I turned back to the stove and served the food on two plates.

"What in the world is this?" Addie asked, her eyes rounding. "It looks amazing."

"It's a spicy barbecue pork with vegetables and rice. Korean," I added.

"And how did you learn to make this?"

"I don't know," I said. "Just thought it sounded good when I read about it, and figured I'd try something different." I didn't add that this was my way of traveling since I'd never gotten a chance to actually do any real travel.

"Well it looks fantastic."

"I'm sure you had a pretty good selection of ethnic food to choose from in New York."

She lifted a shoulder, and nodded. "We didn't really experiment much, though. Luke liked things a certain way. We got into habits, I guess." She didn't sound happy about it. I didn't get it. If Addie was mine, I'd take her anywhere she wanted to go, eat anything she wanted to try.

We ate in silence for a minute, both of us moving slowly, savoring both the meal and the time we had.

"I know it's not my business," I said. "But I'm sorry about what happened with your relationship. It sounds like he took you for granted."

She made a small noise of assent. "I should have seen it a lot earlier. I was complacent, too. Sometimes it's easier to believe things are the way you want them than to do anything to change them and try to make them what you want."

That made sense. And it was true in my life too, maybe.

"I'm sorry too," she said. "About the way Shelly treats you. It's not my business either, but I think you're a fantastic dad."

It was almost embarrassing how good it felt to hear someone say that. I didn't think anyone ever had, actually. "That's seriously my only goal."

"To be a good dad?"

"Yeah. It's the only thing my life is really about. The one thing I have to get right."

"Don't you have to get things right for yourself though, too?" She was holding the big globe of wine aloft, her head tilted to one side and those big dark eyes on my face. I felt seen in a way I hadn't in a long time—years.

"Maybe. When I know Dan is grown. Taken care of."

"So you are going to let your own happiness take a back seat for another, what, like fifteen years?" Her tone made it clear she didn't agree with this plan. But of course, Addie didn't have kids.

"I owe him that, I think."

"I think you owe him a dad who is modeling a full life. Showing him what it looks like to live your fullest, best version of yourself."

"I think this is probably the best version of myself I can manage right now."

Addie frowned at me, and I felt her disapproval. "Michael,"

she said, her voice low and soft, stirring a deep longing inside me. "You deserve to be happy. And Dan wants that for you too."

I felt the flush hit my cheeks again, and dropped my eyes as something washed through me—an emotion so overwhelming I worried for a moment I was going to actually break down and cry.

Fuck, get a grip, Tucker.

I swallowed hard and sought a reason why her words were having this effect on me. And then it hit me. No one had cared whether I was happy in years. Not since my parents had died. Dan might care—but he was a kid. His job was to be selfish. It was his right for another year or two at least. But Addie's words made me feel like she actually cared, and I'd felt so alone for so long, it actually had me choked up.

I covered with another sip of wine and a big bite of pork, and by the time I swallowed, I felt in control of my emotions again.

We talked about other things then, about the way the weather had begun to turn colder, about trying out some of the fireplaces in the cooling house. About the windows we were having replaced over the next week. And as we cleared the dishes and poured ourselves another glass of wine each, I had an idea.

"Want to go on a little treasure hunt?" I asked Addie.

Her eyes lit up and she laughed lightly. "What do you mean?"

"We have the key I found upstairs," I reminded her. "And we have no idea what it fits. Let's hunt."

Her lips formed a line and her chin dipped down a little. "Are you going to make a whole bunch more jokes about it being 'door-key'?"

I shook my head. "No, I think it was just the one."

Addie looked around then, and I thought maybe she was wondering if it might be too spooky to go hunting through the house at night. But already the place had come a long way from the frightening decrepit pit it had been when we'd first come inside. Now it glowed merrily under the warmer bulbs I'd put in, and the floors gleamed underfoot. The dusty smell had been replaced slowly by odors of food and life, and cleaning products. I found myself wanting her to say yes, almost desperate to spend more time together, laughing and enjoying each other's company.

"Okay," she said. "Let's hunt."

We set off through the house, wine glasses in hand as we went through each room, searching for something we weren't sure even existed.

We prowled around the rooms on the first level, stopping to investigate areas we hadn't paid much attention to before—atop dusty mantles, along window casings and in dark corners, searching even in silly places where there was no chance of a keyhole.

"I've got nothing," Addie said, shaking her head and grinning at me as we met in the center of the parlor.

"Me either." I gazed toward the stairway. "Upstairs?"

"Let's go," she said, striding confidently ahead of me. I tried to keep my gaze from the sway of her hips as she ascended ahead of me, but that was an exercise in futility. Addie was beautiful, head to toe, and her backside was no exception.

At the landing, we looked around us, seeking anything that might have a keyhole.

"What if it was like, a safe?" Addie asked. "In the movies, that would be behind a painting or something."

"The only thing still hanging on the walls is that mirror in your room," I said, and we both turned toward the master bedroom.

There was a large mirror on one wall, in surprisingly good condition, considering the likely age of the thing.

"It looks heavy," Addie said doubtfully, putting her wine glass down on the windowsill and then approaching the mirror.

I followed suit, and wrapped my fingers around the sides of the huge mirror, preparing to lift it off the wall.

"Be careful," Addie said.

"Thanks for that. I was going to be very negligent, but you've changed my mind."

"Funny."

I lifted the mirror and felt it detach from the wall. It was every bit as heavy as it looked. And then some. As I lowered it to the floor, Addie sucked in a breath. "Michael, look!"

There, hidden behind the old mirror, was a little safe, stuck into the wall. And the keyhole looked like it matched the key I'd found perfectly. I let out a victorious whoop.

"You do it," I said, handing Addie the key.

Her eyes lit up and she took it from me, fitting it carefully into the lock and then turning it, eliciting a satisfying 'click' from the mechanism.

"Yay!" She cried, and if I hadn't already thought she was cute, I'd be a goner now.

She pulled the little door open, and looked inside. I stepped up close behind her, peering into the dark little space. A wad of folded papers rested within, along with a small box and an envelope.

"Shall we?" I reached in and retrieved the items.

"Let's look at it in the kitchen," Addie said, and I reluctantly stepped away from her, the scent of her still in my nose.

Back at the table with our glasses of wine forgotten in front of us, we spread the items before us.

"Where should we start?" I asked.

"The box." Addie's eyes glowed with excitement.

"Shouldn't we save that for last?"

"Oh no. You're one of those?"

"One of what?"

"I bet you open presents super slow, saving the wrapping paper and everything."

"I do not." I didn't know why this suggestion made me feel slightly indignant. "I just like to savor things a bit. Take my time with things I know I'll enjoy."

Addie's expression changed then, and it occurred to me I could have been talking about any number of things. Addie was clearly thinking the same thing. "Oh," she said, swallowing. And then her hand shot out and she popped open the lid of the box. "Oh wow."

She turned the box so I could see what lay inside, and the overhead lights glinted off the facets of a small but perfect diamond set in a complex silver setting.

"That's beautiful," I said. "A wedding ring, you think?"

She nodded. "Must have been. I wonder whose?"

I shrugged. "No telling how long it's been in that little wall safe. We don't know if even Filene knew about that."

Addie looked skeptical. "I'm starting to feel like she planned all this for us somehow. Like she knew exactly what she was doing."

I grinned. I'd had that feeling too. "Do you ever think that there's a chance we'll get to the end of all this, and she'll pop out and be like, 'I wasn't dead after all!'"

Addie's smile dropped and she stared at me for a second. "Um. No. That's a little morbid."

"No, it would be morbid if I thought she was dead when she wasn't. Thinking someone might not be dead when they are is the opposite of morbid."

"So it's less-bid."

"Um. So are you taking over the dad jokes, then?"

She laughed and slapped my arm playfully. "Anyway, I know what you mean. It all reminds me a little of this book I read when I was a kid. *The Westing Game.* Did you ever read that?"

I searched my meager literary roots. "I don't know."

"It was about this old guy who planned a whole murder mystery around his own death."

"Wait. If he was dead, how did he do that?"

"Exactly!" Addie sounded like this all made sense, but I guessed it did have some parallels to my idea that Filene had somehow planned all this for us.

"Okay, open the other stuff." I pushed the envelope toward her.

"There's newspaper in here." She unfolded the yellowed paper and her eyes widened as she scanned whatever words it held.

"Well?" The suspense was killing me.

"There was a murder," she breathed, and handed me the page.

I read out loud:

"Matthew Elias Tucker, local esteemed townsman, was found shot dead early Friday morning on the edge of his property at 54 Maple Lane by the local constable on his morning rounds. He is survived by his son Elias and his wife Ina.

"It is surmised that the suspected murder is one more dastardly deed in the ongoing feud between the Tucker and Tanner families. As readers surely recall, last summer saw the grisly devastation of the Arnold Tanner's barn and livestock after he attempted to assert his ownership over the property at Maple Lane.

"With no witnesses or any real evidence, it is likely this murder will remain a mystery, but there is no doubt it will fuel the ongoing animosity between the two families."

I finished reading and stared at Addie. "You said ghosts were people who had unfinished things or wanted revenge, right?"

"Yeah." Addie's expression was dark.

"So if Matthew Tucker was killed by a Tanner, right here on this property, then I could see him wanting revenge." I still didn't believe in ghosts, but if there was going to be one, I could see it being this guy.

"And haunting the house where he was killed," she finished, eyes wide.

We stared at the article for a moment and then Addie pushed the other papers toward me. "What's this?"

I unfolded the papers and spread them between us. "It's a land deed," I said, reading. "For plots 54, 55, and 56 in Singletree Township. To Matthew Tucker."

She shook her head. "I don't get it."

I shrugged. "The mystery grows."

"Wait, what's the date on that?" She asked, pushing the deed at me again.

"1828."

She stared at the paper for a long minute. Then looked up at me. "Well, if those plots are the one this house sits on, then that doesn't make sense."

"Why not?"

"Mom found a record of the land purchase. And it was bought by a Tanner, not a Tucker. In 1827, not 1828."

I felt my brow wrinkle. Mysteries were not my strong suit and it was getting late. Plus, I was on my second big glass of wine. "And?"

She shook her head. "I don't know. If a Tanner bought it, why did the deed say Tucker?"

"No idea."

"Tuckers stole it." She said this very matter of factly. Like she believed it. I felt the knee-jerk reaction starting inside me, but pushed it down.

"I thought we'd gotten past all that feud stuff and had moved on to solving a mystery together, Addie."

She lifted a shoulder. "If the shoe fits," she said, but there was a comic lilt to her voice.

"It's too late for this kind of confusion," I said.

She glanced at her watch. "Oh, it is late. And Dan comes tomorrow?"

Though I loved my son, and I lived for the time I spent with him, I felt a twinge of sadness that this close quiet time with Addie would come to an end in the morning.

Normally it would be Shelly's week, but she said she'd picked up some extra shifts and wouldn't be around in the evenings when he might need her. It was confusing—Shelly acted like she wanted to keep Dan from me, but then she also seemed to enjoy the flexibility that having me in his life offered her. That was Shelly. "He does."

And with that, we each went to bed and miraculously, slept the night through with no otherworldly screaming.

22

VINTAGE 'VETTE
ADDISON

Friday morning arrived with a thunderstorm, and Dan was delivered by Shelly, who gave me evil looks the entire time she was in the house, which was much longer than anyone seemed to want her there. Evidently she was taking some different shifts at The Shack, and needed to drop Dan off early.

"Mom," Daniel said after Shelly had interrupted breakfast and then demanded Michael give her a tour of the house to prove it was a safe place for Daniel to be for the weekend, "you can go now."

"That's not very loving," she scolded him, looking hurt. I felt a little bad for Shelly. But Dan had sounded like he was trying for a joke that just didn't go off well.

"I'm sorry," he said immediately, and he gave her a warm hug that softened my heart a little bit toward her.

"All right," she said. "But if anything at all happens, you call me," she told her son.

"I still don't think he needed a cell phone. He's twelve," Michael said, in a voice that suggested he didn't want to rekindle the fight they'd had when she'd arrived, but that he also didn't think the conversation was over.

"How else is he supposed to reach me if he needs me?"

"The same way he always has? On my phone."

"If he doesn't feel safe, he needs to be able to tell me."

Michael took a step back, looking as if she'd slapped him. I had dueling impulses—one, I wanted to go to him, put a hand on his back or his shoulder to comfort him, and two, I wanted to step between them and give Shelly a piece of my mind. Michael was probably the best father I'd ever seen, though I honestly didn't have a lot of experience with fathers in general.

"Fine," Michael said, his voice tight. "He'll call you if he needs you."

"Good."

"Good."

"Bye Mom."

Shelly hugged her son again, shot me a glare, and then turned and left. Daniel disappeared up the stairs.

And it was then that I noticed that the box with the ring, the one we'd left sitting open on the table the night before, was now empty. Had she taken it? Had we forgotten to put it back? Where was the ring?

"Michael?"

He rubbed a hand through his hair, sending it all standing on end as his shoulders slumped. "Yeah?"

"Did you put the ring somewhere? For safekeeping?"

His lips pulled up in confusion and he shook his head. "No, why?"

"It's gone." I pointed to the empty box on the table.

We both stared at it for a minute as Daniel's footsteps overhead thumped and clunked.

"You don't think Shelly took it, do you?" I asked, wondering if he was thinking the same thing.

"She wouldn't," he said. "I mean . . . I don't think she would do that."

I didn't know what to think. "Maybe we should put the rest of the stuff back in the safe for now? Just in case we need it?"

"Yeah," he said, ruffling his hair again.

"I'll look around," I assured him. "Maybe it just fell off the table or something." I doubted this could have happened, but also didn't insist that either his ex was a thief in addition to being a less-than-delightful houseguest or that our ghosts liked shiny objects.

The window replacement was beginning today, and the workmen arrived soon after Shelly had departed, and by the time Michael had taken Daniel to school and headed off to work, the house was abuzz with activity, so much so that I felt comfortable going up to the attic alone to sort through the letters and pictures there. I wanted to see if I could get to the bottom of the mystery surrounding the land deed. If there was a record showing the land had been sold to a Tanner, why did the deed to the land say Tucker?

It was like a stroll through history, pulling open newspaper clippings and flipping through ancient photos. The headlines were interesting, though I didn't have a lot of historical context for most:

PROHIBITION! Jan. 16, 1919 Momentous Day in World's History

Mrs. Ross Takes Office - First Female Governor in US - 1925

Scopes Found Guilty of Teaching Evolution - 1925

There were stacks of papers, many of them discussing banal news of the day, but others sporting headlines that had me remembering high school history:

Herbert Hoover Elected! 1930

U.S. Prohibition Ends - Uncertainty Faces Nation - 1933

I spent the better part of the day upstairs, lost in my exploration through history. There was no rhyme or reason I could find as to why certain events seemed to warrant the keeping of the front page while others did not, but reading about each event felt like peering through a time machine. And when the foreman's voice rang through the house in late afternoon, letting me know they were heading out for the day, it was like being awakened from a strange nap rife with odd and dusty dreams.

I went downstairs to see the workmen off, but before they left, the foreman asked about the garage. "Are we replacing those windows too?"

"Yeah, I think so," I said. "Only, we don't have a key."

He shook his head. "If we're replacing windows, shouldn't matter. We can do it from the outside as easily as inside on these old buildings."

"Oh," I said, feeling suddenly a little less secure than I had before. "Well, okay then."

The total cost to replace all the windows in the house with energy efficient double-paned glass was enormous, but Michael and I had agreed it was important if anyone ever planned to actually live in the house again. And since our six months would take us right through a cold Singletree winter, it would be good for us, too.

"We'll get the rest done by mid-week," he said.

"Okay," I said, and watched the trucks pull out of the driveway as the sun began to set.

I shivered, heading back into the big house alone. With no one else around, I was reminded that the place was most likely haunted, and I checked my watch, hoping Michael might be home sooner rather than later. Before I could become too worried, I heard Michael's truck rumbling up the driveway.

Daniel, Michael and I spent the weekend mostly outside, pulling weeds in the yard, while the window crew continued working on the upper levels of the house.

The guys didn't work Sunday, but they were back bright and early on Monday morning. I'd seen Michael off to the store, and had resumed my weed-pulling out in the yard. My mother had already called to give me an earful about missing Sunday dinner when a voice came floating through the greenery about mid-day. "Ma'am?"

"Yes?" I pushed my hair out of my face and pulled off my gloves, going to meet the foreman in the middle of the yard near the garage.

"There's a tarp in there over the car. You okay with us going ahead with the work? That oughta keep the dust off it."

I glanced toward the garage, where the men had removed the front window. I knew there was a car in there, but I was imagining it was as old and dusty already as the rest of the house. "Probably doesn't matter," I said. "I mean, a little dust won't hurt it, right?

The man looked weirdly uncertain. "I mean, I guess not. Some people are particular about their cars."

"Well, don't like, drop a brick on it or anything, right?" I laughed. "And could you leave the door unlocked when you're done in there?"

"Leave it unlocked?" He looked surprised by this request, and I thought I'd told him we didn't have the key, but I figured he had bigger things on his mind.

"Yes please," I said.

"Sure thing." He walked away, shaking his head, like I was the silliest client he'd had in a while.

Whatever. I went back to the never-ending task of pulling the overgrowth from the yard.

When the contractors finished the windows, I told Michael

and Daniel that the garage was finally unlocked and we went out there together. What lay inside was something none of us had expected. Well, none of us, except maybe Daniel.

We pushed open the creaky door and stood inside, letting our eyes adjust to the dark interior. In the middle of the space sat a car, covered entirely in a shredded tarp. In the space where the tarp had been eaten or just aged away, hints of what lay beneath peeked through. Shiny red paint gleamed in contrast to the dark colorless space around it.

"What is this?" Michael asked, reaching toward one of the shiny patches as Daniel practically bounced in excitement.

"Let's find out," I suggested.

Together, we slid the old tarp off the car.

"A Corvette!" he practically screamed when the car beneath was revealed.

There, sitting in the middle of the ancient garage, a gorgeous older model sports car. I would never have identified it on my own, but evidently Daniel knew his vintage 'vettes.

"Holy shit," he breathed, his voice suddenly reverent. "Dad, it's a 1958 Roadster."

"Language," Michael said, but his tone was so distracted by the bright red car in front of us that I was surprised he'd managed to remember his parental duties at all.

"This is amazing," I said. It was swoopy and cool, and I suddenly understood why the contractor had looked at me like I was crazy when I'd told him not to drop a brick on it. This was not what I'd envisioned sitting out in the garage.

"This is amazing," Daniel said, running a hand gently over the angled fender. "This thing is a collector's item. Super old."

Compared to the rest of the house, this was a relatively young antique, but Daniel's perspective was probably different than mine, considering he was twelve.

"Dad, can we drive it?"

Michael looked unsure. "I don't think so."

"Come on!" Daniel sounded very much his age as he prepped himself for a tween-style tantrum.

"Dan," Michael said, meeting his son's eyes. "We don't have the keys, for one thing. And for another, we need to make sure the thing is insured before we take it out. What if something happened? Besides that, we probably need to get it serviced. And maybe appraised."

"This car is super valuable," Daniel said, nodding in his sudden agreement.

"And I'm not sure a guy like me should be driving a super valuable car," Michael said.

"I'll drive!" Dan volunteered.

"Oh, well, I am definitely sure a guy like you should not be driving a super valuable car."

Daniel circled the car, and then popped open the door and slid into the driver's seat, a huge smile taking over his young face as he took the steering wheel. "Oh, Dad."

Michael stood from where he'd been examining the bumper. "Yeah?"

"The keys are right here." Daniel pulled them from the ignition and held them up, beaming.

"Great," Michael said, holding out his hand.

"So as soon as it's insured, we'll take it for a drive, right?"

It had taken a lot to get Daniel out of the garage, including promises of insurance and impending rides.

THE NEXT FEW weeks passed quickly, filled with days spent directing contractors, stripping wallpaper, and demolishing the existing kitchen. Michael and I fell into a strangely comforting routine, laced with something that felt like friendship—and a little bit like something more.

Daniel came and went—he stayed in the house for a week at a time, and even Shelly seemed to settle into something that felt less like bucking every little change.

The screams still came—only at night—but in some ways I had begun to accept them as part of the house. I'd gotten used to them, and had settled into sleeping in my own room without feeling terrified. Nothing came with the screams, except the occasional scrabbling sound or a crash of something in the attic falling over again. But if the ghosts in the house limited themselves to screaming and staying in the attic, I decided it was the kind of haunting I could live with. The only really disturbing thing about our ghosts was their tendency to steal.

"Your watch now? Was it expensive?" I stared at Michael across the dining room table. We'd taken to eating take out in the dining room since the kitchen was currently being remodeled.

"I'm a high school graduate who runs a farm supply store. Do you think I was wearing a Rolex?" He smiled at me across the table, his eyes gleaming.

"Well, no, but . . . still."

"Yeah. I liked that watch."

"So, let me see if I have the tally so far. The ring, my silver stud earrings, the silver pill container I left in the bathroom, and now your watch?"

"Yes. The ghosts like shiny objects, evidently."

"So weird."

"Everything about this house is weird. Maybe the garage most of all."

"Right?" I said, laughing.

Now, sitting at the table in our increasingly livable haunted house, Michael smiled at me and my heart picked up a quicker rhythm inside my chest. "Yeah, what in the world should we do with that thing?"

I shook my head. "No idea." I'd continued sorting through the documents in the house, but hadn't found any mention of a car collector or race car driver in the past inhabitants. Some mysteries remained to be solved.

Since Michael had had the cable installed, we'd taken to watching movies in the evenings in the parlor, where we'd recently installed a flat screen and a couple very comfortable couches, along with an area rug, a coffee table, and a couple lamps. We figured if we were going to live here for six months, we couldn't sit on the floor or folding chairs the whole time. Michael brought a few things from his house, and I picked out a couple too.

Each night we'd take a glass of wine and sit together, watching the big screen and enjoying each other's company. But it was becoming increasingly hard to just sit—something was growing in the air between us.

"We've been here six weeks now," I pointed out as we settled one night, the movie ready to play in front of us.

"Yeah?" Michael said. "It's gone fast."

It had. The house, and Michael, had become my happy place. I still went home for Sunday dinners and helped Mom at the Tin, and even Lottie seemed to have accepted the strange new arrangement. She'd laid off pushing me about living with a Tucker, and I wondered if it was in part because she had been spending more time with a Tucker, too.

The house, and even the ghostly sounds and occasionally terrifying happenings, felt like my home now. And Michael—well, I wasn't sure exactly what he was, but I knew he was important to me.

I'd spent a lot of time pushing away and denying feelings I had about him that were not partnerly or appropriate to home-improvement buddies. But as the weeks went on, and our friendship grew, it became harder and harder. Especially when we sat close on the couch at night.

I wondered sometimes what he was thinking, why he didn't make a move, or try to at least. But I knew his life was complicated, with Shelly and Daniel. And despite the chemistry I often thought I felt when he touched me, when our eyes met—I forced myself to accept that most likely, I just wasn't his type. If Shelly had been his type, well, she and I were very different.

23

HALF CAT STRIKES AGAIN
MICHAEL

Addie Tanner was exactly my type, and it was killing me. We spent so much time together, working and relaxing inside the old house, that every moment had become a kind of exquisite torture. She was gorgeous and funny, confident and smart—and I knew that a woman like that would want little to do with a small town guy with no prospects for anything better. I mean, yeah, if we sold the house and the car, we both stood to make a decent amount of money. But that wasn't the kind of success I thought a woman like Addie looked for in a man. Her last relationship had been with a world-class violinist, for fuck's sake. (One who also sounded like a world-class ass.)

And though there were very few minutes spent in her company where I wasn't thinking about how gorgeous she was, how smart, how completely perfect—I knew I couldn't act on it. This was a temporary situation, and she was headed back to the big city, back to her incredible life. I knew she'd called her boss to make some kind of arrangement, and she'd mentioned using the proceeds from the house sale to set up a new apartment in New York. She wasn't planning to stay here, and certainly not with me.

"This movie is legitimately awful," she said from beside me one night as we watched a romantic comedy that was so predictable, I was starting to feel like maybe I should write movie scripts.

"Wait," I said. "Any minute his mother is going to burst in and there's going to be a huge misunderstanding about why she's in his room."

Addie's feet were in my lap, and my hands were rubbing up and down her shins, feeling the firm muscle and smooth skin there. This wasn't unusual—we'd become close physically too. But I was pretty sure she didn't realize how hard it was for me. And I mean hard in every sense of the word. Most nights we'd say goodnight and I'd tell her I needed to take a shower before turning in. I'd wait until she was done in the bathroom and then do one of two things: take a freezing cold shower and hate myself for how much I wanted her, or take my dick in my hand and hate myself for how much I wanted her.

"This should be a drinking game," Addie said. "You'd totally be winning. You called that exactly!"

"You want a drink?" I asked her, thinking that maybe getting completely drunk would help cut some of the constant tension I felt around her now.

"Um, sure," she said, swinging her feet off my lap and pulling the blanket up over her lap.

"We've got a bottle of Half Cat."

"Do we have club soda?"

"Think so." I shuffled off to the kitchen, which was in the midst of being completely renovated, to check, and returned after a few minutes with two glasses, a couple bottles of club soda, and the Half Cat.

Addison had paused the movie and waited for me, and in the low light of the parlor, her cheeks glowed ruddy and her eyes danced in a way that pretty nearly killed me.

Whiskey. Immediately.

"Here you go." I handed her the drink.

"Okay, so when do we drink?"

Right fucking now. "Ah, how about any time he calls her the wrong name?"

"Yes, good. And also whenever one of the parents walks into a room where they're about to kiss."

"Okay, and also any time she does that sighing hair flip thing."

"Then I'm going to get hammered."

"The movie's half over."

"You hope," she laughed as I settled back onto the couch, scooting over a bit so Addie's feet could come back into my lap but she could still sit up enough to drink.

An hour later, the credits were rolling and my plan had completely backfired. Addie was tipsy and adorable, and was now snuggled into my side with her hands on my chest under the blanket. And I was as hard as an iron rod and in the midst of the most difficult struggle I'd ever faced as everything in me demanded I take her into my arms, kiss her senseless, and then haul her upstairs to my newly installed bed.

I was this close to doing it. But I couldn't make the first move here. If Addie did, however, all bets were off.

"That was fun," she said, her head just beneath my chin as I switched the television off. Her hair smelled like heaven, and having my arm around her was practically killing me, but I wouldn't have removed it for the world. "I like the part where—"

Addie was interrupted by a screech so loud and other-worldly that we both stiffened and leapt from the couch. Addie hit the coffee table with her shin as she leapt up, and started to topple over it sideways, so I grabbed for her arm and pulled her to me again. This put us chest to chest, and resulted in her body being essentially pressed up against the length of mine.

I knew it the exact second she registered the length of iron in my sweat pants. Her whole body stiffened against me, and I realized how inappropriate it was. She was staring up at me, her eyes widening as my erection pressed shamelessly against her belly, and just as I was opening my mouth to apologize, she pressed herself against me—against it—harder, rolling gently.

The sensation was sheer torture. "Addie, I'm—"

I had no idea what I was planning to say. But it didn't matter, because she didn't give me a chance. Addie pressed herself against me and raised herself up until we were nearly eye to eye. Then she tipped her head back, her mouth opening as a little sigh escaped her.

I inclined my head, my body finally having had enough with my restraint and taking charge, leaving my logic and reason on the couch behind us. We were centimeters apart, but I couldn't let myself do it, couldn't allow myself to take her mouth with mine, no matter how many times I'd dreamed it.

And I didn't have to. She closed the distance, her mouth slamming into mine roughly at first, and then settling into a firm pressure of her lips over mine, and then—oh holy mother of fuck—she opened her mouth and took my bottom lip between her teeth, letting out a little moan as she did it.

Whatever was left of my reserve snapped—there was that first move, after all—and I kissed her then, my mouth claiming hers and my tongue tasting every bit of her that I had access to. For long, delicious moments, we kissed, our mouths confirming that every desire I had for this woman was reciprocated, her hands grabbing at my ass, sliding up under my shirt, and suggesting she'd thought about me just as much as I'd thought about her.

Until she stopped, freezing in my arms and then wrenching herself away and turning her back on me.

"Shit," I muttered, not understanding what had shifted, but knowing it wasn't going to be good.

"I'm sorry," she whispered, still not facing me.

"That wasn't for you to be sorry about," I told her. "From where I'm standing, that was one hundred percent mutual."

She shook her head, finally turning back around, and as soon as I saw her face I wished I hadn't. Her lips were swollen and red from our kiss, her skin heated and pink, but her eyes— were so full of regret that I wished I could unsee her expression.

"I never meant to do that," she said, wiping at her mouth as if she could wipe the kiss away. "I'm sorry. I shouldn't have. I let myself get carried away."

She took two steps backward, and I felt the connection between us sever. There would be no going back, no way to salvage this night or this relationship. I should have known better. I didn't know why, but I knew that one kiss had ruined everything.

"It's no problem," I said, dropping her gaze before something in me snapped in two. "My fault. I overstepped."

"You didn't," she rushed the words out. "Michael, you didn't. You didn't read it wrong or do anything I didn't want. This was my fault. It's just," she laughed here, a light quick sound that made me feel so very small. "It's just that this isn't my real life," she said. "And I have no business leading you on or fooling myself about the possibility of staying here once the house is finished. I mean, we both know that. I don't belong here."

"Right." Darkness clouded my mind. She was too good for this place, for me. I'd known that, so why did it hurt so much? I turned and headed for the stairs. "I'm gonna head up." I couldn't face her now, couldn't bear to look at her. Of course this wasn't her real life. Who the fuck was I, anyway? A deadbeat townie with unrealized dreams and a heart full of regrets. I wasn't the guy a woman like Addie needed. And I'd known it all along. I was so angry I'd allowed myself to believe, even for a second, that it might be different.

"Okay, I, uh . . ." Addie stuttered from where she still stood, in the spot where we'd kissed like there would be no tomorrow. "I'm really sorry, Michael."

"Yeah, you said that." I threw the words over my shoulder, bitterness sweeping in to replace the desire I'd felt. Because if I couldn't get a little bit angry about it, I was pretty sure my heart would break.

"Good night," she said, but I was already on my way to another before-bed shower, already thinking about the punishing pumping my dick was going to need this night if I had any chance at all of sleeping again.

24

HOW TO BE A MORON
ADDISON

I watched Michael retreat up the stairs, knowing I'd shattered everything good between us. How could I have been so stupid? So weak? I should never have allowed the closeness to grow between us, should never have begun touching him, taking comfort in his constant nearness, in his warm smile.

I'd ruined everything, and the stiff posture of Michael's shoulders as he moved away from me told me exactly how angry he was. There would be no salvaging this.

Even though I wanted to fix everything, I knew it would be stupid to let myself become more involved with a man in Singletree. I couldn't stay here. This was not my life. I had a job to return to, friends who would surely be missing me—though very few of them had called, actually, and I'd only gotten a couple of texts checking in over the two months I'd now been gone.

But I'd made my life years ago—I was a city girl, not the girl who stays in the small town. I needed bigger opportunities, bigger possibilities than a small town like Singletree could offer. Lottie had reminded me of this enough times while I was away.

Still, every time I thought about Michael's smiling face, that divot in his stubbled chin—my heart warmed in a way it never really had when I thought about Luke. But when I thought about the anger that had stormed in those eyes after I'd pulled away from our kiss . . . none of it mattered. He probably hated me now, thought I was some kind of long-game tease. And that was for the best. We were supposed to be business partners, nothing more.

I wished Daniel had been there this week, having him in the house would have diluted some of the awkward tension that filled the spaces between Michael and I over the next few days. We barely spoke, only found ourselves in the same room when the kitchen crew needed a decision made or had a question while he was home. But mostly, Michael stayed away, spending long hours at the store while I supervised the kitchen project and the men who were beginning to rebuild the front porch to make it safe. I began to search for affordable apartments in New York during my down time.

The good thing was that with so much activity in the house, I had little time to be frightened. The ghosts, it seemed, had settled down. Or maybe I'd just grown accustomed to the middle of the night screams and the strange scrabbling noises I heard around me sometimes. I wasn't afraid of them anymore, at least, but I just didn't know what a person was to do about harmless ghosts who occasionally swiped shiny objects. We'd probably have to handle it somehow before we could sell the house.

Four days passed with Michael essentially ignoring me. I ate before he came home from work, and waited until he'd gone in the mornings to go down and make coffee in the makeshift kitchen we'd set up in the dining room. It was awkward and horrible.

On the fifth day after our kiss, I spent the day with Mom at the Tin as she went into mass production of her Halloween treats. Halloween was just a week away, and as Mom told me, "these goblin toes won't frost themselves!"

I spent the day covered in frosting and enduring Mom's philosophies about ghost infestation.

"I think what you really need is to get in there with Sally McHord."

I sighed, steeling myself for this idea. "Who is Sally McHord, Mom?" I asked as I placed a toe on the baking sheet.

"She's a psychic," Mom said, nodding her bobbed head sagely. "Very good one, too."

"How do you know if someone is a good psychic, Mom?"

"Yelp reviews," Mom answered. "And she helped George Dews with his malamute."

"His dog?"

"Yes. It turned out the dog really wanted George to stop playing The Beatles. He hated their music, but was having trouble communicating with George. Sally stepped in, and now that George has sworn off The Beatles, he and the dog are doing fine."

"So she is a skilled psychic who can communicate with dogs." This conversation seemed completely appropriate, given what my life had become.

"She's a pet psychic, if you want to get specific," Mom huffed, as if divulging this detail was super annoying.

"Um. Okay."

"I'll bring her up to the house."

"If the place was being haunted by Chihuahuas, that would be a great idea, Mom. But I don't think that's what we have." It really almost wasn't worth the effort of arguing. I felt emotionally and physically exhausted.

"You don't know."

That was true, I thought as I deposited my three thousandth toe on the sheet. I didn't know. I didn't know anything.

"So what's wrong, Addie? Not just the ghosts." Mom was way too observant.

"Everything is good."

Mom put down her spatula and fixed me with a glare that had terrified me as a kid. "Do not lie to your mother. I can read you like a cookbook, Addison. Always could."

That was the truth. I sighed. I couldn't tell her I'd kissed Michael Tucker. Then I'd get an earful of I told you so about getting involved with Tuckers. So I deflected. "I don't know. I just . . . I guess I'm feeling like I need to be getting back to New York soon. The longer I stay here, the harder it is to remember what I really want."

"What do you really want?"

"My life back! In the city!" As I said the words, I realized how empty and untrue they were.

"The one where your boyfriend ignored you, you worked so much you could never see your family, and you hardly ever called home?"

I sighed. "Those were the less good things about that life, yeah."

"Tell me the more good things, then. What did you love about your life in New York?" Mom had stopped frosting, and I laid down my spatula too, taking a sip of water as my mind spun.

"There were a lot of good things. Like every kind of take-out you could possibly want."

Mom's lips formed into a thin line, but she said nothing, so I continued. Mom didn't seem swayed by the take-out options.

"And the energy. There was always something going on, always something to do. The people there were very cosmopolitan—no food in buckets."

"So your dislike of your hometown has to do with The Shack?"

I shook my head, scrambling for other examples. "No, it was just one example, Mom."

"You haven't mentioned friends, people."

"I have friends there," I said, feeling defensive. "But you know, everyone there is very busy. We all have lives. Jobs."

"It sounds horribly lonely, Addie."

For some stupid reason, my mind flashed to the house, to dinners with Daniel and Michael, to the movie nights we used to have before I screwed everything up. "Well, it wasn't. I was too busy to be lonely."

"And too busy to notice that your relationship wasn't working."

Pain sliced through me and I let my eyes slam shut for an instant, trying to absorb it. Mom was right. "That's not fair. And that's not a nice thing to say."

Mom sighed and turned back to the frosting. "I'm your mother, Addie, not your friend. It's my job to say the things you don't want to hear."

I had nothing to say to that because I was still reeling that my own mother would poke her finger in a wound as raw as my relationship with Luke. The worst thing was, I knew she was right.

"The other thing I'll say is that since you've been here, you have seemed increasingly happy. But since I didn't see you for years before you came home, I don't have a lot to compare it to."

Another jab.

We frosted in silence for a little while, and then Mom stuck her spatula into the bowl and declared us done. "Is the kitchen finished yet at the house?" She asked as I gathered my bag and got ready to head back up the hill. The house had felt like a refuge at one point, and I missed feeling like I fit there. Now it was just one more place filled with awkward silences, one more place I didn't belong.

"Should be done tomorrow," I told her. The appliances were being delivered, and that would be it.

"Then we'll do Sunday dinner at your house this week," she announced in a tone that brooked no argument.

"Um. Okay," I said, wondering if that would be okay with Michael. In some ways it would be nice to show off all the work we'd been doing. And it would be more people to fill in the awkward silences between me and Michael. "I'll just check with Michael, I guess."

"It's your house too. You tell him this is a Tanner tradition. If he doesn't like it, he can get lost."

"Mom, it's his house."

"And yours. By the way, his rude uncle Victor should probably be invited too."

"If he's rude, why do you want him there?"

"Aren't we making amends?"

I shook my head. "Not that I was aware of. Last time we talked about it, you were planning some sort of frosting assault on the bookstore windows."

"I think I'm a bigger person than that." Mom refused to meet my eyes.

"Since when?" I stared at my mother. She was hiding something, and I was very curious about what exactly it was.

"Just plan dinner, Addie. I'll bring a roast. We'll be there at six."

"Um. Okay." With that strange conversation echoing in my mind, I trudged up the hill toward the house. The yard had been trimmed and cleared, and with all the new windows gleaming with light from inside the house, it looked much less creepy and haunted than it used to. I slipped inside the gates, which we now left open most of the time, and took the path around the house to the kitchen door.

I let myself in with my key, and stopped for a moment to

admire the new, modern kitchen we'd installed. The counter-tops were a light milky quartz and the angled glass subway tiles of the backsplash gave a nice contrast in a gleaming green. The gas grill had been built under a copper hood, and the cabinets were all painted a very dark forest green that looked almost black in certain light. The wide plank tile flooring set it all off perfectly, and the new pendants hanging over the island looked wonderful. We'd done a good job.

"That you?" Michael's voice came from the dining room. A little thrill went through me before I remembered that Michael was not my biggest fan.

"Yes, sorry. Just got stalled looking at the kitchen."

Michael appeared in the doorway, looking sexier than ever with his flannel sleeves rolled up and his hair gleaming coppery in the kitchen lights. "Looks good, doesn't it?"

"Yes," I agreed, pleased that suddenly we seemed to be talking again. "We did a good job, I think." This was the most we'd spoken since the ill-fated kiss, and I was trying hard to stay on neutral ground, to keep my voice steady, not to scare him away. I'd missed him so much, even the attention he was giving me now felt like a gift.

"You chose all the fixtures and colors," he said. "You have great taste. I wasn't sure about the green, but I really think it works."

I ventured a look at his face, our eyes meeting for a brief second. I thought maybe I glimpsed a longing there that matched my own. "Thanks," I managed as a spark lit me up inside.

"I've got dinner, if you want some," Michael said. "Ordered some Thai food."

The Thai place was in Center County, so he must have driven to get it, or paid a delivery driver a ridiculous amount to bring it. "If you're sure?"

"Yeah, I got way too much."

"Thanks," I said, dropping my things in the mud room by the back stairs and following him to the dining room. Were we finally moving past the kiss?

I sat as Michael filled a plate for me and then set it in front of me before sitting across the table.

For a few minutes, neither of us said anything, and the silence of the old house—which wasn't really silent—filled the space around us.

But then Michael began apologizing. "Listen, Addie. I owe you an apology."

"What? No you don't."

"I should never have made assumptions. You know, the other night."

Was he talking about the kiss? I shook my head, confused.

"I got carried away, is all. Things were so easy with us, and I just . . . I guess it's been a while since I'd spent time with anyone, you know, really had anyone to talk to. And I let myself get carried away with it.

"I realize, of course, that I'm just this small-town hick, that there's nothing here that would be . . ." he trailed off for a minute. "That would be good enough for you."

"What are you talking about?" I asked, starting to really dislike the way this apology was going. Why would he think so little of himself? I was the one who'd made the mistake, and it had nothing to do with where he lived or who he was.

"I know you're too good for a guy like me," he said. "I'll just put it plainly so there's no more weirdness between us, okay?"

"What?"

"You and me. You're this super successful, wildly intelligent, incredibly sexy woman, and I know how stupid it was for a guy like me, a total failure who never even got out of Singletree, to even think you might look twice at him. I should never have let my mind run away with me. I know it was stupid, and—"

As he delivered the second half of this insane self-deprecating tirade, I stood and rounded the table, wrapping my fingers around his wrist and pulling him to his feet.

"Stop it, you moronic asshole," I practically yelled into his face. Michael's eyes widened in surprise, but I wasn't finished. "I can't just sit here and let you say things like that about yourself. For one thing, they're completely ridiculous, for another, you'd have to be completely insane to believe a single word that's coming out of your mouth right now!"

"I . . . what?"

"You are a successful businessman and a fantastic father! You're generous and smart, so giving and gracious, and the most incredibly sexy man I've ever met, and if you don't stop putting yourself down, I'm going to prove it to you." Every cell in my body was firing up thanks to my sudden anger and the proximity of his body.

Michael was inches from me, since I'd pressed myself up against him to deliver these last words. I couldn't believe he would discount himself this way, think so little of himself when he was one of the most impressive people I'd ever met.

He just stared at me for a long second, and then a little glint lit his eye, and he said, "Yeah, I think you'd better prove it."

That was all the invitation I needed. I wrapped my arms around his waist and kissed him again for all I was worth. And the memory I'd been savoring of our first kiss did not do him justice. Michael's kiss now was warm and tender, demanding and hot, and had my body shaking with want and my knees close to buckling beneath me.

After several very intense minutes, his hands went to my waist and he lifted me up until I was sitting on the gleaming dining room table Filene Easter had left us.

I wrapped my legs around him, pulling him closer, and then let my hands drift to the flannel shirt. It was soft and worn, and smelled like Michael, but it had to go. I pulled it from him as his mouth found my neck, and I dropped my head back, gasping.

Michael's hips were hard between my legs, but I wanted to feel more of him, all of him. I wanted to touch that thick length I'd felt between his legs the last time we'd kissed, and my hands began pulling clothes from his body in a frenzy.

We undressed each other clumsily, our mouths seeking constant connection as our hands unfastened and pulled and tugged. Finally, I sat atop the dining room table in my bra and panties, and Michael stood before me, shirtless, his jeans unfastened, but sadly, still on. He took a step back, his chest heaving.

"I'm worried we're making the same mistake."

"I don't care," I said, reaching for him.

"But don't you . . ."

I wrapped a hand over his waistband and tugged so hard he nearly crashed into me, stopping himself with a hand on the edge of the table.

"Take those off," I demanded, pointing at his pants.

He complied, and when he stood before me in his boxer briefs, the very tip of an impressively sized cock pushing out the waistband, I nearly exploded with need. I reached for him, and he moved closer, his mouth finding mine again.

Sensation took over then, words and thoughts giving way to the slide of tongues, the gasp of breath, the slip of hands over flesh. As he leaned into me, kissing me hard, one of Michael's hands dipped from my waist down to caress the top of my thigh, stroking and teasing the skin just along the edges of my panties. I writhed, trying to maneuver myself so that his hand would fall where I wanted it, where I needed it.

And when he finally let his fingers slide over the silk of my panties, gliding over the spot where I ached and yearned to be touched, I let out a very unladylike moan. But Michael must not have been one for ladylike noises, because in the next instant, he was pulling my panties from my body and his fingers were sliding through my slick folds, teasing and circling and finally, pressing right where I wanted them.

"Oh God," I heard myself moan, and my own hands landed at that instant on the hard length of him, causing him to bite out a rasping, "fuuuck."

I'm not sure how we decided that doing exactly that atop Filene Easter's gleaming dining room table next to assorted boxes of Pad Thai and curry was a good idea, but I suppose neither of us was really thinking at that point. And soon, Michael was sheathing himself with a condom I dug out of my purse and kneeling over me, his knees braced on the shining wood of the table.

"Are you sure about this?" he asked, notching himself at my entrance as I writhed beneath him in anticipation.

I answered by pulling him down to my mouth and arching myself up so that my hips met his, opening me to him. And as he slid in, inch by agonizing inch, I felt myself falling apart and becoming some version of myself I'd never imagined. A woman who has sex with hot younger men atop dining tables.

"Oh God," I seemed to keep repeating as I felt myself stretching to accommodate him.

"You feel so good," he whispered, his breath sweet against my neck as he began to slide in and out.

"This. Feels. So. Good," I agreed, sensations spilling through me that I wasn't sure I'd ever experienced quite as fully before.

I forgot the hard surface of the wood behind me, the smell of curry wafting around us. All I felt was Michael, warm and thick and hard. And all I heard was him, telling me how perfect I was, how lucky he felt, how good this was between us.

I arched and pressed and urged him on, both of us straining

for a release that if I was honest, had been building for the past seven weeks between us. And when it came, amid Michael's hard thrusts and my moans and cries as I tried to take more and more of him, it probably scared the ghosts.

My body shot off like a rocket, and the aftereffects went on for what felt like hours, laying there on the dining room table with Michael's hard body over mine, both of us gasping for breath.

"Holy fuck," he breathed, rolling to brace his head on one hand, his elbow on the table.

"Mrs. Easter probably never imagined that going on in her dining room," I said, giggling.

Michael frowned then, and his brow wrinkled as he said, "or you know, maybe she did."

"What?" I suddenly wondered if he thought Mrs. Easter had used this table the same way.

"All that stuff she said. About the feud ending, about finding the past and the future in the house. Don't you think she was playing matchmaker?"

"She wanted us to have sex in her house?"

He shrugged, a sleepy smile covering his face. "No, probably not." He didn't say anything else, but the thought did echo through my mind. Mrs. Easter been playing matchmaker? Was that what this was really all about?

Eventually, the table began to feel hard and cold beneath me, and we slid from the surface to clean up and pull our clothes back on. When we'd cleaned up the food and the table without speaking, I stopped Michael in the kitchen and pulled him to face me.

"That," I told him, "was amazing. And you are the sexiest and most impressive man I've ever met. So I have no idea what exactly is going to happen here, but don't let me ever hear you questioning that truth again."

"If I do though, will you have to teach me another lesson, maybe?" He smiled a wicked smile, and I laughed as we went together upstairs. We brushed our teeth side by side in the bathroom mirror and without a word, we both headed to the master bedroom, where we undressed across from one another and then slid into the soft sheets atop the new mattress and into each other's arms.

"I might need a lesson or two now, actually," Michael said, his breath hot in my ear.

And for the rest of the night, I showed him over and over exactly how sexy and competent he was.

25

BABYSITTER FANTASIES

MICHAEL

I could say I'd never imagined I would find myself in bed with Addison Tanner. Only that would be a complete lie. I had imagined it plenty of times, right before telling myself what a ridiculous fantasy it was and how a woman like that would never find herself in that situation with a guy like me.

But here we were.

And it wasn't just the physical truth of the two of us, waking in the gauzy morning light, pressed against each other's bodies and exchanging sleepy kisses and whispers. The physical was easy enough to write off—it happened. People made mistakes. Hell, I'd been walking proof of that for more than a decade.

It was the words she'd said the night before. The ones she'd worked so hard to make me hear, to make me believe. That maybe I wasn't the guy I'd been telling myself I was this whole time. That maybe I did deserve a chance to find happiness for myself. That maybe successfully raising my son wasn't an all or nothing proposition. There might be room in ensuring his happiness to look after my own. Maybe.

These thoughts were more than I wanted to consider as the

shafts of light reached through the room, drifting languid and soft, just like the two of us in the big king bed we'd had installed.

"Good morning," I said, pulling the woman in my arms closer against me, loving the silky warmth of her skin, the softness of her hair against my cheek.

"Hmm," she said, wiggling her butt in closer to bend of my hips, putting her smack against my quickly waking morning wood.

"Sleep okay?" I asked. I wanted to roll her over, claim her again, talk to her in a way that showed I knew where we stood, how things were. But I didn't know. And in the back of my mind, I feared Addison might wake up and declare the previous night a mistake, just as she'd done the moment we'd kissed.

But instead, she reached behind her and began to stroke me, soft teasing touches mixed with firm grasps that had me groaning and sent my hands searching her body. As her fingers teased me, my own hand slipped down her soft belly, to the apex of her thighs, where I took my time doing some teasing of my own. Addie moaned and pressed back against me again, turning her head now to find my mouth.

When I had her writhing in my arms, I flipped her over and braced myself over her, taking a moment just to stare at the face of the beautiful woman beneath me. Was she really here? How was I this lucky?

"Why are you teasing me?" she whined as the tip of my cock pressed against her entrance.

"Just trying to wrap my head around the fact that I fucked the babysitter last night," I said.

Her mouth formed a little o, and then she poked me in the side, feigning anger. "I was five! I was not your babysitter."

"It's hotter if I think of it that way. You're the sexy and experienced woman, taking advantage of a younger man," I suggested.

She scowled. "I'm not that much older."

"It's just a fantasy," I told her, though in reality I had all the fantasy I needed right here beneath me. "Let me grab a condom." I began to roll off of her, but Addie stopped me.

"No, it's all right. I'm on the pill." Then she hesitated. "I mean, if you're . . ."

"I honestly haven't been with anyone in years," I told her. "But last time I was tested I was clean. And I trust that my hand hasn't been messing around on me."

She slapped my chest playfully, but seconds later, all joking had been put aside as I pressed myself inside her, relishing the feel of every inch of her skin against mine.

I hadn't lied. It had been years. And spending this time with Addison would fuel years more worth of fantasies if it didn't work out, which I was pretty sure it would not—especially since I was still pretty sure she intended to go back to New York. But that didn't mean I wouldn't enjoy every single second of it while it lasted.

The feeling of her against me, around me, with nothing between us, was the most erotic thing I'd ever experienced. And her breathy moans, the way her nails dug into my skin—it wasn't my most impressive performance. And so we needed a couple tries to get it right.

We got out of bed late, and I made coffee in the new kitchen as Addie took a shower. When she came down, I felt almost shy around her, but she came straight into my arms, kissing me like she was mine. And my confidence grew.

"You going to the store today?" she asked when her hands were wrapped around a mug and she was seated at the new kitchen island.

"I am," I said. "As much as I love my cousins, I don't trust them enough to let them open and close the store every day. For all I know, there's another Tanner-sponsored flash sale going on right now."

Addie's face darkened at the mention of the feud, and she blew out a long breath. "Can we just agree right now that as far as you and I are concerned, this thing is over?"

"I've got no beef with that at all. But you and I were not the ones invested to begin with."

"True, but maybe we can lead by example."

"We can try," I agreed.

"Speaking of Tanners, did I tell you Lottie would like to have Sunday dinner here?"

That was new. From what I'd observed, Lottie hated me and everything about this arrangement between me and her oldest daughter. I put down my cup and tried to imagine having Lottie Tanner here for more than a few minutes to check up on us, as she'd done a few times now. It had been uncomfortable. "Uh, no."

"Yes, and she wants your uncle to come."

"Lottie wants Victor here?" This didn't make any sense at all. The two of them hated each other.

"I guess so. She mentioned that she'd bumped into him when she was digging through records recently."

"Records?"

"About the house, the land."

That made sense. Victor had mentioned scouring records so he could prove that the house should belong to the Tuckers only. Fortunately, the trust superseded two-hundred year old land deeds, so it was mostly an exercise in historical trivia for both him and Lottie. "Well, I guess we can invite everyone and see what happens."

"Okay," Addie said, looking uncertain. "Mom's bringing a roast. Maybe we can ask everyone to bring a dish and then you and I don't have to cook."

"But we have this incredible new kitchen," I pointed out.

"And it would be a shame to mess it up," Addie said.

"Okay, fine. I'll ask Victor to make his cornbread." I paused. "Does this mean Emmett and Virge are invited too?" I was pretty sure she wouldn't want a repeat of what had happened in the store. They'd finally admitted to me what they'd said to her.

Addie's face fell, but she recovered herself. "Um, I guess so, yeah."

"I'll make sure we have enough whiskey. This is going to be interesting."

"It is," she agreed.

I kissed her again, long and hard, and then headed off to work. I didn't strictly have to work there on Saturdays—Emmett and Virge were slightly more competent than I let on to Addie. But I wanted to pick up the things I'd been finishing up in my workshop. Especially if we were about to have company.

26

THE GERMAN SHEPHERD'S SADNESS
ADDISON

I spent most of Saturday in a state of dreamy wakefulness, wandering around the house, thinking about Michael. He was humble and unassuming—things Luke never had been—but there was also an edge of sexy confidence to him that I sensed hadn't been uncovered in a while. And the more I saw of it, the more I wanted.

As I tidied up the bedroom and made more coffee, preparing to spend another day out in the garden, I thought about my plans. Maybe I didn't have to go back to New York. Maybe, considering the amount of money this house and the car sitting out in the garage were worth, I could envision a new plan. With that kind of money, I could really do anything I wanted. I couldn't imagine not doing some kind of work, but I didn't think finance was really my calling. I knew I didn't want to bake, like Mom, or teach, like Amberlynn. And it was too late to become a doctor like Paige.

My mind turned over the possibilities, and I felt like a bright new pathway had suddenly been illuminated for me—one that might include Michael. And Singletree.

Just as I was heading out the back door into the yard, my

mother trundled up the path, followed by another woman who was gazing around the property with an evaluative look on her face. Mom was the queen of unexpected visits. There went my quiet day.

"There you are!" Lottie called, as if she'd been looking for me for hours.

"Here I am. Good morning, Mom."

"Addie, this is Sally. I told you I'd be bringing her by."

Actually, Mom had told me Sally was a pet psychic with good Yelp ratings, but it never paid off to bring up semantics with Mom. "Sally, nice to meet you."

"You too, dear. I understand you're having some spirit trouble in the house?" She glanced past me at the house.

"Ah, maybe? We're just hearing some noises now and then."

Sally nodded as if she knew exactly what I meant. "Can you describe them for me?"

I told her about the scrabbling and the crashes and the shrieks, as well as the missing items. "My silver bracelet has recently gone missing too, so that's actually the most concerning ghostly occurrence we've been having."

"Yes, and what do the screams sound like?" Sally's wrinkled face was offset by very large bright blue eyes, and she looked genuinely concerned, which made me feel a bit less annoyed at my mother for overstepping.

"Well, they're high pitched and—"

"I was hoping you might demonstrate."

"Oh. Um, you want me to scream?"

"If you don't mind, dear."

"Ah, okay, sure," I said. Then I cleared my throat and did my best imitation of the otherworldly screaming we'd heard in the house.

My mother looked aghast at this demonstration, and Sally shook her head. I wasn't sure if she had taken my scream as a very bad sign about the potential haunting at the house, or if both women were just disappointed with my rendition.

"Let's go inside," Mom suggested.

"Okay, sure," I said, putting aside the gardening tools and leading the women up the back steps.

"Oh my lord, Addison," Mom cried as we moved into the kitchen. "This is absolutely gorgeous."

"Thank you." It was crazy how much my mother's validation meant to me.

Mom ran her hands over the counters and paused for long appreciative moments at the double ovens and gas stove. "It's amazing," she breathed.

"There was a lot of space," I pointed out. "It just needed updating."

Mom turned to me and smiled. "Filene would love this," she said, a tear spilling down her cheek. I had almost forgotten that Mom and Filene Easter had been friends. Since Filene hadn't wanted a service or any kind of gravestone, it was like she'd become just a distant memory. But for Mom, I realized, that was not the case.

"And Filene," Sally said, stepping forward and regarding us both with those wide blue eyes, "that's the dog?"

"The dog?" I asked, shaking my head. "What dog?"

"The one you're having all the trouble with. I'm getting a very strong German Shepherd vibe in here."

I turned to my mother, narrowing my eyes. She didn't need actual words to know exactly what I was telling her. *This is stupid. There is no dog. This lady is insane. Thanks so much for bringing her over.*

"Now, Addie," Mom said. "Give this a chance."

"Um, I don't know anything about a dog, Sally."

Sally nodded, wandering through the doorway and into the hallway, turning into the dining room.

I hadn't been in the room since the previous night, when Michael and I had gone at it on the gorgeous dining room table, but looking at it now in the light of day with my mother and the pet psychic both gazing thoughtfully at the place I'd lain and orgasmed as Michael had thrust above me . . . well, it made me blush. And then I started coughing and choking when I noticed my underwear hanging off the back of one of the chairs.

Luckily, when I'd recovered, Mom and Sally had moved us into the parlor and then asked if we might go upstairs. I'd snagged the evidence and shoved it into my pocket.

"Honestly, that's where we hear most of it."

"That's where the dog was most content," Sally said, nodding as if she understood everything now.

After touring the entire house to the random accompaniment of Sally's pronouncements about the dog who'd once lived here, we went back down to the kitchen, where I made both ladies some tea.

"So here's the problem," Sally said, when we were all sitting at the island. "The dog never had a chance to properly say goodbye to his owner."

"Oh." I had trouble summoning any enthusiasm into my voice.

"And he's screaming in frustration."

"Oh."

"So you need to pose as the owner and allow the doggy to say his goodbyes."

"I don't really see how that would be possible," I told her. "I don't know who the owner was."

"Oh, he said Elias was his name."

I had no response to that. Elias was actually the name of one of the men who'd lived here. Lucille's father. Maybe this lady wasn't nuts.

"So, like, how would we do this?" I asked, suddenly a little more willing to believe the pet psychic might know what she was doing.

"There's a man here, correct? Your mother said you were living with some terrible man."

I glared at Mom, who shrugged. "Yes, Michael."

"Good. You spend an entire day calling him Elias, and ask him about his dog as much as you can. He should speak fondly of the dog and allow as many opportunities for the dog's spirit to come forward as possible."

"By doing what, exactly?"

"Play with a ball, throw a stick, that sort of thing. Maybe bring out some dog food."

"Ah, okay," I said, still a little overwhelmed by the idea that a German Shepherd was actually haunting us. What use did the dog have for my bracelet? "Thanks," I told Sally.

"Just let me know if it helps, dear. Maybe leave a review?"

"Sure," I said, imagining myself writing a Yelp review about this engagement. "So do I owe you something?"

"No, honey. This was a favor to your darling mother."

Mom beamed.

"Okay, well, thank you."

After a little more small talk and another cup of tea, my mother and Sally departed, leaving me to garden for the afternoon with the spirit of an unhappy German Shepherd at my side.

MICHAEL ARRIVED home just after five, and I'd managed to pick up some drinks and dinner from The Shack.

But even after his truck trundled noisily into the driveway, Michael didn't appear, so I went out to see what he was doing.

Michael was at the bed of the truck, unloading four white

wooden rocking chairs. "For the porch," he told me. Then he put down the chair he was holding and smiled at me. "For you."

Something warm and unidentifiable welled up inside me. I was touched.

I remembered saying how much I'd enjoy sitting out there, and I was shocked that he had remembered it too. "These are for me?" I asked, dumbfounded. I couldn't remember the last time anyone had made such a sweet gesture. "Thank you."

"I wanted to do something nice. To maybe help offset the years of 'not nice' between our families."

"Wait, did you . . ." I looked over the smooth form of one of the chairs. They weren't like any I'd seen online when I'd priced them. "Did you make these yourself?"

He actually blushed and dropped his eyes to the ground. I half expected him to utter the word shucks. But instead, he cleared his throat and then met my eyes. "Yeah. It's the thing I really enjoy, making furniture. I have a workshop out behind the store."

"You're really talented. You could definitely sell these," I told him, unable to stop myself from sitting in one to test it out. "They're gorgeous."

"Thanks," he said, as I stood again.

I stepped closer to him, wrapping my arms around his waist. "This is nice. This is so nice." And then I did what I'd been thinking of doing all day. I kissed him, long and sweet and languorous, out there under the sweeping fall of leaves and the angling rays of the setting autumn sun. And for that one moment, everything in my life was perfect.

We had dinner in the parlor after setting up the new chairs on the front porch. I tested out every one of them, rocking back and forth on the new porch planks while gazing out at the gates that led down to the town square. I could never have imagined a couple months ago that I'd be sitting on the front porch of the old haunted house, happy and content.

"I made a swing too," Michael said, once I'd finished rocking and stood back up to go inside.

"Seriously?" I grinned. The idea of a porch swing made me so happy. It seemed so provincial, so very southern—to sit on a porch swing and drink lemonade. It wasn't the kind of life I'd thought I'd have, the kind I'd had in New York. But it was the kind of life I was beginning to think I wanted.

"Hey," he said, leaning over the porch railing, staring at something. "Come look at this."

I joined him, following his gaze down to the ground, where there was a very noticeable anthill and about forty million big red ants.

My stomach roiled. I hated ants. I hated bugs. "Fire ants?" I asked.

"Yes, I think so," he said. "I'll call an exterminator. We don't want to mess around with those."

I put the ants out of my mind as best I could and went inside to open the boxes of clams and fries I'd brought home, and then turned on a movie neither of us was really watching.

"I told you about Sunday dinner, right?" I asked him, my mouth half full of clam.

"Yeah," he said. "Uncle Victor was weirdly agreeable. The cousins are suspicious."

"Maybe it's a trap," I suggested, grinning.

"Knowing your mother . . ."

"Careful," I warned, though he wasn't wrong to be wary of Lottie. "Oh, and speaking of my mother."

Michael looked at me and then his eyes slid shut. "Just tell me. I can handle it."

"She came by today with a pet psychic. Long story short, I'm supposed to call you Elias as much as possible and you're supposed to spend as much time as you can throwing balls and putting out kibble."

"Should I pretend that isn't insane?"

"She thinks we're haunted by a German Shepherd."

"Right," he said, just accepting this in stride because based on everything else my mother had done, this made perfect sense.

"So what do you say, Elias?"

"What do I get to call you?" He asked.

I put my drink down and turned toward him on the couch. "If you want to go upstairs, you can call me anything you want." It was the boldest thing I'd probably ever said, but this thing between us had me feeling like a different version of myself. A better, more confident, sexier version.

"Let's go," he said.

We practically sprinted up the stairs, and the second I'd crossed the threshold into the bedroom, Michael caught my wrist and pulled me into his chest. For a few beats, he held me close and just looked down at me with those expressive blue eyes, and then he smiled and leaned in, pressing his lips to mine.

The kiss was slow and teasing, a current of control that was at odds with the wild thrashing inside my body every time Michael looked at me that way or touched me. But after a moment, his tongue swept the seam of my lips and the kiss deepened, and he walked with me toward the bed, pushing me back until the mattress hit my thighs.

We broke the kiss only long enough to scoot into the center of the mattress, Michael hovering over me for a long moment. I stared up at him, beginning to feel both impatient and a little uncomfortable under his intense scrutiny.

"What?" I laughed, reaching for him.

"You," he said simply. "You're incredible. I feel so lucky to have had the chance to know you. I would never have imagined this." He shook his head lightly, smiling, and then the smile slid from his face as his eyes darkened.

For the rest of the evening, we didn't talk much, and Michael, didn't repeat his thoughts about feeling lucky—instead, he showed me. His tongue made trails across my body, swirling and laving every part of me, and at one point, when his head was between my thighs, my hands fisted in that thick red hair, I had the sense we weren't alone in the room. And when I screamed my release, I thought I heard the ghost scream along with me—only this time, it didn't frighten me.

But it was a little creepy.

And it definitely wasn't a German Shepherd.

27

WE DON'T JOKE ABOUT COONS
MICHAEL

S pending night after night with Addison Tanner in my arms felt like a completely different version of my life. Somewhere though, in the dark corners of my practical and pessimistic brain, I wondered if it wasn't doomed from the start. She was a Tanner, after all. And the odds were stacked against us. Our disparate ages. Our families. Her career. My failures. Our mutual baggage. My responsibilities to my son. None of that added up to a carefree and successful relationship, but the neutral territory of the house made it feel like maybe it was all possible.

I decided, consciously or subconsciously, not to allow any of the realities of my life interfere with the first real selfish happiness I'd found in years. It was too heady, too addictive for reality to intervene.

Saturday morning we called the exterminator to deal with the ants. He was a tall wiry guy with a permanent scowl named Liam, who showed up almost immediately after I'd called and stood over the anthill shaking his head.

"It's a big colony," he said. "I might need to come out a couple times to really get it."

I shrugged. "That's okay. I just don't like it being so close to the front door."

He gazed up at me then, narrow eyes evaluating me. "Don't mind the ghosts though, eh?"

I smiled, gazing around the rebuilt front porch. From the outside, I guessed maybe the house did still look a little dilapidated. We hadn't had it repainted yet. But the place was sound, and the interior work was almost complete. The electrician had updated the wiring, and we had internet and cable, and a state of the art kitchen. It was hard to look at the old house the way I once had. "I guess I don't."

He nodded, gazing around me at the big house. "What about coons, you mind them much?"

I shook my head. "Come again?"

"I could take care of them at the same time as these ants."

"Did you say coons?"

He crossed his arms and nodded again, not saying anything.

"Liam, do you see raccoons?" I was beginning to wonder if our exterminator was hallucinating.

"I bet you do," he said. "Big old hole up there on the right side under the eaves, right next to that tree." He pointed at something I couldn't see from where I was standing, so I moved off the porch to gaze up to where he indicated.

There was a hole.

"How do you know it's raccoons?" I asked.

"They're predictable." He dropped his arms and began walking away from me, heading for his truck and his gear. "You probably hearin' some screeching? Maybe finding some turds around the place, noticing a dog smell? Missing anything shiny?"

I stopped in my tracks. "Seriously?"

He glanced over his shoulder as he unloaded his gear. "I ain't joking. Raccoons is serious business."

The laugh that came out of me surprised Liam into spinning around.

"I mean it. Serious," he said, chastising me for my humor.

"I believe you. It's just . . . yeah, we have a raccoon problem for sure. Go ahead and take care of it."

"The humane way or the easy way?" He paused. "Humane costs more, mind you."

"Ah," I was tempted to say the easy way, but I knew Daniel and Addie would definitely choose humane. "Better do it the humane way."

"Gonna take a week or so."

I nodded. "That's fine." We'd been living with them this long. "Hey, any chance of finding any of the stuff you think they snatched? They took my watch, I think."

"Gotta find the hidey hole. Likely up in that tree." He pointed. "I can look for ya."

"Thanks," I said, feeling like a weight had just been lifted from my shoulders. Selling a haunted house was not an easy business. Selling a house with a recently resolved raccoon problem shouldn't be nearly as hard. I headed back inside to let Liam get to work, but the more I thought about the idea of selling the house, the less I wanted to think about it. That was the goal, after all. But it would also mean the end of pretty much everything that had made me happy these last few weeks. Addie, our time together.

"Exterminator here?" Addie asked as I headed back inside.

"Yeah, and you'll never believe what he said."

"Zombie ants? Unkillable, right?"

I laughed. "No, he'll get the ants, it'll be fine. It's the raccoons I was surprised about." I told her what he'd said, and her eyes grew wider with every word.

"Raccoons?" She burst out laughing.

"So while it was a credible theory, it's not a German Shepherd."

"I was going to call you Elias all day to see if it helped!"

When the exterminator had finished—clearing us of ants and placing the traps to catch our nocturnal screamers—Addie and I each headed into town and off to our separate tasks. I needed to get into the store and inventory some of the supplies that had arrived this week, and Addie said she owed her mother some help at the Tin.

"Daniel will be here tonight," I reminded her as she set off down the hill.

"So pizza?" She asked, grinning.

"Sounds good."

I watched her disappear down the hill into town, and a deep contentment settled in my heart. What would it be like, I wondered, if this was my real life? If Addie was really mine, and we lived in this big old house and shared our evenings and our years together? What would that be like?

Whatever it might be like, it was unlikely to happen, and I vowed to enjoy it while it lasted.

WHEN WE ALL rose on Sunday morning—in separate beds, since Daniel had come back—each of us had tasks to accomplish. We were hosting dinner, and that meant showing the house off to a whole bunch of people. People who traditionally hated each other. Which was why I'd stocked up on whiskey and wine the day prior.

"Mom's bringing the main course, and everyone's bringing something, so we just need to get dessert done, finish up the rolls, and get a salad put together," Addie said. It didn't sound like a lot, but it seemed to take her all day in the kitchen. I tried to help, and chopped and washed as directed. As we finished up, Daniel wandered in from outside.

"Hey," I said, smiling at him.

He watched me washing dishes and sat down at the counter, looking happy and relaxed.

"So I think we're gonna have a good dinner," I said. "But you know, I don't think there's any pasta." I said. I looked between Daniel and Addie.

"Did we need pasta?" Addie looked worried.

"Oh God, no, don't encourage him. It's a dad joke," Daniel moaned.

Addison turned and raised an eyebrow, waiting for the joke.

"What do you call a fake noodle?" I asked them.

"Don't do it, Dad. I'm begging you."

"An *impasta*," I told them. When they were done groaning, Dan and I went outside.

Daniel and I focused on the yard, and though I had to divert about thirty requests to take the Corvette for a spin (I was still a little uncertain about what we needed to do with the collector car in the dilapidated garage, and definitely wasn't going to drive it around town. If people had forgotten it was there, that was for the best for now), we spent a pretty enjoyable day together.

At four o'clock, the front door knocker sounded through the house, and I went out to answer it, since Addie was in the shower upstairs.

I opened the door to find Lottie Tanner standing with her sister Verda, holding a huge covered pan and the strange little doll that had been fastened to the door since Addie had hosted the stinky sisters to wave burning sticks around the place.

"Mrs. Tanner, hello," I said, taking the voodoo doll and sticking it into my back pocket.

Her face narrowed as if she was going to say something nasty, but then her eyes fell on Daniel at my shoulder, and she managed a smile instead. "Hello, Tuckers. Thank you for inviting us."

"I'm telling you, Lottie, this is a bad idea," Verda hissed in her sister's ear.

"Why don't you come in?" I asked, waving them into the foyer.

"I can take that for you," Daniel said, reaching for the roast pan. My heart swelled a bit with pride.

"What excellent manners," Lottie commented, turning to her sister as if to say, "see? It'll be okay."

"He's too young for the Tucker evil to have taken hold yet," Verda said, giving Dan an evaluative look.

I showed the ladies to the kitchen and offered them each a glass of wine, which they accepted somewhat graciously. Lottie made herself at home in the kitchen while Verda asked Daniel to give her a tour, and she busily oohed and aahed over the way Addison had decorated.

Soon, Addie had appeared at her mother's side, and she looked gorgeous in a thick white sweater and slim jeans, with her hair tied up on the back of her head and glowing skin. We exchanged a few secret smiles when no one was looking, but soon we were both busy hosting a house full of guests.

Wiley and Amberlynn appeared next, carrying a potted plant and a bottle of Half Cat. Then Paige and Cormac arrived with his two little girls in tow and a wrapped package, which Addie set aside until the littlest girl demanded we open it. Daniel did the honors, revealing a taxidermied raccoon. Daniel looked impressed.

"We heard about your troubles, and Cormac has some connections in the taxidermy world," Paige explained. "Thought this was appropriate."

"Um, okay," I said, trying to be gracious about the dead

stuffed animal Daniel was now settling onto the hearth near the front door. "Well, thank you."

My uncle arrived next, with Virge and Emmett at his side, and while my uncle was freshly shaven and acting oddly polite, my cousins scowled around the place and refused to mix, choosing to sit on the front porch with glasses of whiskey and keeping to themselves.

A little later, I was surprised to find Lottie and Victor laughing together in the kitchen, their heads close together. The feud, I sensed, might be coming to an end across multiple generations. I just needed to convince my cousins it was over.

Soon, we were all sitting around the huge dining room table, warm lights glowing on the wall and candles in the middle, right where I'd had sex with Addie for the first time.

I sipped my wine and smiled, feeling a strange sense of wholeness I wasn't sure I'd ever felt before as this huge mixed family gathered around me. I caught Addie's eyes across the table and grinned at her, and my heart soared when her twinkling eyes and beautiful lips returned everything I was feeling as she held her glass up to me.

28

SUNDAY SILLINESS
ADDISON

I would never have believed it, but Sunday dinner with the Tuckers and Tanners all at the table was a success. Verda graciously chose to leave her moose-related gripes at the door, and even Emmett and Virgil were tolerable once they'd had a few glasses of whiskey.

Everyone commented on the way we'd finished the downstairs, and I glowed with every compliment. I'd wanted the chance to design a real space for years, and the apartment I'd shared with Luke in New York had been all him. But here, the fresh paper I'd hung in the dining room and the striking paint in the foyer all worked together to make the house feel coordinated yet fun. It made me happy, seeing my family appreciate my choices—the big plush rugs, the kitschy bright fabrics and framed art.

Daniel was a huge help in the kitchen, even helping me wash dishes once the whole thing was over, and I was developing a fondness for the boy that I'd never expected to feel. I wasn't sure what Michael had told him about us, so I made a point of avoiding longing gazes, and didn't touch Michael when Dan was around.

As the evening wound down, everyone smiling and enjoying good food and good wine—and even good company—we found ourselves formulating a plan.

Halloween was just around the corner, and the old haunted house on the hill had always been a big draw for the kids from town. This year, we decided to let the kids come into the house and see it for themselves.

"We could do a haunted house as a fundraiser for the high school's gym renovation," Amberlynn suggested.

"Oh, that's a great idea," Victor said, and I was surprised to see him throw his arm around Lottie as he said it. She glowed.

"Maybe we should theme it," I suggested.

"Yeah, what if we themed it around the Tanner-Tucker feud?" Daniel suggested. I braced myself—though we were all getting along, it might be a bit early for this.

Surprisingly, Virgil and Verda both nodded at this suggestion.

"Maybe this is a good time to say something," Victor said, standing up and holding up his glass.

Michael and I exchanged a surprised look across the table.

"Lottie and I have been doing a lot of research, as you know," he said, and Lottie nodded. "And we've uncovered some interesting information about the origins of this problem between our families."

He looked around at all of us, and I was beginning to realize that Victor had a bit of a dramatic flair.

"This property was evidently purchased by a Tanner back in 1827," he said. "And we were lucky to learn that Gracie Vanderburg over at the records center isn't the first in her family to deal in county records." He grinned and raised his eyebrows. "In fact, her great-great uncle was a clerk at the time of the land purchase, and he kept some journals that her family still holds."

"Tell them, Vic," Mom interjected, rubbing her hands together in barely contained anticipation.

"I'm getting there, Lots."

They exchanged a look that I was pretty sure meant they'd been doing more than just scouring records together. Good for Mom.

"Anyway, what we've learned is that while Arnold Tanner bought the property and had intended to build on it as a surprise for his wife Esther, he died before he could do so. And since he didn't mention this purchase to anyone, when the clerk died before filing the deed, the property purchase was a bit of a mystery around the land office for a while. Gracie's uncle didn't learn the truth until years later, when his father told him about his friend Arnold's plans. In the meantime, the new clerk found a scrawled note about the deed and misread the name Tanner for Tucker. He filed the land claim under the name Tucker, and unknowingly gave the land away. The Tuckers built a house on the land immediately, thrilled about their windfall. And after a couple years, someone let the beans spill to Esther, and she insisted that the whole thing go to court.

"The documents gave the land to the Tuckers, but the Tanners had gotten themselves all in a dither about it, insisting that justice must be done. And soon after the court found for our family, the house on this property burned to the ground."

Gasps erupted around the table. This whole feud was far more serious than I'd ever imagined.

"And then," Mom said, springing to her feet as if she just couldn't wait another second for Victor to finish up, "the Tuckers retaliated by stealing a herd of goats from the Tanners, and shooting Zeke Tanner in the process. Which might have been an accident, but no one knows. That made our family pretty mad, as you might imagine—especially Zeke, who I guess then started all kinds of sabotage."

Victor nodded, looking thrilled at getting to be the center of attention with Lottie, and he finished up. "The Tuckers rebuilt the house, put up the fence around it, and the feud went on."

"And I, for one, think it's time we decided to end it," Mom said, smiling around the table magnanimously.

"I second that," Victor said.

We all raised our glasses, and as I locked eyes with Michael, we all cheered the official end of the feud.

Between the end of the feud and plans for the haunted house, Daniel could barely sit still, he was so excited. It was endearing.

My sisters agreed to help plan, and Amberlynn said she'd spread the word at the high school and recruit a few kids to help populate the scenes we had in mind.

Everyone left around the same time, floating out onto the front porch and down the lawn, carried by full stomachs and good feelings into the brisk night air. It all seemed like it had gone perfectly, until a scream came from my sister's car.

"Paige?" I dashed out the gate.

"What the heck is this?" She asked, pointing at the evil-looking little statue sitting in the passenger seat.

Cormac was grinning and the girls looked uncertain about what to think.

Daniel arrived at my side. "It's Thaddius," he said. "But I didn't mean for him to scare you."

I gazed at the boy, shaking my head and grinning.

"It's the new feud," he said. "A harmless one," he added quickly when he read what he must have thought was disapproval on my face. "I've read about other families having a gnome like this one. And they take turns hiding him around each other's property, either in hard to find spots or doing funny things. And once you find him, it's your turn to hide him in someone else's house or yard." Daniel looked so happy about this idea, I couldn't shoot him down.

"I love it," Paige said, surprising me.

"Yes!" Taylor was bouncing and clapping her hands, and her sister imitated her perfectly.

"It's a kinder, gentler feud," Cormac suggested, and I nodded. It was perfect.

"You're a pretty smart kid," I told Daniel, wrapping an arm around his shoulder and pulling him into me, and his face broke into an abashed grin.

We turned to find Michael standing just behind us, smiling in a distant way, like he was thinking about something.

After we'd said goodbye to all the guests, and even Mom had left with a smile on her face, the three of us went back inside and cleaned up what was left of the dishes.

"I'd say that was an incredible success," Michael said. "And I think there might be something going on between your mom and my uncle."

"Right?" I asked. "I noticed that too. Good for them."

Daniel made a face, but even he seemed to be happy with the way the night had gone.

"All right, Dan," Michael said, turning to him. "School tomorrow. How did you sleep in your own room last night?" We'd set up a room upstairs for Daniel, with a bed and a desk of his own.

Daniel looked at me and said, "thanks for the room. It's incredible. I know my dad didn't put that together. Why aren't you an interior designer, anyway?"

"I don't know," I said. "I always wanted to be. I even took some classes online a while back. I just . . . got busy, I guess."

"Well, your taste is way better than Dad's!"

Michael punched him in the arm, and Dan turned and bounded up the stairs.

We exchanged a smile, and a quick kiss, and then went our separate ways for bed. And as I settled in for the night—even though I was alone, I felt less alone than I ever had before.

29

FEUDS AND FUN HOUSES
MICHAEL

W e had two weeks to plan a feud-themed haunted house. Luckily, my son was more motivated about this project than I'd seen him about anything before.

"We should totally park the Corvette on the lawn," he suggested as the three of us sat around the kitchen island Thursday night the week after our successful Sunday dinner. Shelly hadn't said another word about sole custody, and so far I hadn't let the kid out of my sight, had made sure all his homework was done, and had generally done everything in my power to prove I was a good father.

My attorney had told me that unless she formally filed for sole custody, it was just a threat—but it was one that got my attention. I'd begun to think that maybe I could be a good father and still have a life of my own, but if anything threatened my relationship with Daniel, it was an easy choice to decide what was most important.

Only . . . looking at Addison across the island as she discussed the intricacies of creating realistic fake blood with my son, I wondered if having her in his life wasn't actually a good thing. Maybe having another responsible and successful adult invested in him multiplied his odds of success, gave him an even firmer ground to launch from. The relationship that had grown between them made me smile to myself when I was doing tasks around the store, had me chuckling when I remembered the two of them laughing together.

If something real developed between me and Addie, how would having her in my son's life be bad? I was so accustomed to pushing away anything that seemed like a distraction for me, anything that pulled my attention in another direction. But with Addie, I was beginning to see things a different way. Of course, Daniel had no real idea what was going on. All he knew was that we had a house together thanks to a very odd legal arrangement.

"So the raccoon is going to leap off the mantle when the door opens?" Addie was asking Dan now, her eyebrows adorably wrinkled.

"Or maybe when people walk by," he suggested.

We spent an enjoyable evening, drawing up plans and figuring out each aspect of our haunted house, and I said good-night to my son, knowing the next day would be bittersweet—he'd go back to Shelly for the rest of the week. But I'd have time alone with Addison. And after sleeping in separate bedrooms for the week, I was ready to hold her in my arms again.

Just before bed, Dan insisted on going out to look around the yard in order to finalize some plans. I was trying to finish up installing some shelving in the master bedroom for Addie, so I told him to use his phone flashlight and be careful. As Addie and I worked together to put up the shelves, I had a strong sense of serenity—everything was working out.

Daniel came in after about twenty minutes, and at first I didn't notice the limp.

"Hey, what's wrong?" I asked him.

"Nothing. I'm good." He shrugged and walked away, but the limp was definitely not a good thing.

"Hey," I called after him. "Why are you limping?"

"Dad," he insisted. "I'm fine."

I should have been more insistent, but hindsight is twenty-twenty.

The following morning, I took Dan to school and went into the store, to find Virgil and Emmett grumpy and muttering with their heads together.

"What?" I asked, almost afraid of the answer.

"That gnome showed up here last night," Virgil said, his face dark as he crossed his arms over his chest.

I laughed. "Oh, the new feud gnome? Thaddius?"

"Laugh all you want," Emmett growled. "This means war."

I shook my head, dropping a hand on the counter loudly enough to startle a customer wandering past. "Sorry," I told her, waving toward the garden pots she was examining. Then I turned to my cousins. "This doesn't mean war, actually. This means that both sides of this stupid feud have agreed to take the whole thing down a notch. We're moving this ridiculous feud to level where it can't hurt anyone's business or prized possessions, to a place where we can continue pranking each other but know that it's all in good fun."

They just stared at me, their faces remaining dark.

"Where was the gnome?" I asked.

"He was sitting out front on one of your Adirondack chairs this morning when I opened," Virgil said.

"That's perfectly harmless," I said.

They exchanged a look.

"Was he holding a sign that said 'Tuckers are Fuckers?'"

"No," Virgil said.

"Was he holding a sign that said, 'Store clearance, everything must go'?"

"No," Emmett said.

"Was he doing anything besides just sitting innocently in the chair?" I asked.

"No," they admitted.

"Good, then if you can handle yourselves appropriately, you have permission to take on the responsibility of placing the gnome next. Harmlessly. Without any kind of vandalism or criminal activity."

Virgil sighed. "Fine."

"Good," I said.

The rest of the day progressed calmly, with Thaddius standing next to the register, adding a bit of spooky charm to the place to honor the approach of Halloween.

❧

THAT NIGHT, Addison was waiting for me at the house with lasagna, garlic bread, red wine, and the most beautiful smile I could imagine.

"This is nice," I said, accepting the glass of wine she handed me once I'd dropped my messenger bag.

"It's our first night alone in a while," she said, and it felt so good to know she'd been anticipating it just as much as I had.

I sipped the wine, feeling all the tension wash through me and away as the lush flavor coated my tongue.

This.

Addison waiting, warm and smiling, this beautiful house, the smell of home cooked food in the air. This was everything I wanted. This feeling of happiness welling inside from a place I hadn't heard from in years, maybe ever. This idea that my life could still take a turn, that there could still be something in it for me beyond the day to day focus I'd found in trying to be a good father to my son. This.

We sat down to dinner, an air of calm anticipation around us in the knowledge that we had the whole night together, the whole weekend. There was no rush.

"Thanks for making dinner," I said.

Addison smiled. "I'm practicing. It isn't something I've done a lot, but my mom said lasagna is pretty much foolproof."

"You're pretty far from a fool anyway."

"That was close to a dad joke."

"Do I tell too many dad jokes?"

"It's part of your charm," she said, and I believed she meant it.

Dinner was a leisurely affair, each of us relaxed and smiling. Our meal was punctuated with light touches as we talked, and with exchanged looks that said we both knew what was to come. It was like extended foreplay, and by the time we were taking the dishes to the kitchen, I couldn't wait any longer.

I put my plate on the counter and then let my hands find the sweet curve of Addie's hips as she faced the sink. I pulled her into my hips and was rewarded with her sharp intake of breath. As my hands explored beneath the hem, finding their way to the smooth skin of her stomach, sliding across soft warmth and pulling her tighter into me, she dropped her head back onto my shoulder. I leaned my head in, burying my nose in the floral sweetness of her hair and then finding the long column of her beautiful throat.

Addie moaned as my lips brushed her skin, and gasped again when I began kissing and licking my way along the side of her neck, moving into the curve of her shoulder to be rewarded with another breathy moan.

My hands had found their way to her breasts, and I cupped the perfect swells in my hands, my balls tightening in anticipation as I pressed myself harder against her. I let out a throaty groan of my own, blinded and deafened to everything but her. But this.

Until.

"Dad?"

I looked up to find Daniel standing just inside the back door, his mouth open slightly and his brow furrowed.

"Dan," I said, but my brain was too muddled with Addie to respond quickly enough. To respond correctly. I should have stepped away, should have sat him down and explained things, but in the next second, his mother was standing behind him. And she did not look confused at all.

"So you lied to me before," she said. "This," she waved between me and Addie, "is exactly what I thought it was. And that doesn't even matter," she went on. "You let my son get injured in this disaster of a house."

"No," I said, feeling like my words were blocks of concrete, heavy and impossible to arrange correctly. "Wait, hurt? Dan?" I looked to Dan. The limp?

"He stepped on a nail out in the yard," she said. "And we just came from the doctor where he had a tetanus shot and had the wound treated in case of infection. The fact you didn't even know about it only makes it worse. And now, this." She waved back and forth between Addison and me. "No wonder you were too distracted to keep your son safe."

Daniel looked as upset and confused as I felt. "Are you okay, Dan?" I asked.

He didn't answer, but stared at Addie, looking hurt. This wasn't the way I wanted to tell him about the relationship I was building with Addie. And I couldn't help but feel like Shelly's presence just behind him was poisoning my ability to defend myself, like there was no way I could really explain anything with her there. And there was really no defending myself if what she said about Dan getting hurt was true.

"I think we all know exactly what's going on," Shelly snapped.

"Just a second," Addison tried, stepping forward, but Daniel's face had shifted, his cheeks reddening.

He interrupted whatever Addie had been about to say, "Why didn't you tell me?" His voice cracked, and I felt my heart crack at the same time. "Why didn't you just tell me? I'm not a kid." His words were directly at odds with the emotion on his face, the trembling lip as he struggled with emotion. He was shaking his head now, refusing to meet my eyes.

"Just go upstairs and get your backpack," Shelly said, and when Daniel had trudged off to retrieve his forgotten item, she pinned me with a glare. "You let your son get hurt and lied to him. And you lied to me. You said you'd keep him safe here, and now he's got a hole in his foot that needed medical attention. What if it had been something worse? I might have made an empty threat before, but you'll be hearing from my lawyer now."

"Shell, don't do this," I said, my voice carrying every ounce of the exhaustion I felt.

"I'm doing it. For Daniel," she said.

I knew two things for certain when she spoke those words.

One, Shelly was serious this time. I'd given her ammunition by not looking out for Daniel. My stomach was shredded with the knowledge that he'd gotten hurt under my care, and that Shelly was right, it could have been much worse.

I also knew that whatever bliss I'd shared with Addison had just come to an end. I'd been deceiving us both, pretending I was free to start something, to enjoy something, to share something with her. But in truth, I was not free. I'd let down my guard and my son had paid for it, and now Shelly had the upper hand. I might lose him.

"Daniel, we'll talk about this," I promised as my son walked past me, refusing to meet my eyes.

"Fine." He pushed through the kitchen door, his backpack

slung over his shoulder, and I felt my heart go with him, crushed and crumpled like his pack.

"I'll talk to you Monday," Shelly said, and her voice held a threat I clearly identified.

I watched them both walk away, and then turned to face Addison.

"Michael, I'm so sorry."

"For what? You did nothing wrong." My words came out harsher than I meant for them to.

"I just—" Addie began.

But I couldn't hear her. Not now, not when everything I'd imagined was crumbling like sand walls as the inevitable tide washed in to reclaim its territory. I'd failed Dan. I'd failed to keep him safe, to be the dad he needed. I'd failed at the one thing I'd vowed to focus on. "I'm just going to go to bed," I said, turning toward the stairs.

"Michael—"

"I'm sorry," I whispered. "Good night." My heart felt like it was sinking through my chest, falling like a rock to the bottom of the deepest ocean trench. I didn't think I'd ever retrieve it from there, and tonight I didn't have the energy to even try.

30

MOM LOVE
ADDISON

I saw the exact moment Michael gave up on us. Daniel walked right past him as Shelly's eyes lasered into Michael's downcast face, and I watched his shoulders fall, his expression dim.

And I knew that whatever this was, whatever this had been, it was done.

I felt awful that Dan had gotten hurt—but then again, he'd come back inside the night before and hadn't said a thing about stepping on a nail. Was Shelly maybe blowing it a little out of proportion? I couldn't doubt her really, she was his mother. But why didn't Dan tell us?

It didn't matter now. Not where I was concerned. That night, as I lay alone in the king bed in the master bedroom staring at the ceiling, I realized what a fool I'd been.

This house had made it easy to pretend. I'd allowed myself to build an alternate reality, one in which I wasn't a financial analyst who lived in New York City. One in which I wasn't a spinster, recently dumped by the man I thought I'd be building a life with. One in which I had everything I ever really wanted.

But I could see now that it was a mirage. One I'd wanted so desperately to believe could be real.

Even Michael was just a flickering falsehood—a version of the man I'd wanted to believe in. One he could never be. Because Michael wasn't free.

He'd told me himself that he lived in a prison of his own making. He didn't use those words, of course, but he existed in a cage he built for himself out of regret and guilt over the failure of his relationship with Shelly. Over the mistakes he'd made as a kid and over the opportunities he'd lost as a result.

And now? He was going to choose to step back inside those bars and pull the door shut again, because he thought that was what he deserved.

No amount of convincing from me—that he was a worthy man, that he deserved to be happy, that he was by far one of the most successful people I'd ever met—would change his mind.

So when I woke the next morning with the sun streaming optimistically through the curtains I'd hung, I knew what I needed to do.

Michael was not in the house when I went downstairs. I'd heard his truck start early, and imagined he'd headed off to the store to punish himself some more.

I had coffee and then headed down the hill to the Muffin Tin.

"Addie!" Mom called as I walked through the door. "Oh no. Oh dear. Here, have a pumpkin creme muffin and sit."

I guessed my distress was clear on my face. Or maybe it was just clear to mothers.

I sat at the end of the counter, watching my mother bustle around and wishing I had the energy she always seemed to have. She put a latte and a muffin in front of me and then stood, her perfectly manicured plump little hands on the counter in front of my plate. For some reason, I found myself staring at her hands.

They'd done so much in her lifetime. They'd done so much for me. Those hands had held me when I was a baby, had carried my sisters and me as children. They'd made countless treats and wiped innumerable tears from our cheeks. They'd hugged and loved, and helped for as long as I had known this woman, and for some reason staring at my mother's hands now brought tears to my eyes.

"Oh, Addie, what is it?"

I put one of my hands atop my mother's and looked at the difference. I'd done nothing in my life. I'd thought I was building some kind of empire of independence, modeling the new self-made woman, showing my small-town family what I could do. But my hands were smooth and unlined, and they revealed the folly in my thinking. My hands hadn't smoothed away tears or held babies. They hadn't made cookies for school bake sales or tied shoes on the ends of pudgy little legs. They'd typed and processed spreadsheets and dialed for takeout.

"Mom," I whispered, and it was a broken sob that came from my lips as I realized the extent of my own failures, gazed behind me at the ignored opportunities, the scattered dreams I'd ignored. "I've done everything wrong."

Mom covered my hand with her other one, shaking her head with tears standing in her own eyes. "Oh, my Addie, no. No, you haven't." She stepped around the counter and pulled me into her arms, and I buried my face in her familiar smell. The Aqua Net of her bob, the gardenia perfume she sprayed into the air and then shimmied through, the flour and sugar and cinnamon that made up her days. My heart broke wide open and I cried.

For what felt like hours, I sobbed into my mother's apron like a child, Muffin Tin patrons no doubt avoiding the scene and hoping it might be over soon. But Mom didn't say a word, she just held me close and let me cry.

And when I'd simmered down to sniffles, wiping at my face and recovering myself as best I could, Mom looked at me and said, "Let's figure out what's next."

For the rest of the day, I stayed at the Tin. Mom and I worked side by side, and we didn't actively talk about what it was I was going to do next. Instead, we cobbled together ideas percolated alongside pots of hot coffee and pieced together in the quiet moments between oven timers dinging and customers paying for muffins. And when I helped Mom close down the shop at the end of the day, somehow I had something that felt like a plan.

"So you'll stay through Halloween, and then go back to the city," she said. "Not because you owe anything to anyone, but because you have unfinished business there."

I nodded, testing her words in my soul and finding that they felt right. I would have left earlier, but I felt like I owed it to Daniel to see the haunted house through, and maybe I owed it to Michael to let him know my plans.

He might not care where I went or what I did, but since we were still looped into the house together, he needed to know the plan.

I texted Michael that I was staying with Mom, and I didn't go back to the house that night, or again until Wednesday evening, the following week. I arrived to find Michael hanging the porch swing in the fading light.

"Hi," I said, feeling like an intruder as I stood on the front walk of what was technically my house.

He stopped what he was doing and turned to face me, and in the shadowed eaves, I could see emotions cross his face one by one. Surprise. Happiness. Regret. Distance. "Hi," he said. He stepped toward me and then seemed to think better of it, remaining on the porch at the top of the steps.

"How are you?" I asked, then nodded at the swing without waiting for an answer. "That looks great. You made that?"

He glanced at it as if seeing it for the first time. "I did, yeah." He didn't add what I knew was true: *for you.*

"So, listen," I began, but Michael spread his hands in front of him as if to stop my words.

"No, no, Addie. I owe you an apology."

Oh God, no. I didn't want that. I didn't want to stand here and listen to him tell me why we couldn't be together, how things would never work. "No, it's fine. I just needed to tell you that I'm leaving."

"You're—oh. You're leaving." When he said the words, they sounded flat. Empty.

"Yeah," I said. "So I'll stay for the haunted house, to help out. And then I'm headed back to New York." My stomach twisted as I said the words out loud. But this was the plan. It was only feeling wrong because Michael was here, looking so sad.

"Okay," he said, and I wished for him to beg me not to go, though I'd known he wouldn't do that. He didn't need me here, and I wasn't part of his plan any more than he was part of mine. What we'd had was . . . wonderful. Magical. But that was only because it had been a fantasy.

"And with the house," I began.

"I'll just finish things up. Get it painted."

"Right." I felt uncomfortable, like I didn't belong here at all. "And so you can finish up your six months, and then I'll live here for three months after you move out. We can sell it after that."

"You're coming back?"

"I'll have to, right?"

He nodded.

"At least part time. I'll talk to Anders to see what's permissible."

"Right." He looked disappointed again. "You understand, don't you?" He said suddenly.

I shrugged. I didn't want to hear what I already knew.

"It's Daniel," he went on, his eyes begging me to tell him it was okay. "I have to do better for him. Be the right kind of man."

The unhappy kind, I wanted to say. But I knew it wouldn't make a difference. "Okay," I said instead. Wasn't I leaving anyway? Who was I to tell him he was doing things wrong?

"I just have to see him succeed. Grow up and establish himself."

"And then?" I asked.

"That's it," he said.

That was it. He refused to make any plans for himself, refused to do anything to claim a piece of his own happiness. Instead, he'd martyr himself in the name of his son, out of fear of his ex-wife, and in the name of being a better man. But he couldn't see that half a man would never be enough for anyone, especially himself.

"Okay," I said. "So I'll see you Saturday afternoon to set up."

"Right," he said, sounding defeated as the porch lights illuminated his burnished hair from behind, making him look like he was wearing a halo. My heart twisted a little, watching him. It hurt for me, for what I felt like I'd gotten a tiny little taste of and then had snatched away. But it hurt more for him. Because if Michael Tucker were willing to accept that he deserved to be happy too, that maybe we were happy together, then I'd fight for it. But he had to fight first.

I turned and walked back out the big iron gates, feeling a little bit like I'd turned back the clock to the first days after I'd been home from New York.

My heart ached. My soul felt wrung out.

And I was tired. So tired.

31

EMMETT SPEAKS

MICHAEL

"I thought you were supposed to be the smart one," Emmett said, shaking his head Thursday at the store as we hauled heavy rubber matting from one place to another to make room for the fall seasonal items.

"What the hell does that mean?" I asked. My voice was harsh, and it matched my mood. I'd been angry and frustrated since the weekend, and having Addie stop by to tell me she was going back to New York just made the entire world look bleak and hopeless.

It was ridiculous. A week ago, I'd felt like every day was a new adventure, like even discovering a raccoon infestation was exciting.

Now?

There was nothing to look forward to but an endless parade of days without Daniel interspersed by days with him. The handoff of my son was the only thing that really marked time going forward and even that might potentially be coming to an end if Shelly had her way.

"It means," Emmett said, coming to stand in front of me with his thick arms crossed and sweat trickling down his face. "That you are a dumbass."

Virgil took up a spot next to Emmett, nodding his stringy-haired agreement.

"The first time I've heard you put more than two words together in five years it was to tell me that?" I asked, pushing around them to stack another heavy mat. The punishing work felt like a debt I owed, and I hoped it would wear me out enough to fall straight to sleep instead of laying for hours wondering what Addie was doing.

"That Tanner chick liked you, loser," Emmett said.

Oh God. Was I really going to have to have a heart-to-heart with these two?

"Okay, thanks for your input." I turned and picked up another mat.

"And you're wrecking it," he pointed out.

"She's hot, too," Virgil added.

"Enough," I said spinning to face them, dropping the heavy mat between us with a thunk. "Enough. I know. I know what I did, and who with, and I don't need you questioning the decision. I need to focus on raising my son, and on making sure Shelly sees me doing a good job at that so that I have the opportunity to continue doing it."

"Why you letting her run your life, man?" Virgil asked.

I clenched my teeth. "Because she is the mother of my son."

"So she gets a say about what you do with him, but not really about what you do with little Mike." Virgil said.

"Little Mike?" I asked just before my brain caught up. "Oh for fuck's sake, guys."

"I wasn't going to say this," Virgil said quietly, leaning in. "But you were acting really happy there for a while. Like super happy."

I was not enjoying this conversation at all. I glared at them both, willing them to suddenly morph into valuable employees. Quiet employees.

"Yeah, like you were in love even," Emmett suggested.

"I am not in love with Addison Tanner!" I nearly yelled it, and Helen Manchester turned to stare at me, her hand midway between pulling a pair of garden gloves from the rack and stuffing them into her bag. "Mrs. Manchester, put those back," I said.

"I won't tell the Tanner girl you're in love with her if you don't tell Tess I took these," Helen suggested.

Tess walked around the endcap of the aisle then, holding a potted plant. "Oh for the love of Warcraft, Gran." She snatched the gloves from the old lady and hung them back up.

"Those were going to be a gift," Mrs. Manchester sniffed. "For you."

"Lovely," Tess chirped, steering the old woman away.

"Look guys," I told my cousins, lowering my voice to a hiss. "I'm not in love with anyone, and the last thing I need is Daniel thinking I am."

The brothers exchanged a look and then stepped into my space wearing identical frowns.

"Our dad loved our mom," Emmett said, his voice more clear and pronounced than I'd ever heard it. "And those years, when she was alive, were the best years of our lives." Virgil nodded. "And now that he is in love again, Virge and I are the happiest we've been in a long time."

I shook my head. "What?"

"Seeing your parent in love isn't a bad thing. It's not selfish for you to fall in love, Mike. It's actually good. Watching Dad fall in love with Lottie Tanner is teaching us how it's done." Emmett said.

There was almost too much there to unravel.

"Mom died when we were little. We almost forgot what Dad looked like happy," Virgil said. "Until now."

"Don't make Dan wait to see what you look like happy," Emmett suggested.

I knew there was a kernel of sense in their words, but I was too angry and tired, and confused about getting wisdom from tweedle dee and tweedle didn't, and I just wanted to crawl into a cave to think.

"I'm going home," I told them.

They shrugged and I spun on my heel and went out to the truck. Only I didn't go to the big house on Maple. I went back to my two bedroom cottage, opened a bottle of whiskey, and sat myself down on the couch. And a couple hours later, I passed out.

🍁

"WELL, THIS IS LOVELY," Shelly said, and her voice seemed to be coming through a barrel of cotton and accompanied by needles poking into my brain.

I shook my head, setting off a ricochet of pain inside as I blinked my eyes open.

Oh yeah. The couch. The whiskey.

It was morning, and I was sprawled on the couch, the half-drunk bottle open beside me. The cushion behind my head was wet, and I could only imagine I'd lain there snoring and drooling the better part of the night.

"Why are you in my house?" I asked with a tongue that felt three inches thick.

"Because I owe you an apology."

That brought me upright. Oh shit. Ouch. "Huh?"

"Daniel made me realize—" Shelly stopped talking, taking a

step back and glancing around. "Listen, could you maybe like, take a shower or something? And then we can talk."

"I don't want to take a shower," I said, though I was just being stubborn. Even I could smell that I would benefit from some hot water and soap. "Fine."

Twenty minutes later, I walked back into my living room to find Shelly fluffing couch cushions, the vacuum pulled from the closet and resting in the corner. "You're cleaning?"

"Just tidying up. I guilt clean, you know that." I did remember that.

"Why are you guilty?" I was a bit hungover and also needed her to narrow it down.

She handed me a glass of water and sat on the couch. I took a seat beside her.

"I've been a shit," she said.

I lifted a shoulder. "I'm used to it."

"Thanks."

"So what's changed?"

"Our son," she said, staring at her hands resting on her knees. "He made me sit down and listen to him the day after we walked in on you groping that Tanner chick."

"Always a snappy turn of phrase at the ready."

"Sorry." She cleared her throat. "This is hard for me, Mike. But I think I was wrong. I think I've been wrong."

"About what?" I could count on one hand the number of times Shelly had apologized. Once was for telling me the corsage I bought her for prom looked cheap. Once was for screaming at me that everything was my fault while she was giving birth to Dan, and once was for eating all the cookies and cream and then putting the carton back in the freezer. That was it.

"I've been unfair." Her eyes raised to meet mine then, and the sparkling blue depths I remembered from high school looked worn, faded. "I haven't been happy for a long time," she said. "And so I didn't want you to be happy either."

She paused and I let that sink in. It wasn't a shock, but it was a shock to hear it out loud. And it was more of a shock to know that Shelly was mature enough to say it.

"I didn't like the arrangement with Addison. Not because of Dan. Because of me.

"But when we caught you guys the other night and I got angry, we went home and I guess we both thought about it. Because the next morning he sat me down and asked me to drop my custody fight. He told me that the last few months have been the best ones he's spent with you—that you've been more alive than ever before."

That crushed me to hear. I'd been failing him all along without even realizing it.

"He said that seeing you happy and being with you while you were full of joy was like getting his family back." Her blue eyes lifted to mine again, and they were shining with unshed tears. "Mike, I feel like we're just screwing this all up with him. He just wants to see us both happy, and I've been too busy being mad, and you've been too busy beating yourself up. All he wants is for us both to be happy."

My heart crumpled into an even smaller ball than it had been before at the thought of Daniel being unhappy. Because of me. Because I was so busy making myself miserable I didn't realize I was making him miserable too.

I dropped my head into my hands. "Fuck, Shell. What the hell do we do now?"

She sighed, flopping back into the couch beside me. "I don't really know. I guess we start thinking about what we really want out of life?"

I let out a humorless laugh. "Right."

"Well, it's easy for you," she said.

I turned to look at her. "What?"

"You just need to tell Addison you love her."

"I don't love her. I just met her." But that wasn't really true. None of it was. I'd known her my whole life, in a way. And I found that I very much wanted to know her for the rest of it too.

"And as long as you keep lying to yourself, Daniel's going to know you're not happy. Do it for him, Mike."

I stared at her, unable to believe this was Shelly telling me to go do something to make myself happy. "You really think I should?"

She nodded. "I was wrong about something else. I thought it would make me unhappier if you were happy. But I think it would make me happy to see you happy."

"Seriously?"

"Well, I mean, it might not look like it. It will also piss me off and make me jealous, but somewhere down deep inside, it'll make me happy too."

That sounded about right. "Thanks."

She sighed and then pulled herself back up to sit straight. "Okay. I better go."

I watched my ex-wife stand and walk to the door, still feeling too rough to even be polite and go open it for her. "Shell?" I called from the couch.

"Yeah?"

"Thanks for this," I said.

As the door shut behind her, I let my eyes slide shut again. For now, I needed to sleep off this hangover. And then? I wasn't quite sure what to do, but I knew it would have something to do with Addison Tanner.

32

DON'T UPEND THE PENS
ADDISON

I called my boss to let him know I was coming back early, and things didn't go quite the way I'd imagined.

"We definitely have a place for you here," he told me. "It just might not be the same place you left."

"What does that mean?"

"Look, Addie. It's just . . . I mean, you upended my pen cup the day you left."

"Is that a metaphor?" I'd been really angry about Luke that day and didn't remember exactly what had happened when I'd stormed around work and told my boss I was taking leave.

"No. It isn't an expression. You dumped all my pens on the floor." He said this in the same tone one might say, "you stormed in here with a knife and took hostages." My workplace was traditionally quite sedate. Upending pens was practically a violent offense.

"Um. Sorry?" I didn't feel sorry. I'd been upset.

"Anyway, I was pretty sure that after that, you wouldn't be coming right back, and we needed an analyst. So we hired one."

That hurt a bit. "So where does that leave me?"

"Junior analyst."

"Roger. I'm thirty-five." I'd spent ten years working my way up to the position I'd left not four months earlier, and now I was going to be demoted?

"And a bit unpredictable."

I would figure this out with him in person. "Fine. Fine. I'll be back Monday."

"Ah, okay. We'll see you then, I guess."

After that less-than-positive interaction, I had to scour my network for a place to stay, finally landing a couch with a friend from college for one week.

Still, I needed to get back to the city. Get back to building the life I'd intended in the first place. Once the house was sold, I could make my city life more comfortable. More permanent.

I just needed to hold to my commitment to help Daniel put on the best haunted house Singletree had ever seen, and then I'd be leaving.

"There you are!" Daniel crowed from the front porch as I strode up the walkway on Saturday, steeling myself to see Michael again.

"Here I am," I agreed. I had worn a white dress, as instructed, so that I could play the part of Lucille Tanner, ghostly and lovelorn.

"Good. Dad needs help with the lights upstairs."

"Ah, okay," I said. "Or I could do something down here. Set up gravestones?" I gestured toward the lawn.

"Emmett and Virge have that covered."

"Oh," I said. It had been my plan to avoid Michael as much as possible, not help him hang lights. And though I didn't want to let Daniel down, I also didn't want to spend my night in an uncomfortable situation with Michael, and I was guessing he would think the same. So I did us both a favor.

I hid. Like a scared little girl.

I was still dawdling around the back door, watching a

surprising number of middle school and high school kids running around setting up, when a tall thin guy with about half a beard appeared from around the back of the garage, squinting as he regarded the organized chaos around him.

"Here for the traps," he told me.

I must have looked semi-official, the way I was guarding the back door in my efforts to avoid Michael. "Sorry, what?" I asked him. Had we planned traps into the event? Maybe Dan and Michael had changed the plans since I'd left. "Traps?"

"The coons." He nodded once, as if to show that we were both now in agreed understanding.

"You are?" I asked.

"Liam. Exterminator."

"Oh, you're the guy catching the raccoons!"

"Yeah. And I got these for you." He held out a bag that held a few things I recognized, and some I didn't. Michael's watch. My silver earring. A couple spoons. The ring we'd found in the little box. And a slim silver bracelet I'd never seen before. "Had 'em in their hidey hole up there. Coons like the shiny things," he said, and winked at me like this was a secret we shared.

"All right, Liam," I said, moving aside. "Do what you need to do, I guess." I watched him disappear inside the house I'd still been too chicken to enter.

It didn't feel like my house anymore. It felt like Michael's house now. I was beginning to question why I had even bothered to come when I heard a familiar deep voice inside. "Thanks," Michael was saying, and every nerve in my body fired at once. I nearly fell over right there on the back step.

I knew I'd see him, of course I did. I just hadn't realized quite how tentative my grasp on my own resolve really was. Just hearing that voice made me want to give up all my plans and beg Michael to give us a chance, to see that we were better together.

But he'd been the one to make the choice. And I needed to

accept that my own life did not lie here in Singletree in a ridiculously large old house.

"Thanks," Michael said again, and too late, I realized he and Liam were coming out the back door. I sprang into the bush next to the door, crouching and then realizing a few seconds too late that the bush had dropped its leaves for winter, and I was essentially kneeling behind a pile of twigs. Michael's head swiveled to where I was hiding, and his face showed his surprise at finding me there. "Ah, hi," he said, his brows knit together.

I stood, brushing myself off to free my gauzy dress of twigs and dead leaves, and tried to look composed. "Um. Hi."

"Caught the coons," Liam told me, holding up two long black boxes.

"They're in there?" I asked, momentarily distracted from the way my heart was beating around in my chest like a trapped bird.

"Yep."

"And where will you take them?" I asked him.

"Out to the woods. Hopefully they'll get set up out there and won't be back to bother you none."

"Oh. Okay." I felt Michael's eyes on me as I quizzed Liam, and suddenly wished I could think of many more raccoon-related queries to keep Liam talking so I didn't have to talk to Michael. But I was out.

"Just bill me," Michael told Liam, and the tall man nodded and left.

"Wasn't sure you'd come," Michael said to me. The blue of his eyes looked deep and heavy in the fading light, and I had an urge to cup his cheek in my hand. He looked weary and sad. Much like I felt.

"I promised Daniel," I said, feeling other words crowding up my throat. But I wouldn't let them out. I was tired of being the woman men gave up easily, and I wasn't going to beg.

"Right," he said. "Listen, ah—"

"No." I interrupted him. "Let's just get through tonight. I'm leaving tomorrow, and then we can just coordinate at a distance. It'll be fine." I spun on my heel and retreated around the side of the house, fully aware that I was acting like a child. But with my heart in tatters in my chest and my sanity similarly frayed, it was the best I could do.

Night fell soon enough, and the purple lights sprang to life around the yard. Daniel and his friends greeted guests at the gates and walked them through the house along the path we'd set up. You could hear shrieks and screams as the jump scares and spooky surprises worked their magic, and I was more than happy to stick by the front gates and distribute candy as our guests left, laughing and smiling over the fun we'd planned. I imagined that in the future, my Halloweens would be slightly less family-oriented. New York City didn't really lend itself to high school fundraisers at big ancestral houses.

As our visitors became fewer and further between, some of the helpers began to depart, until finally it was just me, Dan, and Michael, tidying up the yard and putting the house back together.

I was picking up dropped candy when Michael approached me, the ghostly lighting making him seem almost ethereal.

"Listen, Addie," he said, his voice soft, raspy, almost like it pained him to talk.

"Michael, don't." I didn't think I had the strength for almost anything he might say. But there didn't seem to be any stopping him.

"I can't just let you leave," he went on, undeterred. His strong hand wrapped my wrist, as if to keep me from running, and warmth shot up my arm, making me feel hot all over. And confused. What was I doing?

"I need to tell you why I said what I did, why I acted that way.

I was confused. It's just, I've lived my life one way for a long time, thought about things one way," he paused for a breath and I pulled my arm away. I couldn't think when he was touching me. "And then Shelly—"

"I know," I said. "Listen, I can't do this. I just can't. I can't talk to you right now. It's all too hard." I turned away from him and practically sprinted out the front gates and down the hill to where I'd left Mom's car at the curb. I couldn't get away from Singletree fast enough. I needed a fresh start.

Another one.

33

GHOSTLY DEPARTURES
MICHAEL

I watched Addie walk away, her white dress almost mocking in its ghostly beauty, it's symbolism of a fated love between a Tanner and a Tucker. Maybe something like that only happened once, I figured. And our love was closer to the Romeo and Juliet kind than the Lucille and Robert kind. Star crossed, for sure. Maybe Filene just didn't understand the complications that would arise between us.

"Where'd she go?" Daniel asked as I came back inside the house, which was still draped in cobwebs and fucking creepy.

"She left," I told him.

"But I thought you were apologizing." Daniel's eyes were big and sad, and I realized that he had become very invested in my relationship with Addie—he wanted this to succeed. I'd believed it had upset him when he saw us kissing, that he'd thought I was betraying him somehow, but the opposite was true. And now I was failing my son again because I didn't have what it took to get the girl back.

"Some things are just too complicated to work," I told him. "Sometimes it just isn't as easy as you want it to be."

He shook his head, his big eyes widening farther. "She loves you, Dad. I know she does."

Did Addie Tanner love me? I didn't know. There had been moments when I'd held her close, felt her wrap around me, body and soul, and thought it could be true. But we hadn't had a chance. We'd never said those words, or anything close to them.

"No," I told my son as we sat at the kitchen counter. There was a little pile in the center—my watch, the missing ring, a few other shiny items. "It's for the best. I can focus on you and me now," I said, but I heard the hollow mistruth in those words.

"That isn't what either one of us wants," he said. "I want you to be happy. And I want to eat pizza with Addie and watch movies." His big eyes shone, filling with tears. "I think maybe I love her too, Dad."

My heart twisted inside my chest, aching and pulling, trying to find a quiet corner to curl up in to escape the pain. Every time I closed my eyes, I saw that white dress disappearing again. Addie disappearing from my life.

"I know you love her," Dan said, his tone almost accusatory. "And if you say you don't, you'll just be lying."

I stared at him. He was right, of course. In the weeks spent cleaning and painting, hammering and tiling, I'd lost parts of myself. To this house, to the process, to the chance at something new. But mostly, to Addison Tanner. I did love her. But of course I'd been too afraid to even acknowledge it to myself.

"Maybe," I admitted to my son. "Maybe I do. But it's too late tonight to do anything about it. Let's go to bed."

"Does that mean you'll do something about it tomorrow?" Dan asked, bouncing on his chair as one of his hands reached forward and gently pushed the old ring out of the little pile to rest in front of me. I ignored it.

"We'll see." The oldest Dad answer in the books came out of my mouth without me even thinking about it. It was second nature, routine. And maybe that was part of the problem. I'd been stuck in this routine for so long I couldn't even see the way out.

As Daniel's face fell—because all kids know 'we'll see' usually means no—I stopped myself and dropped a hand on his shoulder. "Dan."

He looked up at me. And I saw then the way his cheeks were starting to sharpen, the dark eyes that were becoming deeper, older even. The chin that no longer had the little boy softness. My son was growing up. Maybe it was time I did the same.

"Yes. Tomorrow I'll do something about it."

His face broke into a wide smile then, and my son said, "I'm proud of you, Dad."

34

THE TRAIN TO CRAZYTOWN
ADDISON

Taking the Amtrak into Penn Station on Halloween had been a mistake. I'd changed out of my wedding dress, but I would have fit in better had I left it on, along with the ghoulish makeup I'd been wearing. The Amtrak was populated with ghosts and zombies, vampires and more Avengers and Super-heroes than I could stomach.

I stuck my nose in a book and pretended to read, but my heart wasn't in it. My heart, in fact, was broken.

Part of me thought I shouldn't have left at all, that if I wanted Michael Tucker, I could tug up my big-girl pants and just tell him so. But the sting of rejection was just too fresh, and he'd basically already told me there wasn't a place for me in his life. I couldn't risk being told, once again, that I wasn't worth choosing.

The closer I got to the city, the more I missed Singletree and all the charm my little town held, even without a certain Tucker. I'd come back because I knew I'd been happy here once. I'd designed a life for myself here once. And now I was trying to fit myself back into that life, but I already knew we'd both changed shapes and I wasn't going to fit. There were new angles and curves to me that hadn't been there before Luke left me, before I'd fallen in love with Michael Tucker.

Still, I had committed. I'd had to do something.

So I stepped onto the platform at Penn, immediately swept up in the fecund subway steam, the swell of humanity pressing up the escalators to the concourse. I let the crowd carry me along, up to the subway entrance, and then I rode the red line up to Eighty-Sixth Street, where my couch awaited. Janet had said I was welcome to come tonight, though she and her boyfriend would be out until late.

And as I stood in the crowded subway car after midnight, swaying as the train jolted and turned, I realized I might be the only person not going out that night. New York City was always pulsing with life, but any opportunity for publicly sanctioned costume wearing was a special day—and the citizens took full advantage of the chance to let freak flags fly high and proud. There were far more costumed subway customers than non-costumed folk at this hour, and it made the entire world feel surreal and a little bit insane.

I walked to the building where Janet lived and spoke to the doorman. She'd left my name downstairs with a key, and I went up to the ninth floor, carrying my heavy bag through her apartment door and finally setting it down in the quiet of her space.

Janet was another analyst at my firm, and she was doing very well. She'd bought her apartment last year, and I'd been here once for the housewarming party. Now, in contrast to my mother's cottage, and the huge mansion on Maple, it looked tiny and meager. And the city outside the windows that had once felt vibrant and wild seemed dirty and exhausting.

Maybe I couldn't do city life anymore.

Either way, it didn't matter now. I laid down on the couch, which Janet had made up for me, and closed my eyes, falling asleep without even brushing my teeth or removing my jacket.

Sometime in the middle of the night, Janet came in, giggling, with a male voice accompanying hers.

"Shhhh," one of the whispered dramatically, and once they'd shuffled through and closed the bedroom door, I got up, got dressed for bed, used the bathroom and laid back down.

I awoke late, to a dreary gray Sunday morning. Janet shuffled down the hall a few minutes after I'd used the bathroom, rubbing her eyes.

"Hey," she said. "How are you, Addie?"

"Well, I'm sleeping on a couch," I said. "So I guess I've been better. Thanks so much for letting me stay."

"It's really no problem," she said. "Hey, could you grab the door when it buzzes? I ordered coffee and bagels. I'm gonna try to wash the alcohol from my skin with a quick shower, okay?"

"Sure," I said.

An hour later, I sat at her small table with Janet and her boyfriend Allen, eating bagels and drinking coffee. Though my mom's bakery was wonderful, this was one thing I really did love about New York City.

"That's pretty," Janet said, touching the slim silver bracelet on my arm.

"Oh, yeah," I said, slipping it off. "It was in the house, the one I told you about." I showed it to her, turning it over so she could see the engraving.

"To Lucille," she read. "Our love defies boundaries. Robert." She raised her eyes to me in question.

"It's this beautiful love story between two people from families that hated each other. Kind of like Romeo and Juliet but without all the suicide."

"Oh," she said, handing it back.

"Lucille and Robert's daughter gave us the house," I explained.

"Some gift," Janet said, eyebrows raised.

"Yeah." I tried not to think about what she'd hoped to give us —the house and so much more.

"More lox?" Allen asked, pushing the little board toward me. We'd sliced onions and tomatoes and dressed our bagels with lox and capers.

"I'm good," I said, leaning back in the chair.

"So what happens now?" Janet asked.

"Well," I said. "I guess I get some version of my job back. At a lower salary and a lesser title."

Janet cringed. "Yeah, sorry. I tried to tell them you were coming back."

I shook my head. "It's fine. I upended pens when I left."

She nodded. She knew what our office was like. "I heard about that."

Allen laughed. "That a pretty big deal?"

"Oh yeah," Janet confirmed. "She might as well have come in with a blowtorch."

"So anyway, I guess I'll just go to work tomorrow. See if anyone knows someone who needs a roommate." Even as I said it, my soul seemed to shrivel inside me. I was a thirty-five year old woman. I wanted a family, a house, a dog. I didn't want to share a one-bedroom apartment with a stranger. But this was my life. I couldn't live with my mother forever.

35

LOTTIE GETS MAD
MICHAEL

I didn't sleep much. Saying you were going to do something was very different from actually figuring out what the thing you needed to do might be. And when the sun rose the day after Halloween, I wasn't much closer to figuring it out. I needed help.

So when Dan woke up, we walked down the hill to the Muffin Tin, and went inside, beckoned by the scent of cinnamon and pumpkin spice. Lottie was behind the counter as usual, though there was no sign of Addie, and I realized I'd hoped maybe I could just show up, say something off the cuff and fix everything. But it didn't seem like that was going to happen.

Lottie's eyes lit when they fell on Dan, but her brows lowered as she looked at me.

"Daniel," she said, still frowning at me. "It's so nice to see you again. What can I get for you?"

Daniel ordered a hot chocolate and a pumpkin spice muffin, and Lottie served it up, avoiding my gaze entirely. She smiled sweetly at Dan.

"I guess I'll have a black coffee and one of those muffins too," I said.

"I don't think you will," she told me.

I laughed. What else could you do when the proprietor of the bakery refused to serve you? "Seriously?"

"I'm mad at you."

"Clearly."

Dan wandered to the window with his breakfast, and I crossed my arms over my chest, feeling exhausted.

"She left," Lottie said, her voice sounding more sad than angry now. "And it's your fault."

"She left? Already?" All the ideas I'd had about bumping into Addie in town before she left for New York fizzed away.

"She left last night, thanks to whatever you said to her."

I was too tired to be defensive, and Lottie wasn't wrong. "I didn't get a chance to say anything. She told me not to bother. She said it was all too hard and walked away from me."

Lottie sighed. "And you didn't go after her."

"She asked me to leave her alone!"

The older woman shook her head, her bob staying frozen around her soft face like a steel grey helmet. "Men."

Just then the bell over the door rang and Uncle Victor came strolling in like he owned the place, quite a feat considering the last time he'd been here, he'd been busily attaching furniture to the ceiling.

"Dan!" He boomed, spotting my son in the corner. "Oh, hey Mike," he said upon seeing me. "It's a regular Tucker family reunion," he joked. And then he walked right up to the counter, leaned across it, and gave Lottie Tanner a kiss that I would have classified as a little too long to be coffee-shop appropriate. Besides that, what the actual hell?

Lottie pulled away, fanning her face and blushing madly, and then she said, "Good morning, Victor," in the sweetest voice I'd ever heard her use.

"Are you two . . ." I gestured between them.

"Yes we are," Lottie said, confirming whatever she thought I was indicating in my speechlessness. "Not all Tucker men are terrible at expressing themselves."

"You're kidding," I said. My uncle had never said a whole lot that I could recall that didn't involve yelling at the football games he watched on television or at Virgil and Emmett.

"I am not, and you had better figure what you're going to do to get Addie to come back here, young man," Lottie said, finally letting loose. "She only thinks she wants to go back to that stinky big city, but I know better. She wants to be here. With you, for God only knows what reason."

I sighed. It seemed everyone knew my business long before I did. That said, I was pretty sure I needed their help. "Okay," I said. "I give up. Tell me what to do."

"Let's get some muffins and sit down," Lottie said, finally giving in and letting me have a muffin. She called Amberlynn from the back to work the counter, and we all sat around the table Dan had claimed by the window.

It was the longest Sunday morning of my life. But when it was over, I had a plan.

36

FORCED MARCH
ADDISON

We spent the rest of the day lounging, watching Netflix and enjoying doing almost nothing at all. But in the back of my mind I felt the pain of losing the life I'd begun to live, the ache where Michael had been, and the detached aimlessness of being dropped back into a world where I no longer seemed to belong.

Janet answered her phone late in the day, and went to her bedroom to talk, Allen giving me a shrug and a head shake to tell me he had no idea what she was up to.

She came back out, dressed to go out and grinning. "We should go to the park," she said.

Allen and I exchanged a look and I considered my sweat pants and long T-shirt. In unison, we said, "nah."

"Well you don't have to come," she told her boyfriend. "But Addie and I are going to take a walk."

"We are?" I asked from where I lay, a tub of popcorn balanced on my stomach.

"We are." She walked over, took my tub and pulled me to my feet. "Quick shower now. Just put your hair up, I guess. No time to fix it."

"What? Who cares about my hair?" Janet must have thought I was really in danger of severe depression or something.

"Go on. Get dressed. Go!"

Fifteen minutes later, I was being dragged downstairs and out into the crisp November air of a late afternoon in the city.

About a block from Janet's building, we turned right on Central Park West and strolled along the outer edge of the park. I pointed to a vintage Corvette parked on the other side of the street. "We found one of those in that old house I told you about," I said, unable to keep my mind from lingering on the house, on Michael.

"Oh yeah? Like in the house?" Janet was glancing around nervously.

"No, there was the garage we couldn't get into forever, and it was so funny because all Michael's son could think about was that there might be a Corvette in there—he loves Corvettes. And when we finally got the thing open, it was a Corvette." Tears threatened and I fought them down. Daniel was not mine, I had to let them both go.

We were much closer to the car now, and I was surprised to see it had Maryland plates. "It actually looked exactly like that one."

"How strange," Janet said, her voice taking on a very suspicious tone.

I stopped walking, feeling the signs of a setup. "What are you doing?"

"Walking by the park with a friend."

"Where are we going?"

"Just walking, Addie. Come on." She pulled me by the hand and we continued on, but seeing the car had me thinking about Michael, about Dan. My heart hurt. I didn't want to walk at all.

Janet's phone buzzed and she glanced at it and then slipped

it back into her pocket. "Let's sit." She pulled me suddenly to a bench and forced me onto it.

"Hey!"

"You know what? I have to go," she said, and she began backing away, grinning at me. Janet was abandoning me in the middle of the walk she forced me to take?

"What? No!" I started to stand, but noticed Janet was looking past me, toward someone coming down the sidewalk from the other direction.

I looked to see Daniel and Michael. It took me a moment to understand it was really them, they seemed so incongruous here in the city. But it really was. My heart thumped madly.

"Addie!" Daniel called, breaking into a run and then flinging his arms around me.

"Dan, I . . . I'm surprised to see you." Emotion pushed up my throat and I fought for control. I looked past the tall boy in my arms to see Michael walking toward me, his hands shoved into his pockets and a tentative smile on his face.

"Hi," he said, as he neared.

Janet turned and trotted off toward the apartment, and I realized that somehow she and Michael must have been in touch. I suspected Lottie. She was the only one who knew where I was.

"What are you guys doing here?" I asked.

Michael opened his mouth, but Dan spoke first. "We drove all the way here. In the Corvette!" His cheeks glowed and his smile was contagious. He kept one arm around my waist as he talked, and Michael stood in front of me, smiling uncertainly.

"Really?" So that was the Corvette parked over there.

"Yeah, Dad realized he was a moron and so we jumped in the car as soon as we figured out where you were and drove all the way here so that he could tell you how much he loves you. And how he wishes you'd come back to the house and how maybe you guys should try being serious and stuff."

Uncertainty fluttered inside me. I met Michael's eyes for a brief moment, and while he hadn't said the words, I could see the truth of them in the deep blue depths.

I laughed, still not sure I could trust the happiness that wanted to blossom within me and hugged Dan, my heart speeding around inside me so fast I couldn't really tell how I felt. "Really?"

"Totally!" Dan cried.

"Addie," Michael said, stepping close enough to take my hand. "Daniel kind of stole my thunder there. But maybe that's good, I don't know if I was going to be able to get the words out."

I looked into those eyes that held my heart and realized it was possible nothing had really changed. If he couldn't say the words, did he really mean them?

"I think maybe you should try," I told him.

Daniel moved away from us, and climbed up onto the retaining wall at the edge of the park.

Michael nodded. "Yeah. You're right." He took my other hand in his, and the warmth of our touch seemed to steel him for what he wanted to say next. He squeezed my hands and met my eyes. "Addie, this has been the whole problem. I've been stuck. I had this image of what my life had to be, what it was supposed to be. And it was all about paying some kind of penance for the mistakes I made before I was old enough to know better."

I nodded, it was good to hear that he recognized all this. But I hoped he hadn't come here just to tell me he'd finally seen that he was an idiot.

"But being with you these last months made me realize something else. It made me realize that there are things I still want. Things that will make me happy. And I realized that I deserve to be happy—and that it isn't a failing to need that, to want that. I figured out that it's actually better for Daniel if I'm not just some dad automaton, going through the motions of life.

It's better if I'm really living." He paused, swallowing hard. "And I've never felt more alive than when I was with you."

A tiny laugh escaped my lips and I sealed them shut. I needed more.

"I guess what I'm trying to say is that I love you, Addison. You make me ridiculously happy. And I hoped that maybe you'd consider coming back home. With me. With us."

I sniffed, and realized with some surprise that I'd begun to cry. This. This was what I wanted too, it was all I'd ever wanted. To be a part of something, to be wanted, to have a family. "I'd like that," I whispered.

Michael stepped closer, slipping his hands around my waist. "I hated it when you left," he said, his voice a rasp.

"Me too," I said.

Michael pulled me close, our chests meeting and our faces inches apart. "God, I love you," he said.

And in the space before our lips met, I told him the truth as I'd just come to realize it. "I love you too. Both of you."

My arms wrapped around him, and I kissed Michael Tucker for a long time there on that New York City sidewalk as leaves drifted on the autumn breeze around us.

As my mind began to settle, I realized there were two people standing next to us, staring. One of them was Daniel.

And because this was how my luck seemed to work, the other was Luke.

"Addison?" His beard had grown in thicker, and he wore a flannel shirt that did nothing to hide the softness that had increased around his middle. He looked worn and pale.

I kept Michael's hand in mine as I faced the man I'd believed I had loved. And I was almost relieved to find that I felt nothing. Maybe a distant fondness for an old friend.

"Luke," I said, unable to keep the giddy feelings for the man at my side from coloring my voice. "How are you?"

"Um. I'm good," he said, looking uncertainly between me and Michael.

"This is Luke?" Michael asked, his voice low, angry.

"I've uh, I've been meaning to get in touch," Luke said, ignoring Michael. "I've missed you."

"Oh," I said, realizing a bit late that this was probably not what Luke had been hoping for. "Yeah, you should give me a call sometime," I told him. I turned and reached for Dan's hand, and he stepped near to my other side, squeezing my fingers. "But right now, we have to go."

"Oh," Luke said, taking a step back, almost as if I'd slapped him. "Okay."

"Good to see you," I called over my shoulder as we turned. "Should we get ice cream?" I asked Michael and Dan, pulling them south toward my favorite tiny dessert place.

"That was your ex, right?" Michael asked. "And you want to get ice cream?"

"More than anything," I said. "As long as it's with you guys." A warm reassuring happiness was blooming inside me, expanding and swelling until it seeped through my limbs and filled me completely. I felt more full and happy and complete than I ever had before.

TWEEN TRUTHS
MICHAEL

y plan had been to drive us all back to Singletree that night in the Corvette, to take Addie back to the house, and to show her what she meant to me in every way I possibly could.

But a Corvette really only has two seats. And Dan wasn't a little kid anymore. He couldn't really huddle in the back for the five-hour drive back to Maryland.

So we ate ice cream and pie at Cafe Lalo, walked slowly back to where I'd miraculously found parking for the car, and said goodbye. And then Dan and I had driven home, the mood in the car far more upbeat than it had been on the drive there.

"Are you going to marry her?" Daniel asked me as we neared the big house I now considered home.

"I don't know, Dan," I told him. "For now, I'm just going to do my best to show her that I care about her."

Daniel grinned on the other side of the car as he gazed out the window.

"It doesn't bother you?" I asked him. "To see me with someone?"

He turned and gave me a serious look. "It might have when I

was a little kid. When I thought that if you and Mom were together, my world would be perfect. Now I know it doesn't work like that. And Mom could never make you happy, not like Addie does. You guys are good for each other. I think you make her happy too."

"I hope so."

🍁

ADDIE RETURNED THREE DAYS LATER, after meeting with Luke to retrieve some of her things from storage and giving her final notice at work.

And when she pulled into the driveway in a little U-haul truck, I felt my heart grow wings and do its damndest to escape my chest.

We moved her things into the house, making it feel even more like home to us all. And then Daniel, Addison, and I watched a movie and ate pizza, enjoying the warmth of a fire in the grate and the feeling of things being complete and whole.

When we said goodnight to Daniel, there was no pretense. We went together into the master bedroom and shut the door. And when I took Addison into my arms in our house, in our room, and made love to her over and over in our bed, I felt the circle of my life close with a resounding click.

This.

This was all I needed. All I wanted.

This was completion.

EPILOGUE
ADDISON

Thanksgiving

Michael and I had the biggest house, so we agreed to host Thanksgiving for both families. It was the same crowd we'd come to expect for Sunday dinners, which had become a tradition at the house too. Only at this dinner, we welcomed Shelly and her new boyfriend Liam, who possessed unusual expertise and knowledge of the world of raccoons.

Thaddius had appeared in the garden Thanksgiving morning, and it felt like the exact perfect thing, given the combination of Tuckers and Tanners we'd be hosting.

We all sat around the table in the dining room, with a few folks around an extra table Michael had made for the occasion. His custom-furniture efforts had expanded, and he'd dedicated a full half of the farm supply store to building and selling custom items. We'd set that smaller table up next to the main one, and Michael stood between them to make a toast.

"I'd like to thank everyone for coming tonight," he said. "This year, I think we all have a lot to be thankful for, mostly the fact that we get to share time like this together. We've put aside differences and painful feuds and realized that the Tanners and Tuckers are more family than we are anything else. We have common roots, many of them planted right here in this house. And all of you are welcome here any time."

"Thanks," Liam said, and Shelly elbowed him in the ribs.

Michael sat, and Daniel said, "I think we should all be thankful that Dad didn't tell a joke this year."

Michael stood back up. "I almost forgot."

I rolled my eyes, but inside I was giddy with love. The dad jokes were corny and awful, but they were so much a part of the man I'd fallen in love with. "Go ahead," I said.

"I almost forgot to tell you about when I was buying the turkey for dinner. There was this lady at the store with me, and she kept saying she couldn't find a bird big enough for her family," he said, looking around at the family. "A stock boy wandered by, and she goes, 'excuse me, do these turkeys get any bigger?' And the stock boy said, 'no ma'am. They're dead.'"

Daniel beat a little da-da-dum on the table as Michael sat down.

"Terrible, as always," Shelly said, but even her jab felt good natured.

"Addison, how is business?" Victor asked as we served ourselves from the heaping plates in the center of the table.

"Just getting rolling really," I said. I was finishing the interior design degree I'd started, but Michael had agreed to let me set up a little office in the front living room of the house, using it as a showroom and a client meeting space. I was going to be designing interiors for other people. "Helen Manchester dropped by, asking if I could give her a better gaming space."

"Oh my God," Mom laughed. "She is addicted to that game she plays!"

"Seems to be keeping her young," Victor laughed.

So my first client was a video-game-playing grandmother, and I was thrilled about it.

Dinner went smoothly after that, everyone eating and drinking and laughing. I found myself sitting quietly, enjoying the feeling of family all around me. And at one point, I looked down the table to find Michael smiling at me as our families laughed around us.

"I love you," he mouthed, and I felt my heart expand inside me.

"I love you too," I mouthed back.

"I have something I need to say," Victor announced suddenly, standing up and upending his water glass on the table.

"Oh!" Lottie cried, mopping up the spill. But Victor stilled her hand, taking it in his own.

"Lottie Tanner," he said, and then he dropped to one knee. "You've made me a very happy man these last few months," he said. "Happier than I thought I'd ever be again. And while I never could have imagined this, I believe now that I cannot live without you. Will you marry me, Lottie?"

My mother fell to her knees in front of Victor and kissed him with a passion that had most of us averting our eyes. When she disengaged, she breathed, "Yes. I will!"

And then Victor presented her with the ring, the same one we'd found hidden in the walls of the house where we now sat. Michael had asked me about it when he'd learned of his uncle's intentions, and I couldn't think of anything more fitting. A family ring to unite the family. It was perfect.

Mom cried as everyone admired the ring and clustered around her.

And there, surrounded by the impossible togetherness of the

Tucker and Tanner families, with Whitewoods and Blanchards and exterminators and ex-wives sprinkled in among us, I found the thing I'd been looking for my whole life. I found my own version of family.

THE END

ALSO BY DELANCEY STEWART

Want more? Get early releases, sneak peeks and freebies! Join my mailing list at delanceystewart.com and get a free story!

The Singletree Series:

Happily Ever His

Happily Ever Hers

Shaking the Sleigh

Second Chance Spring

Falling Into Forever

The MR. MATCH Series:

Book One: Scoring the Keeper's Sister

Book Two: Scoring a Fake Fiancée

Book Three: Scoring a Prince

Book Four: Scoring with the Boss

The KINGS GROVE Series:

When We Let Go

Open Your Eyes

When We Fall

Open Your Heart

Christmas in Kings Grove

The STARR RANCH WINERY Series:

Chasing a Starr

CPSIA information can be obtained
at www.ICGtesting.com
Printed in the USA
LVHW050129300121
677807LV00002B/134